THE WIND FROM THE PLAIN
A Trilogy

II   IRON EARTH, COPPER SKY

Yashar Kemal was born in 1922 in a village on the cotton-growing plains of Chukurova, which feature in this novel. He received some basic education in village schools, then became an agricultural labourer and factory-worker. His championship of the poor peasants lost him a succession of jobs, but he was eventually able to buy a typewriter and set himself up as a public letter-writer in the small town of Kadirli. After a spell as a journalist he published a volume of short stories in 1952, and in 1955 his first novel, *Memed, My Hawk*. This won the Varlik Prize for the best novel of the year. It has sold over a quarter of a million copies in Turkey and has been translated into every major language.

Yashar Kemal was a member of the Central Committee of the banned Workers' Party. In 1971 he was held in prison for 26 days, then released without being charged.

Kemal, many of whose books have been translated into English by his wife, is Turkey's most influential living writer.

Yashar Kemal

IRON EARTH, COPPER SKY

Translated from the Turkish by
Thilda Kemal

COLLINS HARVILL
8 Grafton Street, London W1
1989

Collins Harvill
William Collins Sons & Co. Ltd
London · Glasgow · Sydney · Auckland
Toronto · Johannesburg

BRITISH LIBRARY CATALOGUING IN PUBLICATION DATA

Yasar, Kemal, *1922-*
Iron earth, copper sky
Rn: Kemal Sadik Gogcel
I. Title   II. Yer demir gok bakir. *English*
894'.3533 [F]

ISBN 0-00-271350-0

First published under the title
Yer Demir Gök Bakir, Istanbul, 1963

First published in Great Britain by
Collins and Harvill Press, 1974
This edition first published by
Collins Harvill, 1989

© Yashar Kemal 1963
English Translation © William Collins Sons & Co. Ltd 1974

Printed and bound in Great Britain by
William Collins Sons & Co. Ltd, Glasgow

Chapter 1

Silently they made their way towards the oak-wood. Hasan walked ahead, hunched forward, his hands thrust under his jacket. Ummahan followed close behind, her eyes on her feet.

The world was shrouded in snow, hill and vale lost under a sheer unsullied whiteness. Even the sky was quite white. Only down south, way over the Taurus forest, a pale greenish-blue haze hovered like a flimsy veil spread over the boundless whiteness. A dazzling sun bore down on this frozen expanse, reflecting millions of tiny silver sparks.

The two children were barefoot and stepped over the crisp hard snow as though on live coals.

Hasan looked back.

'The minute we get to the forest . . .' he began, then stopped.

'Yes?' Ummahan asked eagerly.

'Nothing. I've changed my mind. I won't tell you.'

'Don't then!' She shrugged. 'As if I cared!'

'Like hell you don't!'

She did not answer back. He was obviously spoiling for a fight.

'D'you hear?' he insisted. 'I said like hell . . .'

'I heard you, brother. What d'you want me to do if you won't tell me?'

'I won't,' he shouted. He began to run. He ran so fast that Ummahan could not keep up with him.

He's become strange, this brother of mine. Never talking, always cross . . . Grinding his teeth, howling in his sleep . . . Grown-ups always tell of such children . . . How the wasting sickness gets them and they die. Hasan . . . Singing and laughing all day long . . . And now . . . Like a dead tree . . .

When Hasan looked back Ummahan was nowhere to be seen. He could feel the sun now like a warm caress on his neck.

5

'Ummahan!' he called, blinking against the glaring whiteness. 'Where are you? Ummahan!'

'I'm coming . . .' Her thin voice trailed off over the wilderness of snow.

He caught sight of her, struggling up the white slope like a tiny black insect.

'Hurry! I'm going to be late because of you, damn you,' he shouted.

She was sweating. 'Please Hasan, let me get my breath . . .'

'I shouldn't have brought you along,' he burst out. ' "Never set out with a bitch, or you're sure to fall into a ditch!" ' He made his voice as gruff as he could and held his chin wisely in his hand like the village elders. This was sure to exasperate her.

Ape! Piddler! she thought. How he wetted his bed . . . I'll fling it in his face now . . . But then he'll never tell me the secret of the wood . . .

' "You'll get lies all day long and more than you need, but never a shred of sense from the petticoat breed",' he taunted again. Then he paused expectantly.

There was no reply from Ummahan.

She's pretending she doesn't care, the hussy. You just wait, my girl!

' "Neither faith nor loyalty can you find in a whore!" '

He saw Ummahan's eyes filling with tears. A pang of remorse shot through him. 'That wasn't for you,' he blurted out, taking her hand. 'You're my dear, beautiful sister. It wasn't for you.'

'Of course it wasn't,' Ummahan cried triumphantly. 'Would a boy ever call his own sister a whore?'

This irritated him. 'Well, haven't you rested enough?' he said. 'You must have collected all the breath in the world by now. Come on, hurry!' He spurted on. 'When we get to the forest . . .' He licked his lips. 'Aha! Then . . .'

'Who cares?' she retorted, beginning to lose patience.

Hasan, exasperated, shouted. 'A whore, that's what you'll be when you grow up!'

6

'Yes, a whore,' she shouted back defiantly. 'That's what I'll be. Such a whore and oh, what a fine time I'll have!'

He could not believe his ears. A good spanking that's what she needs. But suppose she turns back home and leaves me? He was afraid of entering the oak-wood alone.

'Girl,' he said, 'I ought to trample you underfoot, but . . . Come on, walk!'

'I won't! I'll go and tell Father everything you've said. Every single thing!'

'Go to hell! Don't you know Father's worried to death? If you tell him, I'll hack you to pieces with this axe. Now walk!'

'Only if you promise to tell me the secret of the wood.'

'Walk and I'll tell you.'

High overhead a flock of birds flew past, a scattering of black specks in the emptiness of the sky.

There was a weight on Hasan's heart, an aching pain he had never known before. That flame-like blue bird, the elusive bird of good luck that digs into steep riverbanks to nest deep down in the bowels of the earth like a snake . . . If only he could catch one now! No one but Old Halil had ever been known to trap a blue bird. He used to pin the bird's glossy jet black beak on to some child's shoulder, an amulet against want and poverty for ever . . . But there was no Old Halil now. He had disappeared in the autumn when they had gone down to pick cotton in the Chukurova plain. His son had given him up for dead, and the chapter from the Koran had been read in his memory.

'Dead?' Hasan's grandmother had cried. 'He? Die? That fiend, that limb of Satan whose murder would be sanctioned by all the four Holy Books? Oh no, neighbours! Oh no, he'll never die, that one!'

The villagers had been shocked. 'But Meryemdje, can't the old chap die like any other human being?'

'How dare you read the Koran, how dare you recite the *Mevlut*[1] for that infidel, that renegade?'

Long Ali had tried to stop her. 'For heaven's sake, Mother, don't! He's dead and gone. It's a sin to speak against the dead,

[1] *Mevlut*: a memorial service for the dead.

7

however wicked they were. They've nothing more to do with this world . . .'

'Old Halil isn't dead!' she had continued to repeat obstinately.

The *Mevlut* was held on the barren cotton field, with all the villagers attending. The Bald Minstrel intoned the prayer just as though he were singing a familiar ballad, and the women, as always, were moved to tears by the magic of his voice. Only one person was missing.

'My ears mustn't hear our Prophet Muhammet's holy *Mevlut* sung for that apostate,' Meryemdje muttered as she hurried to the farthest corner of the field near the irrigation ditch. The sound followed her. Her hands over her ears, she hastened on, but the chanting seemed to rise as it floated over the flat land. She flung herself down and bent her forehead to the warm Chukurova earth. 'Oh Mother Earth, please stop that Bald Minstrel from sinning against my beautiful white-bearded Allah! Turn his tongue into wood . . .' She scrambled to her feet and rushed on until she came to a hollow behind a clump of trees. It was like the sun flowing brightly back over the glistening world after a dark spell of rain. The sound had died away at last.

When she returned to the cotton field the *Mevlut* was over. The Bald Minstrel tried to banter with her but thought better of it after one glance at her face.

'My beautiful black earth!' she cried, as she sank to the ground and began to pound the earth. 'It's you I'm speaking to and no one else here. These villagers don't deserve to be spoken to any more. They've made a mockery of our religion. They've annoyed our Holy Prophet. I wouldn't stop here another minute among these infidels, it's only old age that pins me down. I tell you, my clever all-knowing earth, my sultan earth, I'll never open my mouth again to anyone in this village, not even to its beasts and insects! Because I'll have you know, Old Halil isn't dead!'

Long Ali rushed up and clapped her mouth shut. Meryemdje was shrieking and struggling like one possessed.

'That Meryemdje!' the villagers said. 'She's gone raving mad.'

8

'She always was mad.'

'Yes, but it's getting worse as she grows older.'

From that day on Meryemdje was never again heard speaking to anyone in the village.

Hasan was gathering brushwood as though his life depended on it. He piled it on the sandy earth at the foot of a rock that jutted out like an awning, forming a small cave where the snow had not penetrated. Then, to Ummahan's amazement he produced a brand new box of matches.

'So that's your secret!' she cried.

'You're dying to know, aren't you?' he said. 'This is only one of my secrets, and don't worry, I didn't steal them. I earned them by the sweat of my brow.'

It came to her like lightning.

'I know!' she cried gleefully. 'I know how you got them!'

'Say it then, since you're so clever,' he jeered. 'But mind you, if you're wrong I'll give you a good spanking.'

'Those cherry shoots you carried all the way down to the Chukurova, you swapped them for these. That's what you did.'

He was taken aback. Why the little witch, he thought with sudden pride, she's clever our Ummahan.

He struck a match and held it to the sticks. They blazed up instantly and the two children huddled down shoulder to shoulder, as close as they could to the slow-spreading warmth.

'Do you know, Ummahan . . . But first, swear you'll never tell a soul.'

'I swear it.'

'Say Mother'll die if I do.'

Ummahan hesitated. 'Let Mother die if I do . . .'

Hasan's face lit up. 'You see this box? Well, I've got another nine of them. All for those cherry shoots! These matches'll last me ten years, fifteen years . . .'

'Oh, they'll last for ever!' she exclaimed admiringly.

Hasan was pleased. 'Look!' He drew a sling from his pocket. 'I got this too. When it's spring and warm again, we'll be able to shoot birds.'

9

'Oh yes!' she cried. 'Dozens and dozens . . .'

'And then we'll light a fire with these matches . . .'

'I'll pluck them clean and salt and cook them.'

'And then we'll have a feast.'

A warm longing for roasted, fragrant meat welled up in them.

'Just wait till the warm spring days are here. Just wait, dear sister . . .'

She was quick to take advantage of his softness. 'What was it you were going to tell me when we came to the forest?'

'Shh!' he said. 'Later, we've got plenty of time. We'll gather the wood in the afternoon so we don't have to go back to the village till sundown. Do you know, Ummahan, I'm frightened of that village. I'm afraid Adil Effendi will come . . .'

She turned her huge deep black eyes on him and saw the fear on his face. 'So am I,' she said quickly. 'I'm terrified.'

'Poor Father, he's so worried he doesn't know what to do.'

'Mother's afraid too. The whole village is full of fear, as if it were being threatened by a pack of wolves. Only Grandmother's not afraid.'

'But she won't speak to anyone, not even to us. If only that Adil Effendi would come and do whatever he's going to do to us. I wish it were over . . .'

He moved closer to the fire, straining his long thin neck. His huge black eyes shone brightly in his bony face. A faint scar ran down his left temple to his neck like a vein. His hair, roughly clipped by his mother, stood out in ragged tufts. Brother and sister were very much alike, slight of build, slim-fingered and dark-eyed. But Ummahan's mouth was full and red, strangely alive in the wanness of her face, like a bright late-blooming flower on the autumnal steppe.

Hasan's eyes were fixed on the flames. He saw a pack of wolves running and tumbling over each other, fighting a pitched battle. And then, in an instant, all gone! How could they have vanished so fast? Just now that big wolf had been there, ears pricked, tongue thrust out and almost licking the mossy rock wall. And then with a whiff of the wind it had crumbled into nothingness.

But here was a whole forest growing out of the fire, now aflame, burning away riotously, now sunk into blackness and smoke. Hasan sniffed at the acrid fumes with delight, then threw in more twigs and cones. The twigs crackled and a flame darted up, tapering out to the roof of the cave. This is a poplar, Hasan thought, a tall glowing poplar of fire. Then the tree snapped and fell back into the flames, and now he saw myriads of ants, crystal-red, swarming, seething . . . For some reason the ants upset him. Quickly, he piled brushwood over them and suddenly a horse, a gigantic horse leaped up from the fire.

'Look, Ummahan,' he shrieked, 'look how it's galloping!'

Ummahan started.

'It's gone,' he sighed. 'Just slipped by in a twinkling. What a handsome horse it was, with its long flying mane . . .'

'Those flames!' Ummahan laughed. 'Why don't I ever see anything?'

'You wouldn't!'

'At this rate you'll soon be like Spellbound Ahmet.'

'Why not?' Hasan retorted kicking at the sand. 'Is he a bad man?'

Ummahan thought this over. 'No, but he's mad, isn't he?'

'Who knows?' Hasan said. 'Now look. Look really hard and you'll see those horses and insects and people, and even the *jinn* and *peris*, for there are lots and lots of them, you know.' He threw in some cones. 'Now, look well.'

'I never see anything but flames coiling round and round like ropes,' she complained.

'Here it comes!' he shouted. 'A greyhound! See, it's running. It's gone . . .'

'I didn't see it,' she said, downcast.

'What a pity,' he sighed. 'It was such a beautiful greyhound.' Then he took her hand. 'Never mind, you'll see them one day too.'

They fell into silence, lost in their thoughts.

Ummahan was the first to rouse herself. The winter sun was sinking fast and it had turned bitterly cold.

'It's getting late. Mother'll be anxious if we stay after dark.'

11

Hasan rose and walked up and down, up and down, dragging his feet in the soft sand.

'I don't feel like going back!' he said helplessly at last. 'Not ever!' He was thinking of the lucky blue bird. Oh, to catch a thousand of them and hang their darkly shining heads all around the village. That would turn away the evil eye. A miracle . . .

'If only we could be sure that Mother wouldn't cry,' Ummahan said. 'And then . . . If it wasn't for the dark . . .'

'If we didn't get hungry,' Hasan added.

'That's true,' she cried. 'If only we were never, never hungry at all . . . But Hasan, we'd better be quick. Look at the sun.'

He grabbed his axe and ran up to an oak. The blow rang out loud in the emptiness of the wood. A dark cloud was advancing over the steadily fading steppe. It came, black and angry, sweeping away before it the scintillation of the snow, staining the whiteness of the earth and sky. He swung the axe furiously, almost at random. With each stroke, frozen flakes dropped to the ground.

'Hurry, Ummahan! Hurry!'

She was darting to and fro, piling up the sticks and binding them into faggots.

'All right, Hasan. We've got enough,' she said at last.

He threw down the axe and looked at his sister suspiciously.

'You wait here,' he ordered, 'and don't dare turn to look where I'm going, or I'll hack you to pieces here and now with this axe.'

Each time it was the same. Where did he go? What did he do? Ummahan was burning to know. But she never could pluck up the courage to go after him.

He ran swiftly, jumping over the rocks and fallen trunks until he came to a great rock set like an island in the midst of a clump of pines. There he paused, his heart beating loudly. Then slowly, as though touching a sacred object, he lifted a large stone. There was nothing under it except a feeble stirring of yellowish, ant-like creatures. With infinite care, as though he feared it would break and the magic would be shattered, he lowered the stone.

On the way back Ummahan looked at him reproachfully.

'Hasan . . .' she began.

'Shh!' he whispered.

'But you haven't told me the secret of the forest,' she protested. 'You promised . . .'

'Shh!' he said sharply.

Chapter 2

They were all squatting about the hearth. The wood Hasan and Ummahan had brought blazed and crackled, filling the hut with its forest fragrance. Old Meryemdje sat still as a stone, her back to the wall, her head bent. Ali eyed her uneasily, thinking of other winter evenings when his mother would while away the long hours with an endless store of tales and reminiscences. If only she would be her old self again now, in these days of trouble . . . If only . . .

How long was it since the evening prayer? No one spoke. The children were quiet, listless, buried in themselves. Elif had tried to cheer up the household, but she too was silent now. Only the long mournful ululations of the wind from the steppe filled the night.

'Mother,' Ali said in a wheedling tone, thinking of the wonderful stories Meryemdje could tell of the steppe and its wolves, 'what of the wolves now in this cold, with the whole world frozen over? What do they eat? How do they keep alive?'

Meryemdje did not seem to hear him.

'Mother . . .' Now if this doesn't shake her into talking, he thought, then nothing ever will to her dying day. 'Mother, people are saying Old Halil isn't dead. They say he came back here while we were still down in the Chukurova plain and when his son returned to the village and opened the door, who should he see inside but Old Halil fast asleep! And you knew it all the time, Mother! You said he wasn't dead. And now he's ashamed to show himself because he thinks it's his fault the village was late for the cotton picking. He's made his son swear not to tell a soul that he's alive. Yes Mother, just like that . . .'

Meryemdje did not stir. A threatening rumble came from the steppe.

Ali's hut was built in a hollow with the bare earth for its back wall. Uneven stones daubed with mud made up the other three walls. Though the roof was of stout oakwood, the house itself was old, dating back to Ali's grandfather. In stormy weather Ali always feared that the snow-laden roof would cave in. Yet he knew this was unlikely in the winter when the whole house with its walls and dirt floor was frozen hard. Houses collapsed only during the spring thaw.

Their one cow, one calf and three goats were lying by the hay stacked in the far corner of the room. It was cold in spite of the brightly burning fire. What they needed was more livestock to warm up the place with their breath, Ali thought.

'Mother,' he said, 'the crop's bound to be plentiful this year, after all this snow. I'll buy a few more goats and another cow with the money. That'll be more than enough to heat this house, now won't it?'

But he might as well have spoken to a corpse.

His thoughts wandered to Adil Effendi and his threats. I intend going to that village myself, Adil Effendi had told the Muhtar,[1] and take the goats and cows from their hearths and the butter from their firkins, yes everything, down to their women's last drawers. All the villages have paid their debts. Your village went down to the Chukurova just like the others, so how is it they all picked good cotton and you didn't? You're simply lying, and this is the last time you get any credit from me. Why, the villages around here have been dealing with us for nearly a hundred years, ever since my grandfather set up shop, and this is the first time a debt hasn't been settled. The village of Yalak is the first to have broken the age-old bond. You've sown the seeds of evil in these mountains . . .

A voice at the window roused him.

'Ali! Ali, open the door!'

'Tashbash, is that you?'

It wasn't like Tashbash to come visiting so late in the night. Something must be wrong, Ali thought as he opened the door.

'What news, brother?' he asked anxiously.

[1] Muhtar: village headman.

15

'Bad,' Tashbash replied, as he sat down by the fire in the place Elif had left for him. 'Adil Effendi's coming.'

'When?' Ali asked wearily.

'Well, nobody knows exactly. Perhaps this very minute . . .'

'What shall we do? Have you thought of something?'

'What's there to think of? We can't pay, that's all. I haven't been able to buy a yard of cloth this year. My wife's in rags . . .'

'It's the same with everyone.'

'It's no use telling Adil Effendi it wasn't our fault, that we were led into a barren cotton field, that we'll repay him next year with double interest. No . . . Ah, it's that Muhtar Sefer who's brought this upon us, and Old Halil too.'

At this Meryemdje raised her head. Her lips moved silently in a sullen mutter.

Tashbash stared at her in amazement.

'Ali, will Mother Meryemdje still not talk?'

Ali shook his head despondently.

'Well!' Tashbash exclaimed. Then he went on quickly. 'Have you heard? Old Halil isn't dead. He's right in the village, hiding in his son's grain crib.'

'I know,' Ali replied.

Chapter 3

Old Halil had made his bed in the grain crib. He never came out except under cover of darkness, and then only when he had to relieve himself. Day and night he lay there, cowering into a corner every time the front door was opened. He had got it into his head that the villagers intended to kill him, and nothing his son could say made any difference.

'But Father,' Hadji would plead, 'you haven't done them any wrong. Everyone knows it's the Muhtar's fault that we didn't find a good cotton field. Just show yourself once, and if anyone so much as wags a finger at you, then come back here and never go out again.'

'You're only a child,' Old Halil would answer obstinately. 'You don't know those wily villagers. All they want is to get hold of me and tear me to pieces. Ah, don't I know!'

'But you'll just rot away here, in this dark hole, without ever seeing the light of day.'

Old Halil cut him short. 'I'd rather die than come out!'

That day there was anxious whispering about the house. Something was brewing. He read fear on his son's face.

'Hadji!' he called. 'Come here. What's wrong? Tell me, have they found out that you're hiding me?'

Hadji sat down beside him on the low wall of the crib and explained about Adil Effendi and the threat that hung over the village. Old Halil did not believe a word of it, but still it was a straw to cling to.

'You go and tell those villagers,' he said craftily, 'that Old Halil knows how to get them out of this fix. They'll all be amazed to see how. I'll save them, but only if they promise not to kill me. You must make them promise before telling them I'm alive or they'll tear me to shreds.'

'There you go again, Father! Why should anyone want to do that?'

'Do as I tell you. You can't understand these things. You're only a child.'

'Father, are you mad? A child? I'm getting on for fifty! And anyway, everyone knows you're here.'

'They know?' Old Halil cried out in terror. 'I'm dead, finished. Bolt the door! Quickly! Now!' He flung himself down and drew the blanket over his head. 'Murderer! Bolt that door . . .'

Hadji shook his head in exasperation as he went to the door.

'Ah, aaah!' the old man wailed. 'That my son, the apple of my eye, should be the cause of my death! I didn't eat to feed him, I went in rags to clothe him, and in return he's bringing down my house over my head!'

He lay there, moaning, working himself into a frenzy. They might be here any minute, the Muhtar, the villagers, all itching to lay their hands on him, to kill him . . . Then they would go to Adil Effendi and say, 'See, we've done away with the culprit. Such a thing would never have happened in this village but for him.' At any moment now that door would burst open. Leading the crowd would be Meryemdje, her hair bristling like a broom. He could hear her screaming vengeance. 'Kill him, women! Kill him! Tear him to pieces, the infidel, the unholy renegade! Kill him!'

'Ah, Meryemdje!' he cried aloud. 'If it weren't for your poor dead husband, my dear friend Ibrahim, if it weren't for him, I know what I'd do to you.'

And then, as always when the fear became unbearable, he saw himself in his prime, riding below Chiyshar village on a late autumn afternoon through a wood of luminous plane trees. He had just stolen the horse from Göksün on the Long Plateau, a sorrel that galloped like the wind, its colour blending with the russet trees . . . They were skirting a brook, so thickly coated with leaves it looked like a red carpet flowing down into the valley, when the horse had baulked. And then he had seen the wounded man lying half hidden by the undergrowth. Quickly he had got off and ripped up his own shirt to make a bandage.

'I can't go to a town. I can't see a doctor,' the man had moaned. 'I am Memo, the bandit.'

Halil had taken him to Aslan Agha, chief of the horse-thief gang. And there the outlaw had remained until his wound healed.

Memo, the lord of these mountains, ready to lay down his life for Halil. If only he were alive now, alive to teach these villagers a lesson!

He hears them, a howling pack at the bolted door. 'Come out, you godless heathen, you traitor!' And then with a great crash the door breaks open. They come pouring through, but almost in the same instant they reel back, scrambling over each other, yelling with fear. Three hefty outlaws rigged out in cartridges from head to toe are aiming their gun muzzles at them.

'Let them have it, Memo,' Halil shouts. 'Shoot them all down, the rascals!'

But Memo laughs. 'Why waste good bullets! Half of them'll die of fright anyway!'

And now Halil is swaggering up and down the village and the villagers come cringing up to him.

'Please forgive us, Halil Agha. Don't turn the bandits on us . . .'

The door creaked open. His heart began to thump.

'Who's that?' he quavered.

'It's me, Father.'

'Look, Hadji, you must get me out of here. Take me to that cave at the foot of Mount Tekech.'

'But Father! There's a raging snowstorm outside, enough to freeze you if you go next door, let alone to Mount Tekech!'

'You do as I tell you. There, in that cave, with my faithful friend Memo . . .' Something seared through his heart. 'Ah,' he cried, 'if he were alive now, I'd have him mow the whole village down!'

'Father, I've told you again and again no one's giving you a thought. The villagers have enough to worry about as it is. If you'd only go out just once, you'd see how they'd open their arms to you. Why, at the *Mevlut*, when we thought you were dead, they all came and cried their hearts out.'

Old Halil sat up. 'So you mean I'm not important enough, eh? You snivelling whelp, this village is in debt, hungry, naked in the dead of winter, and you think they don't know it's my fault? Shame on you! A fine son for an old eagle like Halil to have!' He slumped down. 'I'm cold,' he groaned. 'Bring me another blanket, quick, and tell that whore of yours to cook me some *tarhana* soup. Piping hot I want it. Let me drink something warm before I die . . .'

He lay there till nightfall, trembling with expectation, straining his ears towards the door. Weren't they going to come after all?

'Father,' he heard his daughter-in-law call, 'the soup's ready. We're waiting for you.'

A tantalizing fragrance filled the house. His stomach rumbled with hunger.

'Is it really night? Quite, quite dark?'

'Quite, Father,' Hadji assured him.

'Go out and have a good look, for pity's sake, to make sure.'

Hadji opened the door, slamming it to again.

'It's so dark outside,' he announced solemnly, 'you could cut through the night with an axe.'

Old Halil skipped out of the crib, nimble as a child. He snatched up a spoon and began to gulp down his soup as though he had been starved for days. When he had had his fill, he raised his head and looked warily at the door. Village folk are cunning, he thought. They'll wait till it's night to get their man. In the dark of the night . . .

He rushed back to the grain crib. 'Hadji!' he shouted in agitation. 'Put a heavy log against the door. Do something to save your poor father from those wild beasts. They're hiding outside in the deadly night, and soon they'll be creeping up, one by one, closer and closer, until there's a human mass heaving at that door. They'll grab me by the scruff of the neck like a rabbit and drag me out into the cold snow. And there, by the light of torches, they'll fall upon me like hungry wolves and at one swoop each will have torn a piece of my flesh. Eh, a meet death for Halil, the eagle of these mountains . . . But then, I'm so old now, they ought to spare me, isn't that so, son?'

'Father! What are you imagining? Nobody's thinking of you. Go to sleep.'

Old Halil was outraged. 'Tonight,' he spluttered, 'this very night, they're coming to butcher me. Rejoice, snivelling Hadji! Rejoice that the morsel I eat in this house will be yours at last.'

Hadji had had enough. 'Oh well, Father, perhaps you're right,' he said. 'Perhaps they do bear you a grudge and mean to kill you.'

This was what the old man had been wanting to hear.

'They will, Hadji, they will, you'll see. Now, come here. Hold my hand. Let Fatma come too, and my grandchildren. Yes, all my progeny, because this is the end for me. Even now . . .'

At a sign from Hadji they all crowded around the grain crib.

'Forgive me everything, my dear children,' Old Halil began, his voice warm and soft with emotion. 'This is to be Halil's fate then, to suffer death at the hands of his fellow villagers!' He patted his grandchildren on the head and stroked his daughter-in-law's hand. 'Forgive me all. Farewell . . .'

Hadji had never seen his father in this fond paternal mood. Could it be that he really felt his end drawing near?

Far into the night Hadji and Fatma sat by the hearth listening to the old man's moaning and muttering. At last he fell asleep and Fatma turned to her husband.

'We can't let him suffer like that. Tomorrow, I'm going to do something.'

'What?'

'You'll see. I never cared for him much. You know how he's treated me all these years. But this evening my heart has gone out to him. Poor creature, I'll rid him of this fear that's killing him.'

Old Halil had never been strict about religious observance, and if he did wake up at the time of the early morning prayer it was not to make the *namaz*, but to stir up the ash-covered embers in the hearth and throw on a few logs. When the others awoke the fire would be burning brightly and the house pleasantly warm.

This morning he felt a sudden longing. Ever since taking up his abode in the grain crib he had not even once tended the fire. Lithe as a cat, he crept out and quickly kindled up a blaze. Then he withdrew into his hide-out again and waited with pleasurable anticipation for Fatma to begin her daily bout of bickering with Hadji.

He waited in vain. The last cock had crowed, and still no quarrel. Not so much as a word exchanged!

'Hadji,' he called, 'isn't Fatma there?'

'She's gone out, Father. She had something very important to do.'

'I was wondering . . .' He stopped.

'What is it, Father?'

'It's just that . . .'

'Oh, for God's sake, why don't you speak out?'

Old Halil's head shot into view.

'See here, snivelling Hadji, how dare you speak to me like that? Only yesterday's little whipper-snapper . . . All I was going to say is . . . Is anything wrong?'

'No. Why?'

'Because . . . It's just that . . .'

'I'll be damned if I know what you're getting at.'

'Just that . . .' Then quickly – 'You and Fatma haven't had words this morning. So . . .'

Hadji laughed. 'We didn't have the chance, Father. She was off before daybreak.'

A horrible suspicion filled old Halil.

'Bolt that door, Hadji,' he cried.

Hadji fastened the door, then lifted the bar again stealthily.

'I'll thank you, snivelling Hadji, not to try and fool Old Halil. You go and bar that door properly this very minute or . . .' Suddenly he let out a frenzied shout. 'They're coming! I knew it!' There was a jubilant note in his voice. 'Can't you hear them? Hundreds and hundreds of feet! The whole village, young and old, children and all, coming to kill me! Help! Help me, all-powerful Muhammet. Don't forsake me.'

The sound of many voices, laughing and shouting, could be heard clearly now, ringing in the morning air, growing louder and louder. A big crowd was approaching the house. Fatma's voice rose above the din.

'Open the door, Hadji.'

'Don't, Hadji!' Old Halil shrieked. 'Aren't you my son? It's your father they're going to kill. That whore of yours has betrayed me. Don't let them in, my Hadji. This year I'll pick cotton for you like five men, I will. And I'll spend nothing at all on tobacco . . .'

'Hadji, open the door!'

Old Halil scrambled out of the grain crib, but it was too late. The door was open and there he stood, exposed in the bright glare of day, a huge crowd facing him. He blinked, then hopped back into the crib, pulling the blanket over his head. Gusts of laughter swept the crowd and echoed through the village. This gave him a jolt. What were they up to now? Mocking phrases mingled with laughter reached his ears.

'Hey, Old Halil! Come out of your hole!'

'Come out and see what we'll do to you!'

'Meryemdje's here too! Meryemdje's after you!'

'Try and save your beard from her clutches, Uncle Halil!'

The children had made up a refrain:

> 'Old Uncle Halil
> His tail's got a frill!'

Then he heard Shirtless's deep voice rising angrily above the others.

'Shut up, will you? Are we here to do the poor fellow a good turn or to make fun of him? Halil Agha, don't be afraid.' Shirtless was standing over him now. 'Nobody wants to kill you. You're all wrong about these villagers. Come.'

Suddenly Old Halil found himself swooped up and deposited like a bundle on the threshold of the house. There he remained, quite still, crouching in the snow, waiting for the crowd to set upon him, to strike him. One blow at least . . . But he knew now that they would not touch a hair of his head. Still he waited. A last glimmer of hope . . .

Shirtless tugged him to his feet.

'There now! You see, Uncle Halil? The whole village is here, and they haven't touched you. Nobody will, as long as I'm alive. Ahmet, my child,' he called, 'come and kiss your Uncle Halil's hand.'

The lad ran up.

'You too, Hadji. Kiss your father's hand.'

Soon there was a long line of smiling villagers waiting to kiss Old Halil's hand.

'All right,' Shirtless said at last. 'Halil Agha's our respected grandfather and the elder of this village, but that's enough now or he'll catch his death of cold. The rest of you come back and kiss his hand tomorrow.'

He swept the old man up in his arms again and carried him indoors.

'There, Uncle Halil!' he said, setting him down by the fire. 'You're the beloved grandfather of the whole village. May Allah never take you away from us.'

The crowd broke up.

Old Halil was burning with shame. Hadji brought him a large bowl of warmly fragrant soup. He pushed it away.

'Take your soup and leave me alone, snivelling Hadji. If I were you I'd never waste this warm good soup on Old Halil. Because I'll have you know Old Halil's your sworn enemy. It's his fault you were late for the cotton. It's his fault Adil Effendi's hanging over you all like the Angel of Death. Yes, my son, no one else's. Ah, there's no blood left in this village! Kissing the hand of the man who's brought all this upon them! You're not worth a decent Moslem burial, not one of you.'

He stalked off to the grain crib and crept under the blanket. There was an aching void in him. He had not wept for years, but now he wanted to throw himself out of the house, to stand in the snow and howl his heart out.

Outside the storm was wild again. Shrill whistlings came from the frozen steppe, which surged like a violent sea.

God forbid that any human creature should be caught out in this weather! Why, a man would freeze to stone in no time! And what of the wolves, the foxes, the bears? And the birds? The eagles in their eyries on the high mountains?

'Oh, almighty Allah!' he sighed. 'They're your very own creatures, the sweat of your brow, the light of your eyes. Safeguard them against this hard cruel winter.'

The bright-eyed martens, the weasels, the deer and wild goats. He conjured up every minute detail of their separate lives, how they gave birth and fed their young and foraged and how they must be running now, hither and thither, frantic under the driving blizzard. Till nightfall he lay there, casting about in vain for something to cling to. Nothing could fill the emptiness in him. They had not killed him, they had not even struck him. He was alone, despised, the laughing-stock of all.

Suddenly, he sat up, galvanized by the horribly insinuating idea that had come to him. He laughed exultantly.

Fatma was calling to him. 'Father! Come and eat. I've cooked you up such a soup as you've never tasted before! *Tarhana*, with lots of butter and mint and red pepper.'

He clambered out and patted his daughter-in-law's head.

'Bless you, my daughter,' he exclaimed as he drank up the soup eagerly. 'I've never eaten anything so good.'

It was nearly midnight, but he was still awake in the grain crib, listening. Let them all be sound asleep and then he'd show them. They'd see what kind of man Old Halil was!

He waited until the first roosters of the false dawn had crowed and then he tiptoed out of the grain crib. He had an ancient shepherd's cloak that he loved and never allowed anyone to touch. His felt-lined boots were ready behind the door. In a trice he was dressed, a bundle of bread and cheese tied to his waist, a store of matches in his pocket, his stick in his hand, and out he went, reeling under the buffeting blizzard.

'Hehey!' he cried as he plunged forward. 'Old Halil's survived many a worse storm, eh, my beauty?'

He resolved to keep going south, always south. The blizzard would batter itself out against the shepherd's cloak, it was perfectly windproof. When the last houses were behind him and the mad winds were flailing at him on all sides, the first doubt flashed through his mind. He chased it away. Think of the villagers' surprise in the morning! No Old Halil?!! Where could he have gone to on this night of devils? Not out to his death in this blizzard, surely? Or could it be that he had been lifted bodily into the sky?

'Who cares!' he shouted out loud. 'Even if you don't make it, you're well out of that village, Old Halil. Let the whole wide sky crumble down on the earth in snow and blizzard. Who cares!'

He struggled forward blindly, the biting snow working its way down his nape. Then he realized that for some time he had been walking back in the direction of the village. Old Halil lose his bearings! Never! But he had to find the Mortar Stone or he would never be able to make his way through the Long Valley. Soon he was going downhill, and suddenly he came upon a quiet spot, sheltered from the blizzard. He breathed with relief, there must be plenty of places like this where I can rest. He sat down on the snow.

Far down below is the Long Valley. It was there they had found Young Veli last spring, huddled up under the thawing snow, smiling as though in his sleep. You felt like giving him a nudge to rouse him. There is no counting those who have gone to their death in the Long Valley. The lost caravan . . . That was long ago. Just that one star in the sky to guide them, and they followed it all the time, and the morning never came. In the spring, as the snows melted, they emerged, horses, mules, donkeys and men, intact, as though making ready to set out on a fresh journey.

He rose slowly, reluctant to face the blizzard again. But his hands and feet were beginning to freeze. I must go on, he thought, or I'm finished. The Mortar Stone can't be far now. If I keep this pace up, I may be out of the Long Valley by morning.

It was when he found himself nailed to the spot, drowning in a stormy sea of snow, gasping for breath, that he knew he had missed the Mortar Stone and had reached the very bottom of the

Long Valley, the place of no return, of death. It's this fear that'll kill me, he told himself, not the storm, not the cold! Death was difficult. Death was the greatest void. He felt it in the marrow of his bones, and the fear of it drove him on. The forest, that was his only hope now. Which way did it lie? He could not think. A warm drowsiness was creeping over him, pleasant, irresistible, the surest way to death, he knew it. But he must sleep. His body felt light at the thought of sleep. Then the ground was no longer under his feet. He had fallen into a crevasse. He struck the ice and the pain shooting up his right arm jolted him out of his numbness.

'Help! My arm's broken. This will be the end of me,' he cried.

But he got up and rushed on, wide awake now. For the first time he really felt the elemental fury of the blizzard. He wrapped himself up more tightly in his cloak.

Chapter 4

'Ah, Sefer Agha, these dreams will be the death of me. I'm afraid to sleep. I'm afraid to go to bed. And it's getting worse every day.'

Zaladja Woman was pleading with the Muhtar again, begging him to interpret her dreams.

'A cloud, Sefer Agha, blacker than any thundercloud, is after me and I'm running like the wind on the Chukurova plain. And then crack, the earth splits open and horses come galloping out with flying manes and tails. I cry to them to stop, but they rush by, heedless. Then I grab a horse's mane just as it springs out of the earth. Swiftly, the horse carries me away from the angry cloud. But suddenly, instead of a horse, I'm riding a poor scraggy greyhound and then it throws me down and I'm all alone on the flat empty plain, and that furious black cloud is upon me, coming lower and lower, pressing me to the ground, stifling me in its swirling blackness. Now tell me what it all means, Sefer Agha. And here's some butter I saved for you and two dozen eggs.'

'Is that all you dreamed?' the Muhtar asked, surprised.

'Of course not. But explain this one first.'

'A black cloud,' Sefer began, 'is always a sign of evil, and the black cloud in your dream is clearly Adil Effendi. The horses fleeing at his approach are the poor harassed villagers. The thin greyhound is a sign that their welfare hangs on a thread just as thin. The blackness that stifles you is a sign of the black evil night that will rain stones on us, that will devastate this village, if people go on listening to that Tashbash and his friend, Long Ali . . .'

It was noon by the time Zaladja Woman had exhausted her store of dreams. She left in a highly exalted state.

28

'It's coming!' she cried to the first person she met. 'The black cloud, coming to destroy the village.'

'Are you mad, Zaladja?'

'Go and ask the Muhtar. A black cloud . . .'

A group of women pressed around her, laughing.

'What have you been dreaming about this time, Zaladja?' one of them jeered. 'Another male deer going to bed with you and turning into a handsome young man?'

Zaladja was incensed. 'Laugh away, laugh away, you bitches. It's Adil Effendi who's coming. He's the black cloud! Let me see you laugh after he's taken away the last of your food and blankets and rugs.'

The women laughed again, but uneasily this time, for every one of them feared Adil Effendi.

It was all over the village in an instant. Adil Effendi was coming, descending upon the village like a thundercloud. Nobody asked where the news came from. Zaladja's dream was forgotten. The group of women swelled, but they were silent now, gazing out at the wintry steppe. The men had begun to gather before the Muhtar's house. They stood about, grim and apprehensive, not uttering a word. Then one of the women caught sight of Old Meryemdje, barefoot on the frozen snow, heading for the Muhtar's house. Soon all the women were following her, muttering among themselves.

'Have you heard? Old Halil disappeared last night!'

'He's gone to Mount Tekech to die. He said so.'

'No, it's because he was afraid.'

'He knew Adil Effendi was coming. That's why he ran away!'

'He couldn't bear to see what Adil was going to do to us.'

'Allah!' an old woman cried. 'Take our lives before we see that day!'

At last the Muhtar appeared at his door. Ever since it had become clear that the villagers would be unable to settle their debts that year, he had felt thoroughly disgraced. That out of the hundred and sixty-odd villages in these parts, his should be the only one to break the age-old custom! How could he ever hold his head up in the town again? He, the son of the famed Hidir, Headman of seven villages! Adil Effendi would come any day now to claim his due. As a mighty eagle swoops down on a covey of pigeons, scattering them in a flutter of flying feathers, so Adil Effendi would swoop down on Yalak village. And then there was no knowing what these villagers might do. A hungry villager can turn into a rabid dog. They might well tear Adil to pieces, and the armed policemen with him as well.

Then an idea struck him like lightning.

'Are the members of the Village Council here?' he called out. 'We're going to hold a very important meeting.'

They were all there, waiting expectantly.

'A great evil is threatening us,' the Muhtar began. 'It's the second time that this village has come to such a pass. There are some of you who will remember. It was during the Chukurova drought, twenty-five years ago. Not only was the cotton crop scorched black, but even grass didn't grow that year. We all went down for the cotton picking just as usual, and what did we see! Parched, lifeless fields, not a green plant anywhere, so we came back home empty-handed. Adil Effendi was young then. Everyone was up to their ears in debt to him, just like today, and one morning he came to the village with twenty policemen and a Government official. Do you owe this man anything, they asked us. Yes, we do, we replied. To deny one's debt is to deny Allah, we said. Well then, they said, Adil Effendi is going to seize your belongings as payment. Let him, we said, it's his due. Those of you who were there will never forget what happened then. Adil Effendi took away everything, our grain, our flour, our *bulgur*, our chickens, our goats and donkeys and cows, whatever he could lay his hands on. And he did something else. He took the drawers of Bald Mustafa's wife right off her legs! You may forget everything, he said, but you won't forget this, and it'll teach you to be more careful about your debts in the future. So, that winter we went hungry. We ate pinenuts and berries off the trees. We devoured the green wheat before the ears had even ripened. A great number of children died that year, Mad Mustan lost three of his children. He wanted to go and kill Adil Effendi, but we held him back. What are you doing, Mustan, we said. If you kill him, who will give us credit, who will sell us food? We'll all go naked without him. So Mustan did not kill Adil after all, and Allah gave him another three children. Now Adil Effendi's coming again, he'll pick the village clean and this time we shall all die of hunger. What's worse, we shall be shamed for ever. I've called this meeting to decide what we're to do. Has anybody got any ideas?'

'Let's get out of here,' an old man suggested promptly. 'Adil will find the village empty and he'll think we never returned from the Chukurova.'

The veins on the Muhtar's neck began to swell.

'And where would we go in the dead of winter?' he shouted. 'And doesn't Adil know we came back? What d'you think he'll do when he finds the village empty? He'll set a torch to it, that's what he'll do.'

'But what else can we do?'

'So that's all the help you can give me!' the Muhtar sneered. 'I thought our villagers were clever. Well then, since you can't think of anything, open your ears and listen to me. And mind you do just what I tell you. If you don't then don't blame me afterwards. And I'll have you know it's Mother Meryemdje herself who came to me early this morning and gave me this idea.'

Everyone stared at Meryemdje. She started up on hearing her name then angrily struck her stick twice on the ground.

'Yes indeed,' pursued the Muhtar slyly. 'Mother Meryemdje, the wisest, the most valiant of mothers. She said to me, Muhtar, my son, Allah has sent you among us as a saint. Give the village my message.'

Meryemdje flailed her stick furiously, but the Muhtar knew she would sooner die than break her vow of silence.

'I want you to go to your homes and hide your barley and wheat, your horses and donkeys, your cows and oxen, your butter and *bulgur*, all your belongings of any worth. Where? Don't ask me! Everyone must find a good hiding-place, I'll do the same, so that when Adil Effendi comes he'll see a village so bare, so miserable, that he'll take pity and go away. Now, are we all agreed?'

The thin anxious faces seemed to come to life. There was a shuffling of bare feet on the frozen snow.

'Well? What are you waiting for?' the Muhtar said. 'I, for one, I'm going off right now to hide my things.'

He turned and went inside, barely avoiding the stick which Meryemdje suddenly hurled at him in a paroxysm of anger.

Chapter 5

A wave of joy swept over the village. Nobody had ever played such a trick on Adil Effendi before. Had they been asked to hide the whole village, houses, trees and all, they would have found a way of spiriting it out of sight. Meryemdje hurried home like the rest and went straight to the worm-eaten chest which half a century ago had held her trousseau. She had just begun to empty its contents into her lap when Ali noticed her.

'Mother!' he laughed. 'Nobody's going to touch those baubles of yours! What they'll look for are things that are worth money, like livestock and grain. So put all that away and don't worry.'

Meryemdje gave him a withering glance and turned back to her chest.

Her most precious possession was an inlaid silver ring, a present from her husband Ibrahim. It was inscribed with the word of the Prophet. Ibrahim and Old Halil had stolen it from the Circassians, but even so it was a holy ring and would bring abundance and good luck to its owner. Now, wouldn't Adil seize upon such a ring? Silver too. Of course he would. It had to be hidden away. And here was the silver nose-ring her grandmother had given her, which she had been given by her own grandmother. Wouldn't Adil want this priceless heirloom? Was Adil a fool?

Two silk kerchiefs, one orange and the other green. Good enough for Adil Effendi's daughters-in-law. Why shouldn't he take them? If Adil were such a fool, he wouldn't be so rich.

A gleaming bead necklace, three glass bracelets, one yellow like solid gold, one green, and one flaming red, a perfectly good dress she'd only worn a couple of times when she was a young married woman . . . Adil might well want it for his wife.

This needle container of carved pinewood, with three needles in it too! A few coloured lengths of cloth, a printed kerchief, five blue good-luck beads on a string . . .

The inside of the chest smelled of wild apple.

She cast a wary glance at the others. They were not looking at her. Quickly, she snatched up from a corner of the chest a small oilcloth package and thrust it into her bosom. Tightly folded in it, like an amulet, was the sum of ten liras, Meryemdje's shroud money. She closed the chest and tied up her treasures in an old cloth. Now, where to hide the bundle? Her eyes probed the room anxiously. Then she saw it, the ideal hiding-place: a sheet of tin plate nailed under the swallow's nest to keep the droppings off the floor. But she couldn't reach up there. Only Long Ali could do it. She looked at him doubtfully. He was busy digging a hole near the hearth. Elif and the children were helping him. Meryemdje edged up, nearer and nearer, hugging her bundle, until she was right under his nose. He held back the upraised pick-axe in the nick of time.

'Mother!' he shouted. 'What on earth are you doing? I might have hit you.'

Meryemdje looked from him to the bundle, but Ali only stared back. She saw that she must swallow her pride. Taking him by the arm, she led him to the swallow's nest and pointed to her bundle. Ali smiled. He picked it up and pushed it out of sight on the tin plate.

'Is that all right, Mother?' he asked.

It was the first time in months that Meryemdje had asked anything of her son. A happy smile flitted across her face. She retired into a corner and took off her dress. She had a needle and thread ready. Quickly, she stitched the oilcloth package on to the inside of the sleeve.

The others had now dug a deep hole. Into it Ali dumped their reserve of *bulgur* and flour, the butter firkin, the pots and the pans. Then he threw in some brushwood and after spreading a goathair mat over everything, he shovelled the earth back and filled the hole.

Now the grain. A pit right under the grain crib, that was it! Nobody would ever think of looking there. Quickly they had

dragged the sacks out, even Old Meryemdje lent a hand, and by
noon the pit was ready. Ali lined it with hay and lowered in the
sacks, over which he piled the bedding, the embroidered sacks
and the *kilims*. Then he put in some more hay and covered the
pit.

Nothing was left unhidden now, except an old pinewood
pitcher, oozing slimily, a large copper pan, a soot-blackened pot,
a couple of wooden spoons, a calabash for drinking, a handful of
salt, enough *bulgur* to last for a few days and an ancient thread-
bare *kilim* on the floor.

Adil could come any time and take these if he felt like it!

But there was still the livestock.

'Elif,' Ali said, 'I'm going to see what the others are doing
about the animals. I'll be back soon.'

Hasan had his problems too. His matches! He had hidden them
in a crack in the wall, but suppose they searched the house? He
tucked the matches under his shirt and went outside. It was
snowing gently. The village was humming like a beehive,
people scurrying to and fro, all of them bent on hiding their
belongings in the best possible place. He stood against a wall,
hugging the matches to his breast. What should he do? There
was not a single person in the whole village in whom he could
confide. Only Ummahan knew his secret. Ummahan?

She was sitting by the ash-covered fire, dozing in the half-
gloom of the house. He touched her shoulder.

'Come outside, sister,' he said, and led her away to a safe
distance. 'I can't think of where to hide my matches,' he whispered. 'Adil Effendi's sure to take them, and anyway if the
villagers see them they'll snap them up.'

'They'll snap them up,' Ummahan echoed. 'Where . . .'

They dropped down on the snow, both thinking hard, not
looking at each other. Suddenly, Ummahan pointed to the big
plane tree on the edge of their yard. 'There!' she said triumphantly.
'There's a big hollow in that trunk.'

Hasan started and stared at the tree.

'I knew that before you,' he bragged lamely at last. 'But that
tree stands out a mile.'

'All the better,' Ummahan said. Her eyes gleamed shrewdly. 'Nobody'll think of looking there.'

'But if anyone sees us . . .'

'Let's wait till it's dark.'

They sat there, snuggling close to each other, and waited impatiently for the night to fall, basking in the excitement of their shared secret.

It was many hours before Ali came back.

'We're taking the animals up to the Peri Caves,' he told Elif. 'There's plenty of space there and each day five men will go and tend them. We'll do it in turns. Come on Elif, bring them out.'

Night was falling now. All the animals had been spirited away. Not a living creature was to be seen save a few dogs and cats. The village seemed to be quite empty. The houses too had been stripped bare. Never had there been such a miserable, destitute village since the beginning of time, nor had the villagers ever been seen in such tattered clothing, not even in the worst years of famine.

The Muhtar and Tashbash were the only ones to have made no change in their attire. Tashbash had not even bothered to hide anything. His house was just as before, and he had not taken his livestock up to the caves. This enraged and puzzled the villagers. The Muhtar egged them on.

'Good for you, my villagers!' he said as he went from house to house. 'It's better to be Muhtar in this village than mayor in Paradise! Let Adil Effendi come now! How poor you are, he'll say. I forgive you your debts. Townsfolk are apt to be rather dense. It'll never cross their minds that we could sweep the village clean in the twinkling of an eye.'

That evening there was rejoicing in every house. At the Muhtar's, the Bald Minstrel put wings to his songs and sent them soaring through the air. Yellow Mustafa made do with a can for a drum as Durduman blew his *zurna* and the young men danced the *halay*. And when Long Ali took up his pipe, even Meryemdje felt like treading a measure or two.

'I've forgiven you,' she wanted to say. 'I've forgiven you, all of you.'

It was past midnight but sleep would not come to Hasan. His mind was on his matches, hidden outside in the tree hollow. Suppose someone had seen him? Suppose Ummahan gave him away? He nudged her fiercely. She woke up with a cry.

'Shhh!' he whispered. 'I've got something to tell you. Wake up.'

'I'm awake all right,' she said crossly. 'What is it now?'

'I'm going to give you one of my matchboxes, your very own. But you won't tell our secret to anyone, will you?'

Ummahan forgot her annoyance. 'No, never!' she cried, pleased.

Hasan leaned close to her ear. 'Let's go out and see if the matches are still there,' he suggested.

They crept out of bed. Ummahan opened the door carefully and they slipped out into the night.

Hasan put his hand into the tree hollow. The matches still rested there, snug and warm. He patted them fondly.

'I want to touch them too,' Ummahan said.

'What for?' he said. 'They're there all right.'

'I only want to see how they're there.'

'Well, all right, look then,' he said grudgingly, not too pleased by Ummahan's sudden possessiveness. 'But be quick.'

As soon as she had taken her hand out, he thrust his own in again, holding it over the matches a long time.

They did not sleep till morning.

Chapter 6

Like a shadow Hüsneh glided along the wall to where Rejep was waiting. In the snow-lit darkness the two bodies found each other and locked in a crushing embrace. A sharp icy wind was blowing from the steppe, but they did not feel the wind, nor the frozen snow burning their bare feet, nor the salty taste of blood on their lips. Then he drew her in to Squinty Hassan's deserted hut. A draught of warm air struck them as they opened the door. Rejep had lit a huge fire and its reddish glow filled the hut.

Hüsneh took off her clothes at once and piled them by the hearth. She was smiling. Her dark-skinned body gleamed like copper in the light of the flames. There was not so much as a wrinkle on the smooth skin of her curving thighs. Her hands over her breasts, her belly tight and quivering with desire, she stood there in the glow of the fire, leaning slightly over the hearth, her right foot tracing vague designs in the ashes. Rejep gazed at her, not moving, a slight smile on his lips, a happiness filled him, a casting-away of a heavy load, he knew not what. As he looked and still made no move, she sank down by the hearth, trembling all over, her dark eyes opened wide in entreaty. Her hair was plaited into two thick braids that fell over her copper-coloured shoulders. He gazed on, letting the sensuous beauty of her body seep into him, and as his eyes devoured her, her trembling increased.

The big fire had warmed up the empty hut as on a balmy summer evening.

It had all started one night down in the Chukurova plain. They had not even felt themselves sinking into the warm soft soil of the cotton field. Afterwards, they had washed in the brook near-by and there they had begun all over again. The whole village knew of their madness.

Suddenly, with a swift motion Rejep tore off his clothes and threw himself upon Hüsneh. He smothered her with kisses. Her neck, her ears, her round shoulders under the thick braids, her smooth thighs he kissed and bit until her trembling ceased and she lay there almost in a faint, yet drawing him to her. And now the strength of their passion was such that it seemed to pass on to the fire burning in the hearth and to the dirt floor wet with their sweat. The fire was burning now in unison with their passion and the earth panted beneath them. His blood flowed into hers and hers into his. The two bodies were one now, merged into each other, never to come apart till death, never, for all eternity. And when they came apart their bodies were weightless. The faintest breeze could whiff them up like a white dove feather and waft them high and away.

It was nearly dawn when they put on their clothes again. As always Hüsneh could not bring herself to look at Rejep for it seemed to her that if she did, all the flavour, all the magic would be lost. She sat down by the hearth and fixed her eyes on the flames. Her long lashes shadowed her cheeks, her face was moist and pink, her lips ruby-red.

Rejep could not take his eyes off her. It had been so ever since they were children together. He had always been lost in worship before Hüsneh. He wanted to say something, something that would please her, but what? How? His heart tightened.

'This year,' he said at last, 'after the cotton picking . . . we'll run away. Down in the Chukurova plain . . .'

Hüsneh smiled slightly, but said nothing.

'Things will be better there for us. If you wish, we won't come back ever. I'll learn how to work a tractor. They give lots of money to tractor-drivers down there. Hamit, the foreman, said he could make a driver of me in a couple of years. But we can't go now, in the dead of winter. We'd freeze and die on the way. Why, even the wolves wouldn't stir out of their lair in this cold. We'd never make it across the Taurus mountains and reach the Chukurova safe and sound. Just let's wait till the warm spring days are here again.'

Her eyes on the smouldering fire, that faint smile on her lips, soft and still, as though she weren't there at all.

He rose, smiling too, picked up a few sticks and threw them into the fire, which flared with a wet pungent smell. Then he went and sat beside Hüsneh and gave her a kiss behind the ear. Something warm rose inside her. The spell wove itself, denser, tighter, drawing her ever more strongly towards a paradise of bliss.

'Tomorrow Adil Effendi will come,' he went on, 'with fifty policemen at his heels. He'll search the village from top to bottom and won't find a stick. He'll go away furious and he'll never give us credit again. But who cares! He's not the only shopkeeper in these parts! How the villagers hid everything away today! Only I had nothing to hide. I looked and looked and found nothing, not a pin. That cut me to the quick. I'd never felt being poor so hard. No, we won't come back from the Chukurova next winter. I'll work on a tractor. I'll buy a bed and blankets, and one of those trunks with an inlaid mirror, and a radio . . . and . . . and when whoever is Adil Effendi in those parts comes to raid the village we'll have something to hide like everyone else, won't we?'

A warm translucent creek. Under the lofty plane-tree the water ripples gently over gleaming white pebbles . . . Hüsneh felt herself melting, blending into its peaceful radiant flow.

'In the Chukurova there are big gardens. The trees are heavy with golden oranges. One night we'll sleep in one of those gardens, won't we?'

Her moist rosy face, her eyes on the blazing fire, that rapturous smile . . .

'Perhaps we won't wait till it's cotton time. As soon as the warm spring days are here again, on the day of the spring feast of Hidirellez, we'll take to the road. When the world is green and fresh and in flower.'

His hand went to hers and pressed it. Her eyes still on the fire, she slipped her warm hand under his shirt, laying it over his heart.

'Just wait till the warm spring days are here again,' he repeated.

Hüsneh spoke at last, as in a dream. 'The warm spring days . . .'
There was a sharp irrepressible longing in her voice.

The morning cocks began to crow. She rose, her eyes on the
ground.

Hand in hand they went out.

'Just wait till the warm spring days are here, just wait.'

Chapter 7

The morning was sunny and bright, the sky cloudless, perfectly blue. Not the faintest breeze stirred the air. The boundless stretches of snow sparkled and flashed under the sun as though an immense flood of light flowed over the steppe.

All over the village, in front of the houses, small groups had gathered here and there. The conversation centred on Adil Effendi. They could talk of nothing else. He would soon turn up, they had not the slightest doubt about it. Had somebody brought news from the town? Had Adil Effendi sent word he would be there on such a day at such a time? Not at all. But still they knew, and kept re-enacting the scene of his arrival. Their eyes had the cunning gleam of satisfaction at having outwitted the enemy.

'When Adil Effendi comes . . . Oh, you poor Yalak villagers, he'll say, I should have collected alms for you from the towns-people. I've seen misery in my time but never anything like this. I'm ashamed to ask you to pay up. That's what he'll say.'

'So you've forsworn the old tradition and denied your debt, he'll say. That's nothing! When a man's so poor and his home so bare, he'd forswear not only tradition but his very faith.'

'That's exactly what Adil'll say!'

'And then d'you know what he'll say? Come to me, he'll say, you wretched, luckless people, and I'll remedy all your mis-fortunes.'

'No man's without a heart. And even if Adil's heart is made of stone, it will melt at the sight of us.'

A group of villagers straggled out beyond the houses to the south, where the road to the town lay deep under the snow. There they stood, watching out for the traveller who would be coming up the valley. Meryemdje was among them. She sat on a mound, her neck craning forward, a statue of expectation.

Tashbash was waiting too. He was curious to see how all this would end. Would Adil ever believe the spurious evidence of those empty homes? Adil was not born yesterday, he wasn't one to let anybody throw dust into his eyes. He'd know what was what the minute he entered the place. These villagers! How could they be so stupid! Just playing a game, that's what they were doing. A whole village playing a childish game and deceiving themselves. And what if Adil did believe them? They'd never get a stick of credit again.

All through the morning they waited, laughing and chattering, their hopes high. But in the afternoon boredom set in. Their happiness wore off and one by one they dispersed to their homes. Only Meryemdje remained on the edge of the road, her neck still stretched towards the valley. When the sun was gone and it was too dark to see any more, she got up and made her way back, leaning heavily on her stick.

'Now, why didn't he come today this Adil Effendi?' she mused. Then she smiled. 'And why should he? Just because we hid our things today, that doesn't mean . . . Maybe he'll come tomorrow.'

Meryemdje had enjoyed the day's suspense.

That night the villagers slept peacefully.

The next morning they awoke convinced that this was the day. A group of women, Meryemdje at the head of them, made their way to the edge of the village and kept up a watch on the road that led to the town. Again, when evening came, Meryemdje was left there alone, waiting.

'It's only because we expected him today that . . .' she muttered to herself. 'He'll come tomorrow.'

That night also they slept peacefully.

The next morning it was bright and sunny. The sky was cloudless and blue. With a few children and some old women Meryemdje hobbled out of the village and again took up her position on the roadside.

Chapter 8

Ever since the livestock had been stowed away up in the Peri Caves, a strange loneliness had settled over the village. The houses were never warm now, their emptiness was frightening. It was no longer a village, but a desolate place, like a lone mountain top or a dark forest.

Meryemdje loved their little calf and missed it more than she could say, but she could not bring herself to stray too far from her treasured belongings hidden under the swallow's nest over their door.

'If only that accursed man would come and get it over with,' she kept saying to herself.

That morning she left the house as usual, but instead of taking up her watch on the roadside she turned her steps towards the forest. Hasan and the other children tagged after her, and several women thinking something was afoot, followed. They crossed the forest and reached the Peri Caves where a group of villagers was tending the cows and stacking hay and clover.

'Where's our stock?' she intimated by a sign.

A young woman who was milking a cow pointed out a cave to her.

Inside it was warm, with the long-forgotten smell of May in the air. The calf was lying on a bed of clover in a corner, beautiful to her even in the dim light of the cave. She held its head fondly and kissed it on the eyes. The calf leapt to its feet. If Meryemdje had not been bound by her vow not to utter a word again to any living creature in the village, she would have soothed the little calf with loving words. Then she thought: these caves aren't part of the village. They belong to our great Allah. She could address the cave, where the fairies had their abode. Who knows but that

Spellbound Ahmet's fairy wife might be hovering near her this very moment.

'Cave, cave,' she said aloud, 'I'm speaking to you and not to my purplish calf. You're my great Allah's cave, a gift to the fairies here below. You know how much I've missed my dear calf. God forbid he should ever be taken away from us. I think he's missed us too, isn't that so, cave? I'm telling you, cave, let that fellow come and be done with it. Then I can take my calf straight back home.'

She kissed the calf again. 'Keep well, cave,' she said. 'And look after my calf. I must go now. That man might have come.'

When she went out she saw that most of the women of the village were there.

'Everyone's got a purplish calf they love,' she mused. 'And to think those women are mortally afraid of the Peri Caves. And not only the women, but the men too are scared of coming here.'

She started back, the children trailing after her again. With her stick she motioned to the women to get going, but they were engrossed in their goats and cows and paid no attention to her. She was piqued.

'Don't come then,' she muttered. 'Inshallah, Adil will be there and you'll miss everything. Inshallah . . .'

The children skipped about her twittering like birds. 'The best of a human being is in his childhood. May you grow well, my little ones, may you have long lives, my own white doves.' She wanted to say this aloud, but that accursed vow sealed her lips. Whatever had possessed her to do such a thing! What if they had held a funeral ceremony for Old Halil? As if it mattered to her! But now he had vanished again. Maybe he was lying dead, buried under the cold snow. Oh no, Old Halil was not one to die! Just wait and see how he'd pop out from under the snow at the time of the spring thaw, alive as you and me. . .

The village was just as they had left it. No one had come. As she walked home she was accosted by the Muhtar.

'Listen to me, Mother Meryemdje. I'm telling this to you because for me you're more than my own mother. There's a foul-mouthed traitor in this village, a villain who's given us away to

45

Adil Effendi. Has anyone seen Tashbash these past four days? Why didn't he hide his belongings like the rest of us? Even I did, I the Muhtar of this huge village, the son of the famous Headman Hidir? Think what a disgrace it is to have my house bare like this! But I did it for my villagers. What's good for my villagers, I said, is good enough for me! That's what I said. And indeed, I hid everything away, even the gold-plated dagger of my father Hidir. But Tashbash never hid so much as a rag. Why? Now can you wonder that Adil hasn't come yet?'

Meryemdje shook her head doubtfully. Would Tashbash ever do such a thing?

It was soon all over the village. But people hesitated. If such a rumour had been spread about the Muhtar or that crazy Shirtless, or Batty Bekir, they would have believed it. But Tashbash? Now, that was quite another matter.

And so the Muhtar's attempt to stir up the villagers' resentment against Tashbash came to nothing.

A couple of days later he learnt that the plot of the Yalak villagers was an open secret bandied about in all the neighbouring villages and even in the town. He was not surprised. He knew that nothing could be concealed for very long in these villages. But he felt ashamed and blamed himself. The village was dishonoured, and he as their Muhtar would never be able to show his face in the town again. He'd be the laughing-stock of the whole country. It wasn't as if the townspeople themselves did not cheat the tax-collector, and in the villages, when it was time to assess the livestock, was there a single man who did not hide away at least part of his animals? But this they did against the Government and not Adil Effendi who helped them with credit and loans in times of need. No, there was no doubt that Adil Effendi had got wind of everything. He knew, and he had probably spat in disgust. 'Ah, man is just an animal,' he must have said. 'I've done so much for these people all these years and this is how they reward me!'

As for the villagers they seemed to have been driven mad with waiting. The women did no cooking, the men hardly bothered to tend the livestock, the children stopped playing. Nobody did any work. The village was dead. Young and old, from seven to seventy, everyone hung around in a sullen silence, watching the town road. A strange feeling of shame had succeeded the malicious joy of having hoodwinked Adil Effendi. His absence weighed over the village like a gloomy pall turning the wait into an intolerable outrage.

Even Hasan was worried to death. He kept a nightly vigil over his matches in the tree hollow. One night his father caught him sneaking out of the house with Ummahan.

'What are you up to in the dead of night?' Long Ali asked. But he could get nothing out of them. The two children just stood there, struck dumb.

'Well, do as you wish, you little pests,' he shouted at last. 'Go out and see if I care if you catch your death like Old Halil!'

After this, Hasan resolved to carry the matches back inside to their old hiding-place. But he was uneasy. At night, he would take them to bed with him and in the day if he left the house he would tuck them into the sash of his shalvar-trousers, where they bulged conspicuously.

'If only that man would come,' he sighed. 'I wish he'd come and be done with it.'

The same words were on everyone's lips.

The Muhtar was disgusted. He felt he had to do something before people began to get out of hand. One morning he rose with the sun and dressed in his best coat and town trousers. He shaved carefully and put on a necktie. Then he summoned the watchman.

'Watchman,' he said when the man was standing at attention before him, 'you're the best watchman this side of the Taurus mountains. I'll chop off this head of mine if there's a better man than you. Now, I want you to call out a proclamation to the village. Make it so urgent that everyone'll come flocking to my door, young and old, down to the last man, to find out what I have to say. D'you understand?'

The watchman rapped out a salute like a soldier, faced about expertly and made off at a run. He had a beautiful voice, as warm and powerful as the Bald Minstrel's. It was not long before the

Muhtar's front yard filled up. Everyone was there, even Tashbash. They held their breaths as though a stifling dust-storm was upon them. But the sky was clear, the sunlight fell brightly over the spotless snow, washing the whole world clean, even down to the rags they wore.

When the Muhtar appeared, he was assailed on all sides.

'Speak, Muhtar!'

'What is it?'

'Tell us quickly.'

Meryemdje stood in front right under the Muhtar's nose, staring at him as if she would eat the words that came out of his mouth.

He squared his shoulders and stroked his chin like the Hodja of Karatopak. Then he coughed twice and cleared his throat importantly.

'And truly, my friends and neighbours . . . And truly, my soul's companions, my brother comrades . . .' he spoke out in sonorous tones, 'this is a bad time for us.'

'Terrible,' they cried.

'We hid away our belongings, and that was bravely done. Not all the policemen of the Turkish Republic, nor even the holy divining hodjas could have discovered them. I am justly proud of you. But something went wrong. The news of your heroic deed has spread abroad and reached Adil Effendi's ears. That's why he hasn't come! We've waited in vain. And truly, we cannot wait any longer. One more day and we'll burst.'

'We'll burst,' they cried.

'We'll burst and do some madness. Yes, we've had enough. Enough! By hook or by crook we must find a way to make Adil come. We can't live with this blot on our honour. Such a disgrace is unworthy of the noble race of the Turk.'

He had worked himself up into his best speech-making form, but he checked himself. It would not do to exhaust the villagers' patience.

'So listen to me now and pay attention. Go straight back to your homes. No one ever hid anything in this village. All our belongings must be out in the open by tomorrow. Anyway, we're sick of shivering in empty houses. Even today the news will reach Adil Effendi. Yes, my friends, there's a foul-mouthed squealer among us, an enemy, who'll carry the news to Adil like the wind. And if he doesn't this time, because he wishes us ill, then I'll send three members of the Village Council to town to fetch Adil. You can go now and godspeed to you.'

Chapter 9

Meryemdje was not pleased with the turn of events. Muttering imprecations against the Muhtar, the villagers, the whole of creation, she made for home post-haste and planted herself under the swallow's nest. She was bursting with impatience, as if Adil Effendi would turn up this minute, ask for Long Ali's house, discover the hiding-place and seize Meryemdje's things. Then Hasan came in. She beckoned to him anxiously.

'Ah,' Hasan said regretfully, 'if I were just a little bit taller I could reach up there. If I were only two years older. Now, when Father comes . . .'

Meryemdje grunted. Then she pointed to a large log in a corner. They hurried to it and each grasped one end, but try as they would they could not move it.

'Let's roll it,' Hasan suggested.

Ali and Elif found them still struggling with the log.

Ali laughed. 'What are you going to do with that log?' he said. 'You want your bundle, Mother? Just a second.'

He stood on tiptoe and reached for the bundle. Meryemdje let go of the log to which she had been clinging tenaciously and clasped the bundle like a mother her long-lost child. She sat down on the threshold and took out the old dress of her youthful days, slipped it over the one she was wearing, then fastened on the earrings and put on the bead necklace, the bracelets and the ring inscribed with the words of the Prophet. The two silk kerchiefs, orange and green, she tied over her white one. Thus attired she sallied forth into the village.

'Mother Meryemdje's going to be a bride again!' people chaffed her.

Ah, if only Meryemdje hadn't sworn not to speak to them. She'd give them a piece of her mind!

'Elif,' Ali said thoughtfully to his wife, 'one never knows what may happen. We'd better leave some of the grain hidden in the pit. As for the butter, let's not take it out at all.'

It was the same all over the village. Without consulting each other people seemed to have come to a mutual understanding. They brought out a few odds and ends, but left their more valuable belongings buried in the ground, firmly convincing themselves that they had nothing to hide. As for the livestock in the Peri Caves, most people had got used to that. It was a very good place and there they would remain from now on. It wasn't as if they were buried and hidden away.

And so they settled down to await Adil once more, this time with heads held high and conscience at peace.

For the Bald Minstrel this was the day. The mood came upon him once or twice a year. Then he would adorn the neck of his *saz* with three tassels, one blue, one yellow, and one red, in place of the ordinary single white tassel. When the villagers saw the three tassels that evening they began to flow to the Bald Minstrel's house. They knew this would be one of his special, joy-ridden days when he would regale them with unheard songs and legends and stories never told before.

It was a night of white frost. The stars, cold and far apart, were buried deep in their frozen glitter. The full moon streamed over the houses, the lonely trees and the hurrying villagers, casting long shadows over the white snow.

'Throw more wood into the fire,' the Bald Minstrel ordered. 'More, more! Let the flames flare up, let the fire go mad.'

This was one of his needs. Summer or winter, he could not sing his best without a roaring fire at his side.

They heaped logs into the hearth.

The Bald Minstrel laid his *saz* across his knees and sat on in a trance, eyes closed, erect and silent. This was not an act. He could have deceived them once, twice, but not for ever.

Gently he took up his *saz*, touched a chord, once, and started playing, rapt, timeless. Suddenly he broke off.

'Today,' he said, 'you shall draw a moral from my tale.' His eyes swept the crowd. 'Hehey, tufted cranes!'

'Hehey, tufted cranes!' they responded with one voice.

'In the name of our father-bards, Karadjaoglan, Pir Sultan, Dadaloglu, hehey, tufted cranes! Today, in the name of the Kurdish bard Abdal-é-Zeyniki, hehey storm-tossed mountain peaks!'

He struck another chord, once.

'Abdal-é-Zeyniki was valiant among men, a great bard, but blind in both eyes. He was not like other minstrels. As a running water never tires of flowing, never stays in its course, so it was with Abdal. He sang on the road, in the city, in the plain, in the forest, everywhere. And if there was no one to sing to, he would sing for the birds and beasts and flowers, for all the living things of creation. A single one of his songs lasted forty nights. He sang in Kurdish, but the Turk, the Arab, the Persian, the Russian, the Englishman, all were able to understand every word. This was a mystery that no man could understand. He would take up his *saz* each evening at the close of day and lay it aside when the sun showed its tip over the mountains. He burned for a love he had never seen nor ever touched, and before starting his song he would always sing one song dedicated to her. At midnight, he would stop and sing to his love again, and then once more at break of day. And thus he would end the night. Hehey, tufted cranes!'

'Hehey, lonely cranes,' came the crowd's response. 'And hehey snowy mountains.'

The Bald Minstrel bent over his *saz*.

This is Abdal-é-Zeyniki treading his way on the flat deserted road, Abdal the wandering bard of the lofty mountains, the wide plains, of birds and beasts, and of men, good and wicked. A black heavy night weighs upon him. He walks groping at his night, clinging to his night. He is blind, he cannot see his path. He is aged, alone in a desolate world where no creature but he breathes or moves. On and on he walks. In one hand he carries his night, in the other a knife with a luminous point, and as he walks he cleaves the night in two. Suddenly his foot trips against something alive, warm, soft. A bird. But why does it not fly away? He picks it up and holds it to his breast until he comes to a village. What bird is this? asks Abdal. What is wrong with it? It's a crane, they tell him. The tip of one of its wings has been torn off. It will never fly again.

This world is full to the brim. If I had my eyes I would blow the flowers open and stir the waves of the sea. I would make the clouds rain, burnish the stars and rouse the sun in the east. I would put fresh wings on insects and colour them bright. I would build nests for the birds of the air and feed their young. But a dark heavy night bows me down. I must fulfil my lot in darkness.

This crane, if it could fly, would soar over deep seas and high above big cities. It would travel with other cranes in the wake of spring from land to land and never know hot summer or winter hoar, and its feathers would ever bear the scent of spring. Now, perhaps for the first time, it will see the winter, it will know snow and cold.

This bird's fate and mine are one.

So Abdal takes the wounded bird and retires into the mountains. It is the last of autumn. Winter is setting in. Overhead, shrill-screeching flights of cranes pass by, heading for the land of spring.

Abdal sets the crane before him and with the sunset he takes up his *saz*. But now he does not sing to his love. He sings only for the crane, sings to it of men, of high mountains, of the mother earth, of flowing waters, of the ant on the ground, the fish in the sea, the stars in the sky. For days, for months on end he sings, sings tirelessly, and the crane is always there, listening.

It is dawn. The sun is about to rise. Abdal knows it in his bones and he ends his song. Suddenly a great light bursts before his eyes. The brilliance is too much for him. He throws himself face down on the ground, unable to bear the shattering of his long-accustomed darkness. He crouches there, eyes closed, senseless with terror. When he dares to raise his head the world opens before him. The first thing he sees is the wide deep blue of the sky. He gazes up at it, rapt, spellbound. Then he lowers his eyes to the ground and there are the ants and flowers and grass that he has never seen, the rich voluptuous earth, the life-giving mother. Marvelling, he bends and kisses the light.

And the crane is there before him, a lovely tufted crane. He puts out his hand to touch it, to caress it, but with a flutter of wings the crane rises into the air. Abdal gazes after it in wonder as it dwindles into a dot and vanishes in the infinity of the sky.

'And so, for ever after,' spoke the Bald Minstrel, 'our father-bard Abdal-é-Zeyniki sang only of the light and brightness of this world, and always he cursed the darkness. Let them rejoice, those who draw a moral from this tale. Hehey, bright lights, hehey tufted cranes, Abdal's cranes! Let mankind rejoice.'

The Minstrel was tired. He touched a chord, once, kissed his *saz* and laid it aside.

Chapter 10

Long before sunrise as the east began to glow and cast its rosy light upon the white snow, the village was awake as though preparing to greet a day of festivities, and soon after sunrise the village square was alive with a colourful array of women decked in all the finery they could muster. The little mirrors that the young girls attached to their headdress on special occasions flashed in the early morning sun. Arm in arm a group of young men made their way to Long Ali's house. 'Take your pipe and play us a tune or two, Uncle Ali,' they begged. And Ali promptly followed them to the square where the youths lined up for the *halay* dance. Farther off young girls were dancing and singing to the beat of a tambourine.

The village had shed all its cares. Adil Effendi was coming at last. He would be there that very day, they were certain of it, and those bitter weeks of anguished waiting would be over and done with. Blithely the morning wore on. At noon, a rumour set them rushing with sudden cries of joy for the town road. But not a living thing was to be seen. They straggled back, somewhat chastened, but still hoping. In the afternoon, there was another false alarm. But when darkness began to fall they knew that there was not a shred of hope left. Utterly spent, all the blood drained from their veins, they crept back to their homes in a deathlike silence.

The Muhtar was worried. Hands on hips he paced the house from one end to another. The younger of his two wives crouched in a corner hushing the baby she had borne him on their return from Chukurova. Outside a storm was brewing. The wind came howling ever more furiously from over the steppe, the frozen snow crackled, the world shook.

The Muhtar's uneasiness increased. He must do something, he

must think of a way out. Suppose he told the villagers that they need not pay off their debt after all? 'And let Adil tackle me about it, if he will! By God, why not? I'll tell them their debts have been written off, that they never existed. But what if Adil comes along with a posse of policemen? Ah, but Sefer, the king of muhtars will find a way out of that one! After all, Adil's only got that little yellow book of his to show. He could write anything he wished in there. Can you produce a promissory note, I'll ask him, certified by the notary? No? Well then, we don't owe you a jot. That's what I'll say, and then just watch Adil dance with rage.'

He was pleased with his idea, but his uneasiness persisted. He paced the room more quickly, almost hurling himself from one wall to the other.

'I'll do it!' he shouted out loud. 'I'll cancel the debts, whatever happens.'

He was afraid. There was no knowing what the villagers might do now, after this long frustrated wait. He would never be able to retain his hold over them. They might turn against him like angry waters breaking a dam, and join Tashbash, his arch-enemy. Everything was going wrong for him.

Look at what's blowing outside now! Why, this storm's going to uproot the whole village and sweep it right up to the top of Mount Tekech! What a storm! The very earth is shaking.

A sinister fantasy gripped him, dragging him on against a dark wall of fear. The villagers waking up one morning to see Adil Effendi there, in the middle of the village, motionless, his head and shoulders white with snow. The villagers quaking with fear, trembling, trembling, until the trembling is no longer with fear but with rage, and closer, closer they creep to each other like sheep flocking together, pressing together, tighter, tighter . . . One solid compact mass gathering momentum . . . A thunderbolt striking Adil Effendi . . . When the mass breaks apart, there is no Adil at all! A spot of blood on the ground, a leg maybe, a bit of an arm, half a nose . . . Where has that large man vanished to? The police are nowhere to be seen. Panic-stricken, it didn't take them long to decamp. The villagers are tired. There is no more Adil. Arms dangling lifelessly, heads hanging, they stand about, irresolute, a ready prey to lead by the nose.

'Ah Adil, you scoundrel, see what you've done to these people.' The pacing became more frenzied. He felt himself choking, the world darkening and he flung himself out into the night. The blizzard caught him with a slap and rooted him to the spot. The darkness, the stinging snow, the freezing cold . . . Sefer retreated hastily and closed the door.

Suddenly he remembered the girl. 'Pale Ismail's daughter! It's ages since I've talked to her.'

At the thought his body tingled warmly. 'Quick,' he said to his wife. 'Put the baby in its cradle. Go straight to Pale Ismail's and bring back his daughter. That poor girl, we haven't been able to do anything for her. Be quick!'

By now the woman had got used to it. She knew what Sefer was up to and that if she delayed one minute things would go ill for her.

'Quick,' he shouted after her. 'Bring her at once!'

The passion in his voice shook her. She braced herself against the blizzard and ran.

Sefer could hardly wait. He was trembling all over, but he was afraid. What if his desire died away before the girl arrived? He opened and shut the door a dozen times, letting in blasts of snow. His older wife and the children had come in at the shouting and were staring at him fearfully.

Sefer was irritated. 'Get along, all of you,' he roared. 'To your beds! Don't let my eyes see a single one of you.'

'Don't shout like that, Sefer,' his wife said. 'What's wrong with you now? All right! We're going! What's wrong with you?'

He fell silent. The pleasant tingling warmth was slowly draining out of him. 'Oh my God . . . The girl . . . quick!'

The door opened. She came in followed by his younger wife. Eagerly he took her by the hand, and at her touch his body came alive once more, the tingling reaching deep into the very marrow of his bones.

'Come,' he said, 'come, my lovely girl, my unfortunate angel whom I've left unavenged all this time. Come and let us find a remedy for your woes, let us bind your wound.'

He led the girl to the fire and made her sit down. Then he squatted beside her. 'You there,' he said to his younger wife, 'take the baby and go inside.'

His wife picked up the cradle with the baby and retired into the back section of the house.

'Now, tell me . . . Quickly, quickly!'

By now the girl was used to it. She knew what she was expected to say and she was no longer ashamed as in the first days of her misfortune.

'Speak, my girl, speak. Tell me, my gazelle, tell me all so that...'

She even felt pleasure now in telling her story and would let herself be drawn by Sefer's excitement.

'Well, you know Ibrahim from the other village . . .'

'Skip the part about Ibrahim. I know that.'

'We were winnowing the grain close to each other that year...'

'Skip the winnowing. I know all about that.'

'He set a trap for me. He said he would marry me and . . .'

'No, no, skip all that and come to the part about the cave, when they brought you to the cave, he and his companion. You remember? The cave all filled with bats hanging heads down. Now, you went in, and then?'

'We went in and Ibrahim tried to strip me of my clothes. I wouldn't let him. We struggled and night fell. And then his friend came. He attacked me too, but I didn't surrender to them.'

The Muhtar's face began to burn. 'Go on! Go on, quickly!'

The girl was taking her time. She smiled at him through half-lidded eyes, enjoying the sensuous warmth that poured through her limbs.

'Go on, go on!'

She knew what she was about and paid no heed to him. Unhurriedly, she began to speak again.

'His friend left us. I can't be bothered with this god-forsaken girl any longer, he said, you do what you like with her. I was glad he was going. You see, I had my eye on Ibrahim all the time. Then Ibrahim threw himself on me, and what should I see, he held a knife and with it he ripped through my clothes, and I was left naked. They had lit a fire at the mouth of the cave and into the fire he threw all my clothes and held me pinioned until they were burnt to ashes. Then he attacked me again. I tried to hold him off. He was naked too and his body was burning, burning my flesh. Oh, how it scorched into me! I felt myself growing limp . . .'

Sefer quivered all over. 'And then? Then? Quickly, what did you do then?'

She would not let herself be rushed. Slowly, drawing the utmost pleasure out of every word, she went on.

'I was going mad, mad. Ah, there is nothing in the world so pleasant as a man's naked flesh upon yours, burning into your body. I kept myself from fainting because I wanted to feel him taking my virginity. He held me tighter and tighter until my bones were cracking. He forced me to lie down in the dust of the cave and came upon me . . .'

She was trembling too now, like Sefer.

'He came upon you . . .' Sefer prompted her.

'His arms pressed me to the ground, his breath burnt into my flesh. I tried not to let myself go. It was his eyes, the fiery look in his eyes that broke me down. I couldn't hold him off any longer. I let myself go.'

'Stop!' he cried, beside himself, crushing her hand in his. Then he snatched her up in his arms. She was as light as a bird.

Outside, the blizzard boomed over the steppe.

Long Ali was squatting by the hearth talking to his mother.

'Isn't that so, Mother?' he said. 'Adil Effendi, who's got possessions far and wide, who owns a whole marketful of shops in town! He's got more important things to think about. He knows we'll pay him off some time. He's probably forgotten all about us. It seems to me we're mistaken, hiding our things one day, bringing them out again the next. Adil would never come to strip a village for a few paltry debts. That was long ago, when he was a poor beggar. But now . . . we're just making mountains out of molehills, isn't that so, Mother? The hare's got a grudge against the mountain and the mountain's not even aware of the hare, isn't that so, Mother?'

Meryemdje would not open her mouth, but she was seething.

My poor brainless son, where's the man who would renounce his rights? Where's the man who ever has enough though he own the whole world? Of course Adil will come! And he'll strip the village bare too. You can find a way out of death, but not out of this. Aaah, if only I could speak out and give you a piece of my mind!

'Isn't that so, Mother? A man so rich, the whole world his for the taking, why should he come and strip the village bare?'

He will, he will, you just wait and see. And bursting with joy as he does it.

Ali rose suddenly. His mother's obstinate silence was making him more and more nervous. He stood irresolute, listening to the fury of the blizzard. Then quickly he went to the door and opened it. The violence of the blast almost struck him down, but he struggled out and fought his way towards Tashbash's house.

'It's me, brother Memet,' he called.

The door opened.

They squatted down beside the hearth. The oakwood logs had burnt down to crystal-red embers that flared into little white flames at each blast of the wind down the chimney.

The house consisted of a single room, but it had a large fireplace and over it Tashbash had woven a hood of weeds which he had plastered with mud. The walls, coated with white earth, were very different from the slapdash mass of stones of the other houses in the village. All along the base, from the ground to a yard up, Tashbash had painted flying cranes, wind-swept trees, flowering woods, leaping deer, horses, a whole living world. Right above the chimney hung a picture of Mustafa Kemal, a fur *kalpak* on his head, his eyebrows slightly lifted, a faintly sardonic look on his face. Whenever Tashbash glanced at the picture he felt a strange pang of something like pity. To him, Mustafa Kemal was a good man, a brave man. But why that faintly sardonic expression? Mustafa Kemal had laboured hard, had given his all to his nation, yet the religious hodjas had branded him as a godless *giaour*. He had done a great many things, surmounted many obstacles, still there must be something missing, some deed unaccomplished that had proved too much for him. Otherwise, why that subtle smile, as if mocking himself and the world too?

Tashbash looked at Ali. 'What's wrong?' he said.

'We've got to do something, brother,' Ali said. 'Something for these villagers or they'll die of shame. Why don't we two go to town tomorrow, straight to Adil Effendi and speak to him. Try to explain . . .'

Tashbash sat up and glared.

'These villagers!' he spat out. 'They can go to the devil for all I care, and their mothers and wives and children as well. I wouldn't lift my little finger for them. They've only got themselves to blame. If they'd done as I said, if they'd stood up to the Muhtar this year instead of letting themselves be led again into that field where grass doesn't grow, let alone cotton, they wouldn't be in this state now. No, my friend Ali! From now on I wash my hands of them. Never again. I wouldn't stay here another day if I could help it, and as soon as it's spring again I'm going to settle in another village. I don't know about you, but I'm stifling in this place.'

He was boiling with impotent anger. Neither of them spoke another word until midnight.

Tashbash had never been able to digest the last-minute defection of the villagers and their submission to the Muhtar. It drove him mad. To think he had worked a good six years to lay bare to them Sefer's double-dealing! And he had proved it to them beyond doubt, but still they had let themselves be cozened by him in the end. It was unbelievable.

When Ali rose to go, his legs were numb. He limped to the door.

'Farewell, brother,' he said. 'You're right, absolutely right.'

'Goodbye, Ali,' Tashbash said. 'Don't worry. Let them pull at the rope until it snaps.'

Ali sped home through the unremitting blizzard to find Elif waiting there behind the door. It was her habit when something was wrong. She would open the door the minute she heard Ali and look at him reproachfully.

'What's the matter?' he cried in alarm. 'What's happened?' Then he saw that his mother was lying near the fireplace, her eyes closed, drops of perspiration on her brow.

'She went out, Ali. I thought she was just going to relieve herself and I must have fallen asleep for, suddenly, I realized it was far into the night and she wasn't back. I went out and looked everywhere around the house. Where could she be in this storm? Then I woke the children and we began to search from house to house asking for her, when all of a sudden I thought, can she be running away from the village like Old Halil? And I ran towards the town road, and there by the rocks at the beginning of the road I saw a dark shadow on the snow. Mother, I said, but there was no answer. I called again and again, then I went nearer and there she was, a tiny trembling ball. I lifted her on to my back and brought her home.'

Ali sat down beside his mother and took her hands in his.

'It's all right now, Mother,' he said. 'Elif, put some *tarhana* soup to cook over the fire. A hot soup'll do Mother a world of good.'

For the first time a sound came out of Meryemdje. She moaned and moved, lying on her side.

Chapter 11

There was not a vestige of last night's blizzard. A bright clear day had dawned. The frozen snow glittered blindingly. The single poplar tree, way off in the middle of the distant steppe, looked much nearer, it seemed only an arm's length away. And the air was warm too, as on a flowering day in May.

Hasan emerged from the house, a happy smile on his face. His trousers were rolled up to his knees and he was carrying his little axe and a rope.

'For heaven's sake, Hasan,' his mother said, 'see you bring back some stouter wood this time. The last lot melted away the minute they caught fire.'

'I want to go too,' Ummahan cried.

'Go, who's keeping you!' Hasan said. 'So long as you don't come with me! The huge big forest's there, all for you.'

'Mother!' Ummahan wailed. 'I want to go with him. Say something to him.'

Elif gave Hasan a stern look. 'Take the girl along,' she ordered. 'What's wrong with her bringing back a load too?'

'It isn't that,' Hasan said. 'It's that she rattles on and on till my head bursts.'

'I shan't open my mouth,' Ummahan promised.

As they set off they were joined by the neighbour's children.

'Where are you going?' Hasan asked the eldest boy.

'To the forest to cut wood.'

Other children joined them and by the time they were out of the village the group had grown considerably. Each carried an axe and a rope. No one spoke. They went quickly on their bare feet, almost at a run, as though fleeing before a monster. They reached the forest, out of breath, but no one stopped to rest. The boys fell to wrestling and the girls played hide-and-seek. After they had rolled in the snow to their hearts' content, too tired to go on playing, scratched and bruised, they set about gathering the wood. Like a swarm of locusts they hacked the trees bare on their passage and in a short while the faggots were bound and ready and the children sitting on them, wondering what to do next for it was only a little after noon.

For no particular reason a fight broke out between two of the boys. The other children did nothing to stop them. They just looked on and realizing that no one was going to separate them, the boys stopped by themselves.

Then Hasan attempted to creep away from the group unseen. Hiding behind rocks and trees, he made his way stealthily, with infinite precautions, but the children had noticed him. They were all eyes, including Ummahan who was watching from behind a tree. Now he was crawling along the ground. The children held their breath. Suddenly, he jumped up and vanished behind a huge mass of rock. As though they were one body, the children shot forward and took up closer positions behind trees and rocks. There he was, standing beside a long, poplar-tall rock. He had lifted a huge stone and was looking beneath it, intent, spellbound. After a while they saw him carefully ease the stone back, as though he was handling a sacred object. Then he walked away.

The children bounded out of their hiding-places. The first boy to get there grabbed the stone and raised it with some difficulty. The others watched, enthralled, wondering what they would find, but all there was to see was the black rich earth, streaked with pale yellowish roots. One thin flimsy root still clung to the upright stone, taut as a bowstring. They stared wide-eyed, then turned away, lost in thought, leaving the stone erect. What could have been there that they had missed?

Hasan had seen the children discover his stone. As soon as they were gone, he came back and slowly, caressingly lowered it into its place. Then he knelt beside it, motionless.

He was roused by an outburst of wild shrieking. All around him the children were leaping madly, jumping on to each other's backs, rolling in the snow, working themselves into a frenzy. He rose and looked at them darkly, hands on hips. He saw that Ummahan was deep in the fray. 'I'll show her,' he thought vengefully. 'Tumbling about with all those big boys, and without even asking me.' He turned his back on them, found his faggot, heaved it up and made for the road without a word. One and all the children picked up their faggots and rushed after him. The first to catch up was Veli, a dark wizened boy with hunched up shoulders that gave him a permanently frightened air.

'I saw it!' he said. 'It had eyes of fire and its head flashed like the lightning. The minute the others arrived, it became invisible. Yes, indeed.'

Hasan flung him a scornful glance and turned away with a disdainful curve of his lips.

Veli was enraged. 'Why don't you answer, you son of a donkey?' he cried. 'You dirty grandson of mulish Meryemdje! As for your father, he's so long he'll soon be piercing the sky! Whoever saw such a man!'

Hasan quickened his step. He knew instinctively that if he quarrelled with Veli now, all the children would fall upon him and beat him to pulp. But Veli ran after him and clung to his arm.

'I didn't mean that, Hasan,' he said anxiously. 'I thought you didn't believe me and . . . I *did* see it, didn't I?'

Hasan was silent.

'Look,' Veli said. 'Has it got to do with the man from the town? Will he come?'

Hasan paused, fixing his eyes, fiery with anger, on Veli.

'He'll come,' he said darkly. 'He'll come and set the whole village afire.'

At that moment a fearful clamour rose in the direction of the village.

'It's him!' Veli cried, terrified. 'He's come and he's butchering everyone.'

'He's come! The man's come!' The children flung down their faggots and huddled close to each other.

The sun was sinking fast and the western peaks were all aglow. A cold knife-like wind was blowing ever more strongly from over the steppe. No one spoke. No one moved except to press more closely together.

And then, as suddenly as it had begun the noise was cut short to be replaced by an even more terrifying stillness. The children dared not look at each other.

Veli spoke in a whisper. 'He's killed them all, hasn't he, Hasan?'

Hasan drew a deep sigh. 'Every single one,' he said.

The sun had long disappeared and a biting frost had set in, but they were still crouching there, still straining their ears towards the village.

At last Stumpy Memet's son could stand it no longer. 'I'm going home,' he announced. 'Let them kill me too, if they will. We'll die of cold here anyway.' He paused. 'Isn't anyone coming with me?' he blurted out resentfully.

No one stirred.

He stamped his foot and stormed off. But as the group of children receded into the gloom, a paralysing fear gripped him. He could not take another step. He was freezing. Without a second thought he pelted back and slumped on to his faggot. His teeth were chattering. Soon everyone's teeth were chattering too.

It was Durmush who had the idea. Durmush was just eleven. His yellow hair stood straight up on his head and his eyes, like streaked grey marbles, looked out at the world unblinkingly.

'I'm going to light a fire,' he shouted, stamping his bare feet wildly on the snow. 'I don't care if they see us. We'll be dead of cold by the morning.'

Hasan stood up. 'Let's go to the forest,' he said. 'We can light a fire there, behind the rocks, and nobody'll see us.'

Not another word was spoken. Barefoot on the frozen snow, desperately struggling in the teeth of the stinging north wind, the swarm of children was making back for the forest.

'Here,' Durmush cried, pointing to a sheltered spot among the rocks. 'There's no wind here. Come on children, go and gather wood quickly, quickly. Hasan, where are your matches?'

A rain of sticks poured into the clearing. The wood kindled

instantly. They threw in more and more, and hunched around the fire almost squeezing themselves into the blaze. Gradually, they grew warmer, the blood flowed again into their frozen feet and hands. And with the quickening of their limbs, their fear mounted. None of them had ever spent a winter night in the open before.

Veli was the first to voice the common terror. 'What if the wolves come and devour us all?' he burst out.

'Wolves don't come where there's a fire,' Hasan said.

'They might,' Veli insisted.

'They can't!' the others shouted him down. Veli fell silent. Another word and they would have pounced upon him.

But the fear was there. The wolves would attack them any minute now. They kept their eyes fixed on the flames. No one spoke. No one stirred except to throw more wood into the fire.

Wolves are particularly fond of children's flesh. That's what the grown-ups always say.

Hasan kept casting fearful glances into the darkness beyond the fire. It was the same with the others. Weird shadows moved about the rocks, fleetingly. They imagined they saw snarling wolves creeping nearer, in and out of the trees. Behind them, strange figures, holding long rifles. Suddenly, one of the children leapt to his feet screaming in terror.

'They're coming! Listen!'

They hurled themselves into the deeper recesses of the rocks, a panting, clambering mass of pounding hearts. One or two children burst into tears. And soon they were all howling at the top of their voices.

The sounds were drawing nearer. The children heard human voices calling. Their sobbing abated.

'Children!' They recognized Durduman's voice. There was an answering chorus of snivelling, blubbering cries, and suddenly Long Ali came into view, followed by Batty Bekir and Osmandja, and the other men of the village. Cries of joy echoed among the rocks as the children threw themselves into their fathers' arms.

Then there was a deep silence. The villagers squatted around the fire, warming themselves and lighting cigarettes. Nobody asked the children what had happened to them, why they had remained so late in the forest, and the children said nothing at all.

Later, they told the story of the stone, and clung to it as to a lifebuoy.

The next day, at the first crack of dawn, Veli's mother was bending over her son, her eyes wide as saucers.

'Hasan lifted the stone, but before that he looked around to make sure no one was following him. I'd always wondered what he was up to, going to the forest day in, day out. That was fishy, wasn't it, Mother? Well, he lifted the stone and looked underneath and then put it down again. When he'd gone, I went to look and the moment I lifted that stone a blinding light blazed out and I couldn't see a thing. I called to the children. They all looked and someone said there was a whole bazaar of gold buried down there and the stone was the gate to it. I didn't see anything because the light had blinded me. So we decided to sit there and wait and see what would come out of that gate. If they hadn't found us . . .'

Without even stopping to cook the morning soup, Veli's mother made off at full speed for the forest, only to find that all the women and most of the men had already got there before her. Not a single child was about. She cut through the crowd. There was nothing to be seen at all, except a bare hollow, a gaping blackness in the surrounding snow.

'Where is it?' she cried.

'Are you blind? There, right before you!' people told her.

She stared. 'But that's only where the stone was,' she said. 'Where's the stone?'

They pointed to the foot of the long rock, where the stone had been cast off. She drew near and touched it lightly, lovingly. 'So this is it?' she said. Then she turned to the others. 'Who threw it here? Shame on you all! How d'you know there isn't something in this stone? They don't show themselves to us, ever. They only let themselves be seen by children, because they're as pure as angels. I can't move it. Come on, help me put it back. Quick, before some ill fortune befalls us. Have you gone out of your minds, all of you?'

The women were struck with fear. With great care they carried the stone back and deposited it safely into its hollow.

Meryemdje had been standing at a distance leaning on her stick, watching them. Now she walked up and tapped the stone with her stick a couple of times, then smiled.

'Huh,' she muttered under her breath. 'These fool villagers! Hasan's always been like this, playing with stones and birds and bees.'

The women strained their ears, but did not catch a word of what she was saying. Giving the stone another rap Meryemdje turned away, laughing secretly. And suddenly the crowd burst into motion after her, talking their heads off. As they were drawing near the village a quarrel broke out between two women and for a while it looked as though it would be a worse brawl than the day before, but somehow no one wanted to fight today. The women had had their fill yesterday evening when, returning from the fountain, Hidir's daughter had dropped her jug and it had smashed to smithereens. 'What a pity!' Mahmud's wife had exclaimed. 'Such a beautiful jug . . .' This had infuriated Hidir's daughter. She had hurled a curse at the older woman who had cursed back, and before anyone knew it, they were at each other's throat. The girl's relatives had flown to her aid, which led to the woman's relatives joining the fray. In the end, the whole village had been involved in the brawl which had lasted until nightfall. That was the noise which had terrified the children on their return from the forest.

Today, the women kept quiet, thoughtful. 'That stone . . . there's definitely something under it.'

Veli's mother, for one, had no doubt about it. 'They didn't see it,' she whispered to her son. 'Not one of them saw the gate under the stone. We'll wait till things are quieter here and one night we'll go there together, the two of us, without telling anyone and we'll find the golden gate.'

Veli's eyes shone with anticipation.

The affair of the golden gate preyed on everyone's mind and

there was not a soul in the village who did not plan to visit the forest secretly one night. But a new turn of events was to divert their attention and during the next few days the incident was forgotten by all. By all except Hasan. Whenever he thought of the stone a warm love surged within him, a joyous feeling like an intimation of spring.

Chapter 12

Tashbash was in a raging fury. His wife had hurt her head during the brawl at the fountain and now she was laid up, burning with fever. Suppose she died? What was he to do with all those children? He had rushed off to fetch Meryemdje who knew how to brew healing ointments. But Meryemdje, curse her, persisted in remaining dumb as an oyster. If she would just say something.

'Mother Meryemdje, how's the wound?'

Don't worry, it won't kill her, Meryemdje reassured him with a shake of her head, as she bustled about the hearth, throwing things into the soot-blackened cauldron over the fire.

On one side of the fireplace was a cupboard for the bedding and on the other a store of neatly stacked wood, and beyond, suspended from the ceiling, the large flat wicker basket where the *yufka* bread was kept. Three small children with frightened, woebegone faces crouched beside the hearth. A good half of the house was taken up by the livestock, a couple of cows, a bullock, a calf, the oxen, the goats and the chicken coop. Facing the door was a pile of fodder. The acrid animal smell of sweat and hay and fresh cow dung which usually pervaded the whole place was now drowned in the spring-time fragrance of a pinewood forest, the powerful penetrating scent of Meryemdje's healing ointment, brewed from a thousand flowers and herbs.

Ah, Tashbash thought, if only this fragrance would seep into the walls, the doors, the sooty ceiling, into the animals and the hay and the ashes in the hearth, if only it would settle here and never go, never for a thousand years! If only the whole village smelt like this always, if only the falling snow, the blowing blizzard . . . Meryemdje removed the bubbling cauldron from the fire. Swiftly she spooned out some of the steaming salve on to a piece of cloth and applied it over the wound. The woman let out a shriek, then clenched her teeth.

'I'm burning,' she moaned. 'I'm dying.' Her face twisted with pain.

'Mother Meryemdje . . .' Tashbash whispered.

Meryemdje's heart thrilled warmly. Ah, how I wish I could speak to you, my Tashbash! There's none in these mountains knows the secret of this ointment but your own Mother Meryemdje. It comes to me from the great House of Yellow Tanishman, to whom Allah himself revealed the formula of herbs and flowers to be used. So don't trouble yourself at all, my own Tashbash, my good clever son.

She made ready to leave.

'How right you are not to speak to these villagers, Mother Meryemdje!' Tashbash said. 'They've asked for everything that's coming to them.' Meryemdje shot him a pleased look and went her way with the sprightliness of a young girl, her bare feet tripping over the snow.

The very thought of the villagers was enough to drive Tashbash into paroxysms of fury now. If he had possessed a gun he could easily have burst out of the house and killed every single one of them. He went to his wife and laid a hand on her brow.

'How do you feel?' he asked.

'A little better,' she replied faintly.

Now, what was this woman's crime that these scoundrels should do this to her? But wait! Wait and see what's in store for them! Wait and see how they'll soon fall foul of each other and cut each other's throats . . .

Those who saw Tashbash these days said he had gone out of his mind. And it was true there was something strange about him. Ever since that fatal night at Sögütlü on their way down to the cotton picking, when the Muhtar had thwarted his plans and drawn the villagers over to his side, Tashbash had never been the same again.

At first, when they had come to the arid cotton field into which

72

the Muhtar had led them just for the sake of the bribe he would get from the owner, Tashbash had thrown up his cap in triumph and laughed wildly. 'Didn't I say so?' he had shouted. 'Didn't I tell you that Sefer would gull you again? Well, let me see what cotton you're going to pick now! Go ahead and pick if you can find a single boll of cotton on a plant!'

'He's right,' they had said. 'It's the plain truth. Everything's turned out just as he said. There's something about this Tashbash . . .'

And all through the cotton picking, he had jeered and gibed at them, his every word more venomous than a rattlesnake, and they had swallowed it all without a murmur. But when the cotton picking was over and it was clear that they would all return home empty-handed, a sudden change came over Tashbash. He fell into such a state of despondency that knives would not open his mouth. This lasted until they were back in the village and the fear of Adil Effendi had taken hold of them. Then his tongue loosened, but it was only to pour abuse on the whole village, young and old.

'This Tashbash has gone really mad,' they said fearfully. And they avoided his path as much as they could.

His wife's wound was the last straw. The villagers felt they were in for trouble. But they knew Tashbash was right, so what could they do but let him curse away to his heart's content?

'The flying bird itself shuns this village now. Thanks to you! There is a blight upon it, upon its very stones and plants, upon its ants and smallest insects. Thanks to you! The rain will never more freshen its earth. The snow will come down in flames. Thanks to you! And for ever, dearth in place of plenty, evil in place of blessing. Your crops shall wither, there will be no more red-eared wheat. Thanks to you! Pestilence and floods and earthquakes shall lay waste this village. And one day, creeping up from that great wide steppe you will see a thousand green heads, a thousand forked tongues, a thousand red eyes . . . Hundreds and hundreds of serpents come to scourge the village! The air you breathe will be poison. Poison the water you drink, the food

73

you eat, the beds you sleep in. The earth under your feet, the blue sky over your heads, the clouds, the stars, everything will be poison to you. All thanks to you! Even the birds of the air alter their course now, at the sight of this village. Because even they feel the fear and abjectness here. Many a time have I seen swarms of bees arrested in mid-flight as though bumping into a wall and turning away with a panic buzzing . . . Fleeing far, far from this village as though it were hell itself . . .

'Serve you right! Yes, it'll serve you right, all of you, when Adil comes and seizes everything, down to your women's drawers! So Sefer Effendi tells you to hide your belongings and you hide them, he tells you to bring them out again and you do so, without a murmur? So you let him play with you? In the end Adil will come and take your women away too, and sell them in the town, and for nothing! Serve you right, a hundred times right! Just imagine it, a troop of women with bare rumps in the middle of the town market! How will you like that? Where will you ever be able to show your faces again? Why you wretches, can't you be men enough to go and tackle Adil Effendi yourselves? And if the worst comes to the worst, can't you take his bald pate and crush it between two boulders? What's this fear, this shame, this cowardice that's come over you all, that's tainted the very stones and earth of this village?

'Hear me well, oh you craven creatures! Spring will not come this year, out of fear. There shall be no sprouting of grass and plants, no flowering of shrubs and trees in the mountains and the forests. The birds shall not hatch, the horses shall not foal, nor the sheep and goats yean. Your women shall be barren. Your streams and fountains shall flow like blood. And worse, worse things still shall plague you because you would not listen to me all these years.

'For the last time I tell you, shake off this abject fear. Be men! When you were soldiers you saw the world, the big cities, the men who live there like men. You saw the big wide seas. Have you ever given thought to what lies beyond those seas? Have you ever asked yourselves how the sun rises and sets, what is behind the sun? How the wireless works, how the bird flies? Have you ever thought of that?'

Bear with the lash of his tongue if you can! Slowly the fear of Adil Effendi fades, to be replaced by a worse fear, an almost holy dread of Tashbash. When he opens his mouth to speak, people tremble as though his words would come true that minute. They avoid him. They would like to kill him. Even the children at play echo this dread.

'That man Tashbash should be killed . . . That man Tashbash should be drawn and quartered . . .' But no one ever touches him, as though the hand lifted against him would be paralysed in mid-air, as though even to draw near him with a wicked thought would be enough to burn a man to cinders.

As his wife's wound festered, Tashbash's ravings grew wilder. And the more he raved, the more the villagers' fear and respect grew. His voice, bitter and venomous, echoed in their ears night and day, crushing, overwhelming.

Chapter 13

Swiftly Hüsneh slipped out of bed and groped her way to the door. Outside, the snowbound night shone, palely translucent, earth and sky merged in a perfect whiteness. She speeded to the deserted hut. The fire was burning in the grate, and Rejep waiting for her. She threw herself at him hungrily. They never knew how they came together, their naked bodies taut in an ecstasy of sensual joy, twisting, sweating, copper-red in the flush of the flames, two human beings interlocked, wholesome, yearning, timorous, lusty. And she let out the cry she could not keep back.

'I won't stop here another day,' Hüsneh repeated. She clenched Rejep's hand. 'The women are going to be struck barren here, and when spring comes the flowers won't bloom and the green grass won't sprout. There will be pestilence. Earthquakes will make a shambles of all our homes. We've got to get out quickly. Now! This moment! No one will ever find us. Look, I've brought a bundle. The night is clear and as calm as a spring night. If you won't come, I'll go by myself. Barren! Sterile! The women will be barren! And even if they do give birth, their children will be still-born. No, I can't live here any more. And you, what have you got to lose when you don't even own a stick worth hiding from Adil? Now, now, quickly. Let's escape.'
Rejep was trying to talk to her, but she would not listen.
'Now, now!' she urged him vehemently. 'Snakes will rain upon us, a hundred thousand red-eyed venomous snakes . . . The crops will wither, the cows will not fatten, the women will be barren! Come on, quick, quick . . .'
'But in this snow, in the dead of winter . . . We'll freeze to death. When the spring comes, then . . .'
'There won't be any spring. Come on, quickly, quickly!'

'But Old Halil . . .'

'He never died! They'd have found his frozen body if he had. Old as he is, he ran away in the teeth of the snow and winter. He knew. Come, come quickly.'

'When the spring comes . . .'

'It won't come!'

'When the snows melt . . .'

'They won't melt. Come on!'

'But Old Halil's body may be lying buried under the snow. That's why . . .'

'There isn't any body to find!'

Her bundle clasped in one hand, she tugged at Rejep with all her might, urgent, irresistible, as though they were hemmed in on all sides and must flee for dear life. Suddenly he was engulfed by her panic, hypnotized, ready to follow her into hell itself.

They were outside now, running in the white luminous night that was like no other night. On the road, fleeing, not knowing how they had set out, unconscious of how they had come so far.

Hüsneh kissed Rejep's hands again and again, delirious with joy.

'We're going! We're escaping from that hell! Shall I tell you something, Adil Effendi'll be there tomorrow . . .'

Rejep did not speak, he did not think, he let himself be led, bewitched.

'Early, before sunrise he'll be there and he'll strip the village bare, not a crust of bread will he leave. We'd have died of hunger if we'd stayed there. Now they'll all die of hunger . . .' She pressed Rejep's hand to her breast. 'They'll die! They'll be struck barren . . .'

They were nearly freezing when the sun rose. Turning to the east Hüsneh lifted her hands to the sky and prayed.

'Thanks be to our saviour . . .'

A golden flood gushed out from the east, lighting up the wintry steppe and the distant slopes and casting two long shadows over the snow. The shadows raced ahead, very black, furrowing the snow. They had come to the foot of Mount Tekech and still not a single village was in sight. Nothing was left now of Hüsneh's exaltation. She was holding on to Rejep's arm for dear life, utterly spent. But he had shaken himself out of his trance.

'Don't be afraid,' he said. 'I know there are villages behind that ridge. We'll soon get there.'

'But there's a storm gathering,' she said almost in tears. 'And I can hardly stand up any more.' She pointed to Mount Tekech. Black clouds were churning about its crest. 'Look . . .'

'It's not so far,' he encouraged her. 'We'll get there in spite of the storm.'

'They'll die, they'll be barren,' she kept muttering as she staggered forward. It gave her strength. 'Barren, barren, barren!'

'What, for God's sake, are you saying over and over again?' he asked.

The sun was blotted out now.

'Quick,' she gasped. 'Quick! Let's not get caught in the storm.'

It was growing darker and darker. There was not a bird or a beast, not a living thing on the wide steppe. They were alone, two human beings struggling against ruthless nature.

Rejep was angry.

'Barren, barren! Who's going to be barren? Are you mad? God damn that village! God damn that Tashbash!'

'But they will be barren, my Rejep,' she insisted in a faint voice. 'Barren. Are we getting near to any place?'

The news was on everybody's lips even before sunrise. Hüsneh's mother flung herself on to the snow, thrashing about and shrieking with grief. As for Rejep he had no one to lament for him.

There was a subdued effervescence all about the village. Tashbash was on the threshold of his house, seething, for he sensed the undercurrent of relish among the villagers.

'May you sink to the bottom of the earth, all of you,' he shouted suddenly. 'It's because of you that the poor things ran away in the dead of winter. They'll never reach a village. You'll find them dead and buried under the snow.'

It was all around the village in an instant.

'Dead and buried under the snow! Frozen to death . . .'

'If we'd known that they were so much in love . . .'

'Burning with so strong a passion . . .'

'Strong enough to throw themselves into the wild winter night . . .'

'Everyone knew that they were in love . . .'

'That they met in that empty hut . . .'

'But that it was so far gone! . . .'

From the summit of Mount Tekech lowering clouds swirled eastwards over the steppe. A black wind was blowing ever more forcefully, the mad harbinger of the coming blizzard.

'We must look for them.'

'We must save the lovers . . .'

'There's a storm coming!'

A couple of mounted men came forward. 'We'll find them,' they said, and they galloped down into the valley.

'I swear by all that's holy,' declared Hüsneh's father, 'I won't say a word of reproach to them. Just let me have them back safe, and I'll sacrifice my only calf for them. I'll talk to them, laugh with them . . . Oh God, only save her!'

By mid-morning it began to snow and by noon a freezing blizzard had blotted out the whole world.

Tashbash's anger swelled with the blizzard.

'Better to throw oneself into the blizzard and die than live here!' he shouted. 'The flying bird itself shuns this village.'

And he hurled terrible imprecations at the villagers.

Chapter 14

Such a blizzard had developed, lashing over earth and sky, that not a soul remained outside.

It was Shirtless, watching the storm through a chink in his door, who saw him first. He rubbed his eyes and looked again unbelievingly, but the long thin figure had flitted past like a leaf borne on the blizzard. Then he saw it gliding back.

'It's Spellbound Ahmet, the poor idiot!' Shirtless cried, his eyes glued to the chink. 'He'll freeze to death . . . But no, the *peris* will protect him. Maybe even now they've spread their wings over him . . .'

The figure vanished again in the darkening storm and Shirtless crossed over to sit by the fire.

'There's only one way out and that's to kill this Adil Effendi,' he thought, stretching his legs wide. 'The drawback is that he's an old man. The noble race of Shirtless has severed countless heads, it has raised towers of skulls, but never has it lifted a hand against an old man. Yes, Adil ought to be removed from the face of the earth, and what's more, when the Last Judgment comes, whoever had done it would be sent straight to Paradise and no questions asked. So it behoves me, the last representative of the noble Shirtless race, to finish him off, but . . .' He called to his ten-year-old son. 'My Son,' he said solemnly, stroking his beard, 'what is the race of Shirtless in this world?'

The child trotted it out as though he had been wound up.

'The Shirtless race is king of the kings of the mountains. And I am the last representative of this great race, friend of the poor, enemy of the aghas. The Shirtless race has always taken from the rich to give to the poor. The race goes back to the famous bandit Köroglu's friend, the bravest of the brave, the son of the black-smith, the man who crushed four horseshoes with his two fingers . . . It's against all law that this Adil Effendi should go on living, but the ancient tradition of the Shirtless race forbids them to shed the blood of old men.'

Shirtless drew his son to him with pleasure.

'Well done,' he said. 'Ah, if only we could drink the blood of this Adil, the glory of the Shirtless race would ring up to the skies.'

'Ohhoo! If he were just a little less old,' the child bragged, 'the house of Shirtless would tear him to pieces.'

'Ah,' his father sighed as he went back to the door, 'what a chance the house of Shirtless is letting pass . . .'

The child knew he must be silent now. He tiptoed to the ox and began stroking its long horns, for Shirtless, unable to stand the absence of his animals any longer, had brought them back home from the Peri Caves.

He put his eye to the chink and what should he see but Spellbound Ahmet approaching his house! It's the *peris*, he thought complacently. Spellbound, they said to him, you must go and visit the noble house of Shirtless.

He opened the door quickly. 'Welcome, brother,' he called. 'Welcome to the knightly house of Shirtless. It's the *peris* have sent you, or you'd never cross anybody's threshold.'

The idiot stopped dead. His tattered clothing was white with snow.

'Why don't you come in, brother?' Shirtless said, moving up to him. 'Why . . .' But Spellbound Ahmet's gaze nailed him to the spot.

'Dead and buried under the snow!' Spellbound cried out suddenly. 'Frozen to death . . . the lovers . . .' He glared at Shirtless, and then went on in a low mocking voice: 'Race of Shirtless, race of swine! Humbugs all of you! Got your name because one of your forefathers gave his shirts to the poor, did you? A lie! It was because he was so poor that he couldn't buy a shirt in all his life. Knights, hah! When did your people ever own a horse? Humbugs! Cowards! Towers of skulls! Bah, when did you ever kill a fly? And why towers of skulls? Is that a thing to boast about? May your tongue dry up! For the sake of this child . . .' He let

out a long howl. 'Gone are the lovers! Buried under the snow . . .'
He whirled about and vanished in the blinding blizzard.

'He's mad,' Shirtless mumbled to his son. 'Madmen tell a lot of
lies. Everyone knows the Shirtless race has sown terror in these
mountains for centuries. Madmen are like that . . .'

Spellbound Ahmet drifted into Köstüoglu's house.

'Dead and buried under the snow,' he cried. 'Frozen to death
are the lovers! And you, Köstüoglu, are alive, you slimy lazy-
bones. Of what use is your life to anyone? Worse than Slowcoach
Halil you are . . . Gone are the lovers! Dead and buried under the
snow!'

The next house he blew into like a cold gust was Slowcoach
Halil's. He found him still busy digging in the pit where he had
hidden his belongings, picking at the earth as though with
tweezers.

Spellbound stood over him, watching. 'May your task be easy,'
he said. Then, without warning he spat in his face. Slowcoach
gaped at him, mesmerized. His blank gaze sickened the idiot.

'Gone are the lovers! Frozen to death!' he bawled, and threw
himself out of the house.

Köstüoglu and Halil were cousins and renowned for their
sluggishness. Köstüoglu's very gait was deliberate and prudent.
He never stepped on an ant or an insect, or even on a dead leaf,
and it was the same with Slowcoach. Köstüoglu would leave his
house before dawn and reach his field at midday, and by the time
he had yoked the oxen and ploughed a couple of furrows it was
already evening. And it was the same with Slowcoach. When
everyone else picked twenty kilos of cotton, these two would
only manage a kilo apiece.

When he came to Pale Ismail's house, Spellbound was a frozen
heap of snow. His long yellowish hair and beard, even his eyebrows were stiff with frost. At the sight of him the whole household was struck with fear.

'Don't be afraid, I won't eat you,' the idiot said slyly. 'You'd
better watch your horns, Pale Ismail. They're growing. The
Muhtar's doing things to your daughter, but you, you don't say a
word. Oh no, you hope he'll take her to wife. Just to be father-in-

law to a Muhtar you'd give her to that man who's got two wives already. Why don't you marry her off to Veli's son and gladden the poor lad's heart? You're wicked people, all of you, and this village will be struck by pestilences and floods. Gone the lovers! Dead and buried under the snow!'

Nobody dared answer a word.

Next he was inside Snappy Mustafa's house.

'Dead the lovers!' he howled. 'Buried under the snow, and you're lying there, warming your balls before the fire! You've become a slave to that scoundrel of a Muhtar. You're not a man any more, you toadeater!'

Snappy Mustafa had a sharp temper. The idiot knew it well. He backed out of the house quickly and ran for dear life. 'Holo hooo!' he yelled. But Snappy caught up with him and dealt him such a blow that he was left sprawling on the snow. As soon as he came to, Spellbound threw himself into the nearest house and began all over again.

Night was falling when he plunged into the Muhtar's house. There he ranted on, raking up scandals dating from the lifetime of the Muhtar's father. The idiot had an extraordinary memory. The Muhtar, who had visitors from a neighbouring village, was powerless to stop him.

'As for you,' Spellbound said finally, 'you'll die, and by the hand of Tashbash too . . .' With that parting shot, he dashed out.

Now he made for Tashbash's house, but slowly, with reverent steps. He paused before the door and kissed it three times. Tashbash's little boy let him in. By this time, he had become one large hoary mass of snow, with long icicles sticking out of his hair and beard. Meryemdje, who was sitting by the wounded woman's bedside, stared at him, fascinated. It was the first time she had seen him since they had returned from the Chukurova. Long Ali, Zaladja Woman, Ökkesh Dagkurdu, Mangy Mahmut, Durduman and the Bald Minstrel were sitting about the hearth talking. Tashbash squatted silently in a corner, his back to the wall.

Spellbound came up to him, his head bowed. 'Gone are the lovers, dead and buried under the snow!' he moaned, his voice a low bitter lament. Tashbash's eyes filled with tears. Spellbound lifted his head and looked straight at him. 'Spring will not come this year. Our crops will not ripen. Our women will be barren. Floods and earthquakes will wipe out the village. Curses and serpents will rain upon it. If it is still standing, it is thanks to you, o my Tashbash. For your sake . . .'

He bent down and kissed the ground before Tashbash three times. Then he gave a sudden bound and was gone. The blizzard blasted in through the open door and the fire sizzled as snowflakes fell into it.

It was not long before the whole village knew that Spellbound Ahmet, who had been cursing everyone all day long, had kissed the ground three times in the presence of Tashbash. That night they hardly slept at all, agog with speculation.

Chapter 15

Depend upon it, there's something about this Tashbash. I'll put both these hands into the fire and swear to it. Otherwise, why should God's own fool, Spellbound Ahmet, the Peri King's own son-in-law, prostrate himself and kiss the ground before his feet? And with such holy words too. And what about the terrible things Tashbash has been saying? Ever since the world began, only from the mouths of saints have such weighty words come . . .

People could talk and think of nothing else but Tashbash. From a distance they watched his house surreptitiously, gripped by a growing dread. The children would tiptoe up to the door, holding their breath, then streak off, shaking with fear.

Tashbash realized something was wrong, something that concerned him, but he did not know what. One day, he went out to go to Long Ali's, but found himself forced to retrace his steps, unable to bear the looks of fear and suspicion that bored into his back.

Why are they behaving so strangely? he wondered. Even the children are shy of me, scattering like a flight of partridges before my path, and children, mirror-like, always reflect what grown-ups try to hide. What are they up to?

'He said stones will rain upon us! Stones!'
'How does he know?'
'He said that throughout this land of the Taurus the women will be barren, the animals will not give birth, the grass will wither, the green of the mountains will turn into brimstone.'
'How does he know?'
'He said that if we go on like this dark clouds will close over us, we shall never more see the light we love.'
'How does he know?'

85

'There's something about this Tashbash. We all hid our things like the Muhtar told us, but he didn't. He knew Adil wouldn't come.'

'How did he know?'

Tashbash was becoming more and more a burning question in the minds of the villagers. That he kept to his house only added fuel to the fire.

Zaladja Woman now began to dream about Tashbash nightly. She, as usual, attempted to make the Muhtar interpret her dreams, but he flew into a thunderous rage and ordered her out of his house.

'Don't you ever come to me with your dreams about Tashbash! To dream about him brings bad luck,' he shouted.

But Zaladja had to tell someone and she found ready listeners among the villagers. It was true that nobody could interpret her dreams like the Muhtar, but still it was gratifying to have people lend such eager ears.

'A black tent is spread over me, and all around me darkness. Then the tent begins to come down, lower and lower, until it is pressing me to the ground. There I lie, breathless, stifling, fainting, when suddenly the blackness is torn apart, as though with a sword, and light pours through the tent, and in the light is a hand! A beautiful hand . . . Whose hand can it be? What is the face behind it? My eyes are dazzled as I draw nearer. A face bathed in green light . . . Whose? Tashbash! I throw myself at his feet. And then I wake up. I rush to Tashbash's house, and what should I see there?'

'What? What?'

But this, Zaladja will not reveal to anyone. And an uneasy suspicion takes root among the villagers. What can it be that appears at night about Tashbash's house? They press her to speak.

'Don't force me, for pity's sake,' Zaladja replies darkly. 'My mouth will be twisted, my hands and arms will wither like a sapless tree. For God's sake don't make me speak.'

In everyone's mind a dream is taking shape, a new world, half real, half fantasy. No one dares tell what he thinks, and as the

86

days go by, Tashbash slowly retreats into a distant, magic world. He takes on stature.

'What was it? What was it Tashbash said? One night you will lift up your heads and there will be no stars, no moon. They'll have taken them away. And in the morning you'll rise up and what will you see? No more blue sky, no forests on the Taurus mountains, nothing, gone for ever. As for Adil, Tashbash said he may come, but then again he may not . . .'

'How did he know?'

Chapter 16

The Muhtar was having a hard time of it. Only the thought of Pale Ismail's daughter kept him going. He had firmly made up his mind to take her as his third wife, this girl who had come to be the only bright spot in his existence. Whenever the weight of his cares became unbearable he would send for her or he would visit her father's house himself.

Adil had no intention of coming, that was certain. And matters were going from bad to worse. This Tashbash business . . . they were well on the way to making a saint of him. These villagers will catch at the slightest straw when they're in trouble, and if they find no straw, well, they'll produce one out of the blue and then cling to it for dear life. Tashbash, clever, cunning fellow that he was, had been quick to take advantage of their despair. He had begun by pouring forth imprecations just like the prophets in the holy books, and this had served to plant the fear of God into them. Then he had put Spellbound Ahmet through the mill. That kissing of the ground before Tashbash had been the crowning point. Imaginations had been fired well and properly. If this went on, and it looked as if it would, Tashbash, his arch-enemy, would have himself recognized as a saint. He'd be the uncrowned lord of all the Taurus, with everyone at his beck and call, ready to die for him. And there was no doubt that the first thing he'd do would be to have the Muhtar driven out of the village.

Sefer and the four members of the Village Council put their heads together to see what could be done to stop the Tashbash landslide.

'We have no evidence to bring the law against him,' Mealy Muslu said. 'He never even stirs out of his house, and won't let anyone in except Old Meryemdje.'

'He's a sly calculating fellow, knows what he's about,' Sefer said. 'But when I've done with him, he'll be worse off than that other bogus saint, Murtaza.'

'There's no proof,' Muslu insisted. 'We can't do a thing for the present. And anyway, it isn't like Murtaza's case. Murtaza was just a poor dumb beggar. Tashbash has got half the village behind him. He'll know how to swing his power at our expense, especially now that people are sick to death of everything. He's a menace.'

'A menace,' the Muhtar agreed despondently. 'We'll wake up one morning soon and find everybody kissing the ground under his feet. No, the only thing to do is to get Adil Effendi to come. That'll give them something else to think about. Adil's got to come and you're going to fetch him, the four of you. You'll set out for the town right away. Tell Adil that Tashbash is just the first spark. This is going to turn into a fire that'll spread all over the Taurus. So he'd better look sharp and get here before it's too late. Godspeed to you. Tell Adil I kiss his hands and don't forget to do the same as soon as you come into his presence. He likes that.'

'See here, my friends,' Adil was saying. 'Nothing can induce me to come to your village. Nothing! Not at any price! Because . . . You know the reason why as well as I do. You just tell my friend Sefer, with my compliments, that matters have got out of hand. He'll know what I mean. Let him watch his step with those villagers and not tread on the tail of the sleeping serpent. I know exactly what's been going on up there. I've been kept informed day by day of the doings of those ungrateful villagers. No one's ever got away with Adil's money and I'm just biding my time. So tell Sefer it's no use sending me messages every other day, for I won't come, not now. I ask you, and mind you tell Sefer this: why did those villagers dress up as for a festival, and with songs and dances wait for me on the road? Whoever heard of anyone greeting a creditor like that? Tell Sefer I wasn't born yesterday, and anyway what kind of a friend is he? Does he think I don't know those villagers are armed to the teeth with clubs and even guns? But I'm not afraid of them. They can plant a cannon before each house for all I care. Haven't I always been good to them? Why should they have anything against me? But I know what's in their heads, I can guess. Let them thank their lucky stars I haven't descended upon the village with a hundred armed men to claim my due, that I haven't left them naked as the day they were born, without a crust of bread, or even a haircloth under them. No, I thought of how I've been doing business with that village for the past forty years. Those villagers are my children. It's for their sake that I work so hard. Would I ever let them go naked and hungry in the winter? I know they weren't able to pick good cotton this year and that's why they haven't paid their debts. Now what's there to get angry about? Let them come to me, my shop is open to them. They can take whatever they need on credit. I know they'll pay me back next year. I have great faith in the people of Yalak. But they're to come only one at a time. Because if they come in groups . . . it's not that I'm afraid, I fear no one.'

Adil's house was a two-storied blue-washed building with eight rooms and a vast hall. On the ground floor were the stables from which came a strong stench of stale manure. He was seated with his back to the wall, dressed in navy-blue trousers and soft slippers. A gold chain dangled from his waistcoat pocket. His whole body, the enormous paunch, the crinkled pendulous throat, the tiny sunken greenish eyes, the thick short hands, the set of golden teeth, betrayed his nervousness. He seemed to be trapped in a cocoon of fear, fear that conflicted with angry frustration.

'No, I fear no one but Allah. So tell Sefer to be careful with those villagers. They're half-crazy as it is and there's bound to be trouble. For heaven's sake, do everything to placate them. And give my compliments to Old Halil. I'll never forget his service in coming to warn me about what was brewing up there. Just for that, I've written off all his son's debts. Now, don't forget, the villagers can come to my shop and take whatever they fancy, and at cost price too. I won't press them for payment. And tell Sefer not to insist, because I won't put my foot in that village at any price. And if he asks the reason why, tell him, I can't reveal it to anyone.'

Chapter 17

Barefoot Murat told the story and the Bald Minstrel bore him out.

'There's something different about this Tashbash race, but what would you ungrateful villagers know about that! I could tell you a thing or two . . . If any of you'd listen to Barefoot Murat . . . Did you know that all the male children of this family are called Memet? Look, isn't our Tashbash's name Memet? So was his father's. He calls all his three sons Memet, and his forefathers ever since the beginning have been Memets. Now, there's something about that, some secret of divine wisdom, as our Muhtar would say. But, most important, and there I hit the nail on the head, how did that family come to be called Tashbash[1]? Have you ever asked yourself that, you stupid sons of Adam? Why Tashbash? You don't know, but I do, and now the time has come for me to open my mouth.

'One day, the Holy Man of the Mountains, the great Tashbash, a forefather of our own Tashbash was going up the mountain, when what should he see! A man with a body of stone, but on top of it a head that talked and laughed and wept, with large black eyes and a forelock falling over his sweating brow. It was a spring day with the mountains and the trees and the flowers singing softly. The great Tashbash drew near and said: whatever has happened to you? And the young man told him. A wicked sorcerer, he said, fell in love with my sweetheart. He cast a spell over me and carried her away. You are the Holy Man of the Mountains, our great Lord Memet. Find a remedy for my woes. And the Holy Memet said: I will. He stretched his hand out into infinity and plucked a sprig of pomegranate from Paradise. Then he knelt and prayed all day, and when it was evening he struck

[1] Tashbash: Stonehead.

the stone body three times with the sprig. And the stone thawed out into human flesh. Our Lord Tashbash was beginning to rejoice when what should he see! This time it was the head which had been petrified! God, what have I done, our holy Lord Memet cried. He threw himself down and prayed again till the soft winds of morning blew on the mountain, and he looked up, but nothing had happened. The stone head was there, hard as ever. Then he got angry and said: Let my own head be turned to stone instead. And lo and behold, he found himself with a head of stone, and the young man was free to go and seek his sweetheart.

'You may well ask what he did then, the holy Lord Memet, the great great grandfather of our own Tashbash! He had no mouth to pray with, no eyes to see with, no ears to hear with. He was all alone on the mountain with his stone head. But his was a holy body. The wolves and birds of prey, the serpents and scorpions, the tigers and bears could not touch it. Time passed and one day two roses began to bloom out of his palms. Ah, if the great Lord Memet had been able to think he would have laid his hands directly on his head and been saved, for this was the magic of the roses! But how could he think with that brain of stone? But then a blackbird alighted on his head and started pecking at his eyes. His right hand shot up and where the rose petal touched his stone head a bit of flesh appeared. The bird pecked away harder than ever, and the holy man put up both his hands and, behold, his head was a human head again! Our Lord Memet fell to the ground, exhausted, and slept for three days and three nights.'

'Barefoot Murat,' Puffy Poyraz protested, 'that's the story of Mollah Ahmet. He was the Holy Man of the Mountains, and the birds and beasts brought him food for he was their saint. What's it got to do with Tashbash, you yarn-spinner?'

'You don't know anything about it. You wouldn't understand anyway,' Barefoot Murat replied. 'That holy man wasn't Mollah Ahmet, it was Mollah Memet, the ancestor of the Tashbash clan.'

'God damn you for a gossiping fool,' Puffy Poyraz cried, 'and the biggest liar on earth.'

'You're the liar,' Murat retorted. 'A thousand curses on your descendants.' He turned to the villagers. 'Who's right, Puffy or me?'

'You are,' they replied. 'Puffy doesn't know or else he's lying on purpose. If it hadn't happened that way up on the mountain, why was the family named Tashbash? Ask Puffy Poyraz that! Some people are too feeble-minded to be alive.'

Everyone was against Puffy Poyraz.

'That wasn't Mollah Ahmet, it was Mollah Memet Tashbash. What have we to gain by denying a man's noble antecedents?'

'And he's the very ancestor of our own Tashbash.'

'Some upstarts may want to deny it, much good it'll do them!'

'We've got brains in our heads, although some half-witted people don't bother to think! Why wasn't anybody else called Tashbash?'

'Of course it's true! We have it from our fathers and grandfathers that it was so.'

Puffy saw that nothing he could say would be of any use. They were all on Barefoot Murat's side.

The story of the stone head got around. Everyone related it at least twice to his neighbour, and then, out of nowhere, sprang a new story, that of Mount Erciyes[1] and the dragon, the imaginations of the villagers took fire.

Even Tashbash got wind of it. 'I never heard that there ever was such a person in our family!' he said. 'It was no ancestor of mine who went up Mount Erciyes. It was the famed Lokman the Physician, as everyone knows.'

The villagers were furious.

'He's raving mad, the son of a dog! Unworthy of his great race. And anyway, if he'd been a man would our village have come to this?' But then they thought it over. 'What could he say, poor creature? He didn't want to blow his own trumpet, our good Tashbash. He couldn't do anything but deny it . . .'

Once upon a time, long long ago, there lived a physician called Lokman Tashbash. His name was Memet too, but everyone

[1]Erciyes (pronounced Erjiyes): the ancient Mount Argaeus, near Caesarea, now Kayseri.

called him Lokman the Wise because he had found cures for all
the diseases on earth. The world was a happy world in those
ancient times, a world in which people lived without ever being
ill. They suffered from only one complaint and that was death.
How had Lokman Tashbash found all those cures? Well, he was
a great traveller. From east to west there was not a country he
had not journeyed in, and everywhere he went the plants and trees
and flowers, the earth, the flowing waters, the rocks would speak
to him. As he went his way a little flower would raise its head:
stop a minute, Lokman Tashbash, stop for I've something to
whisper into your ear. I'm a panacea for all eye diseases, ask my
name. And Lokman would write down the name and fill his large
leather saddlebag with the flower. It was the same wherever he
went. The flowers, the plants, the whole of nature spoke to him.

You must know that Lokman the Physician was born in this
village like all the Tashbashes. And many of his cures he found
in the plants of the Taurus Mountains. One day he set out to find
the cure for death. First, he went to Mount Erciyes. There, right
on the summit, blooms a magic flower. Its colour changes from
hour to hour and it glows as though a light burns within it.
Whoever approaches this flower and smells its fragrance, even
from a distance, becomes immune from all evil and sickness.
Even death will come suddenly and painlessly to him. He will live
in bliss for the whole of his life long and never know want or
poverty. And should a man find a way to come under the shade
of the plant, should he touch one of its petals, that man will gain
immortality. You may ask then, why doesn't everyone do just
that? This magic flower, whose petals are as long as a poplar, is
guarded by a dragon whose mighty body is coiled all about the
peak of Erciyes. It never sleeps except for one second in twenty-
four hours, but when is that? Is it at night? During the day? No
one knows, and so the magic flower has never been touched by a
human hand. But can't one slay the dragon? Never! Should you
find a way of hacking it to pieces and afterwards grind its flesh at
the mill and burn it and scatter the ashes to the winds, when you
go back to Mount Erciyes you will see the dragon just where it
was before and has ever been. Is it possible to kill a dragon who's

lived in the shade of the magic flower since the world began?

Well, our Lokman Tashbash waited on Mount Erciyes for years and years. And then one day he hit upon the moment when the dragon fell asleep. He slipped past the beast and his hand touched the flower, but just as he was making away the dragon woke up. But even a dragon would not kill our Tashbash Lokman. No, the dragon didn't kill him, but it undid the immortality charm. If only the beast hadn't opened its eyes just then, Tashbash Lokman would have been among us to this day.

After this, Tashbash Lokman set about looking for a certain flower, a flower that had never been seen by anyone. His ear alert, he went in search of it about the world. Finally he returned to the Taurus, and what should he see! More flowers, more plants than anywhere else in the world. So he set about looking for the elusive flower here. One day he came to the flatland that overlooks the city of Tarsus. He was tired, and old too, by now. He came to a lofty plane tree with a spring bubbling beneath it, and after taking a draught from the spring he lay down and went to sleep, using a stone for a pillow. It was still dark when he awoke, but the east was lighting up. Suddenly, with a loud crack, a light burst forth at the foot of the plane tree, so bright you could count the legs of an ant, and a voice said: I am the cure for death. Thank God, cried Lokman, this too has been found. And he wrote it down quickly in his little book and hurried into the plain. When he came to the bridge at Misis, he summoned all the people, saying: I have found the cure for death. And the people gathered around him until the earth was dark with the expectant multitudes. Tashbash Lokman took up his little book, but just as he was about to read out the cure a white wing knocked the book out of his hands and it fell into the river Jeyhan.

Such a man was Tashbash Lokman, the noble ancestor of our own Tashbash. His great soul never erred.

The Muhtar knew exactly where it would all end. Experience had shown how in years of famine or pestilence, saints would arise out of nowhere. Murtaza was the last example, still in the madhouse where he'd ended up, the poor fool, egged on by those unscrupulous villagers. But in this case, it was surely Tashbash himself who was cunningly weaving his background of fairy stories. First, one of his forefathers was turned to stone, next another popped up in the guise of the famous Lokman the Physician. Why should there be all this harping on Tashbash's family and ancestors if he wasn't at the bottom of it? He was playing with these people in their distress, these people who were ready to believe anything, to cling to any ray of hope.

Ah, if only Adil would come and say, you don't owe me anything, my friends, that'd cook Tashbash's goose. It was touch and go now, a matter of days before they'd start looking on him as a saint. What could he do to distract their attention? And that Zaladja Woman, fanning the flame with her dreams, couldn't he persuade her to have another kind of dream, and so gain a day or two? Or . . .

Chapter 18

He couldn't have hit on a better idea. Everyone knew about Pale Ismail's daughter. A wedding was just the thing to draw their attention away from Tashbash, if only for a couple of days, until the Council members returned from town with news from Adil Effendi.

In his excitement he summoned Pale Ismail straight away, forgetting to send out the matchmakers first.

'Don't hold it against me, Ismail Agha,' he said, 'making you come over like this; these are bad times and I'm in a hurry. The truth is that I want your daughter as my third wife, with Allah's will and the Prophet's blessing. I'll send my first wife and Zaladja Woman to your house right away to fetch the girl and the Bald Minstrel will perform the wedding ceremony. What do you say?'

'If it's with Allah's will and the Prophet's blessing, on my own head be it,' Pale Ismail said. 'But I brought her up and I fed her and clothed her all these years. Aren't you going to give me any dowry?'

'She's not a virgin,' the Muhtar replied crossly. 'You know it as well as I and so does the whole world. Who would ever take her for wife? You ought to thank God I don't ask you to pay me for having her.'

'Well, if it's Allah's will,' Pale Ismail said hastily, afraid the Muhtar would change his mind, 'the girl's yours to do what you like with. Send the women and let them bring her to you.'

Sefer was pleased at this quick surrender.

'Look, Ismail Agha,' he said, 'we've got to think of your reputation too. People mustn't look down on you. So I'll give you a cow with its calf for dowry. You'll return the cow to me in the spring. And you'll tell everyone you got five hundred liras, so that people won't say a Muhtar took a girl for nothing. Also, tomorrow I'm going to give a big feast in your honour. I'll slaughter four goats and cook ten cauldrons of *bulgur*. Your daughter will have a wedding feast as good as anyone's. How's that?'

'Thank you, Muhtar,' Pale Ismail said. 'It'll do.'

That evening the Muhtar took Pale Ismail's daughter into his house as his third wife, and the marriage was sealed by the Bald Minstrel.

Early next day the goats were slaughtered, large cauldrons set over the fires and the food for the feast laid out. All the village had been invited. They ate enough to burst and all the talk centred on Tashbash and his glorious forbears. The Muhtar was furious. His plan had failed dismally. The feast had only served to bring everybody together and make it even easier for them to talk of Tashbash.

He tried to argue with them. 'What kind of a tall story is that? How can the great Lokman the Physician be Tashbash's forefather? Have you lost your minds? Tashbash is playing with you.'

But he was wasting his breath. The villagers did not even bother to answer him.

The next morning he decided to talk to Long Ali. Three times he went to his house, but Ali was not there. Finally, he found him in the village square.

'Ali,' he said, 'have you heard what is going on?'

'No,' Ali replied innocently. 'What's going on?'

'You ask me what! Don't you know a terrible disaster is threatening this village? They're making Tashbash into a saint! Haven't you heard? The great Lokman the Physician is supposed to be his grandfather. And what's more, Tashbash is spreading these tales on purpose. He's doing all this to destroy me. Lokman the Physician! I wouldn't be surprised if a couple of prophets crop up among his grandfathers soon! You can tell him this, be he saint or even prophet, I'll destroy him. But there's something else I've been wanting to talk to you about, Ali. I'm growing old. My time has passed. A younger man ought to be Muhtar here and I've chosen you. This is a promise. You'll be Muhtar after me. I'll lay my hand on the Koran and swear to it if you like. But Tash-bash is an obstacle in your path. He's always wanted to be Muhtar himself. It's your duty and mine to warn the villagers and put an end to this business before it's too late. If the Government got wind of this Tashbash affair, what do you think would happen to this village?' He gripped Ali's shoulder and looked straight into his eyes, 'You're a sensible man, tell me, how can Lokman the Physician be an ancestor of Tashbash's? Whoever heard such a thing? Where is it recorded? Well? Speak!'

'I don't know,' Ali said.

'Have you lost your mind too? The great Lokman this piddling Tashbash's forefather? You don't believe it?'

'I don't know.'

'But think! That holy man who discovered the cure for death! Could he be related to this down-at-heel fellow?'

'I don't know.'

'Was Lokman the Physician married that he should have a grandson like this shameless scoundrel?'

Ali flared up. 'How d'you know he wasn't? Is it written in a book that he never married?'

'Come to your senses, Ali. Put your hand on your conscience. Is it likely our wretched Tashbash is even remotely connected with such a great man?'

'One never knows,' Ali said bluntly. 'The heart of the brave lies hidden under his cloak, they say . . .'

The Muhtar gave his shoulder a shove and let go of him.

'You're all banded together! It's a Sheikh Sait[1] revolt you're plotting against the Government. Go ahead then, make a saint of him so that he can be a plague on our heads. But I know what I'll do to you both!'

'Go ahead, don't spare your efforts, Muhtar Sefer Effendi,' Ali said, turning his back on him.

---

[1]Sheikh Sait: a Kurdish religious leader, chief of the Naksibendi dervishes, who in 1925 led the Kurds of the eastern provinces of Turkey in a revolt against the Ataturk Republican régime. The rebellion was crushed and the Sheikh captured and hanged in Diyarbakir with forty-six of his followers in June 1925.

'Damn your pig-headed race,' the Muhtar shouted after him. 'Mulish Meryemdje's offspring! Just you wait!'

He was desperate. No question of waiting for Adil now. Something must be done, and quickly, or he was lost. In matters of life and death, there were two people he could trust. One was Batty Bekir and the other his especial henchman, Ömer, a brave and loyal lad, but with a tendency to make a mess of things. He dispatched the watchman to fetch Batty Bekir.

'We're in trouble with this Tashbash, brother Bekir. The hare will be away and over the hill before we know it and then we may well beat our breasts, and with stones too, it'll be too late.'

'Too late,' Bekir agreed. 'It's a calamity.'

Sefer melted at this sympathy.

'A calamity,' he sighed. 'And when it explodes people will not dare lay a hand on him. Nobody, not even you or I, though we know him for an upstart, nobody will approach him without first invoking the name of Allah. So, before the hare slips over the hill, we must get rid of him. And it must be done tonight. It's either him or us. What do you say? Can we do it, just the two of us? Is your gun loaded? Are you willing?'

Bekir's face had turned yellow. His lips were trembling. The Muhtar noticed it.

'What's that, my friend?' he mocked. 'You're pale as a corpse all of a sudden. Not afraid of Tashbash, are you?'

'I'm afraid,' Bekir admitted feebly.

'What's there to be afraid of about that dog?'

'What if he really does descend from Lokman the Physician? What if he really is a holy man? Will God ever forgive us? Besides, we'd never be able to fire at him. A man's arm would wither, his hands . . .'

'God damn you all for a pack of women-hearted fools,' the Muhtar shouted angrily. 'Get out, out of here! Go back into the arms of that whore whom you call your wife! Why, you fool, would Allah ever make a saint of a miserable wretch like Tashbash?'

A doubt stirred in Sefer, but he repressed it. He remembered how the policeman who had taken Murtaza to the madhouse had been killed soon after in an accident on the Gülek Pass. Everyone had said it was because he had treated the saint so cruelly.

'Never! Tashbash couldn't be a saint any more than the devil could be a prophet! Have you ever seen him making the *namaz* prayer?'

'No, but they say these saints make their *namaz* secretly.'

'Well anyway, one thing's certain, he can't be a saint. Never!'

'It's you who are bringing up this sainthood business,' Bekir pointed out. 'No one ever said he was. It isn't as if all Lokman's descendants were saints, is it? What put it into your head?'

What indeed? The Muhtar hesitated, trying to figure it out. Nothing was wrong really. Why was he working himself up like this?

'Haven't you heard anything said about him? Aren't people talking about him as though he were a holy man?'

'No. They're simply afraid of him. Terribly afraid.'

The Muhtar sighed. 'That's just it!' he said. 'This fear is bad. It points straight to what I'm saying. But still, let's wait another day before we stain our hands with blood. Only do this for me. Take Ömer with you tonight and from a distance fire a few shots over the village. Be careful nobody sees you.'

'I'll do that,' Bekir said, relieved. 'I'll shoot away all night if you like.'

The Muhtar was left alone with his thoughts.

If Tashbash were at the bottom of this, he'd produce a miracle very soon, if not . . . Impossible! It must be his doing. Only a fool would swallow this as genuine stuff. Let's see, why not go and talk to Tashbash and ferret the truth out of him? God knows, maybe the villagers were really making it all up behind the poor fellow's back. They were capable of anything those rascals, even of declaring that the Prophet had risen from his grave and had come to Yalak village. If only it were so, then he was saved. He could deal with Tashbash easily. If not . . .

He rose, then stopped. What if Tashbash refused to talk to him? Better wait till nightfall so that nobody would see him going to his enemy's house.

Some time after the evening prayer he set forth. Arriving

before Tashbash's door he cleared his throat and called out, making his voice as gentle and ingratiating as he could.

'Open the door, Memet, brother! It's the Muhtar. I've come to have a few words with you.' God, what was happening to him? His legs were turning to cotton, his heart knocked loudly.

Tashbash opened the door, surprised.

'Come in, Sefer Agha,' he said, looking at him curiously. What could bring the man to him at this time of the night?

'Have you heard what's going on?' the Muhtar began as soon as he was seated. 'These villagers are going to get you into trouble. Look, my friend, I don't bear you any ill will. I couldn't, not to any of Allah's creatures, and especially not to a Moslem. Each one of my fellow villagers is my own brother. And that's why I've come to warn you of the danger threatening you. Let me go, I said, and extend a helping hand to my brother Memet, let me save him from this calamity. That's what I said. My conscience spoke. I couldn't help myself. Sefer, I said, run to Tashbash's aid, pull him back from the brink of the abyss, even though he thinks you're his enemy.'

'I'm much obliged to you,' Tashbash said suspiciously. 'We understand each other.'

Sefer smiled. 'Is it true you don't know what's going on?'

'What is it?'

'You really don't know?'

'I swear it.'

'You haven't heard the story of the rose growing out of your grandfather's hands and when the petals touched his head of stone it turned into a human head again?'

Tashbash laughed. 'That's a fairytale they used to tell long ago. Why are they bringing it up now?'

'There is more. You know the famous Lokman the Physician, father of all doctors? Well, he's supposed to be an ancestor of yours. Don't tell me you haven't heard of that?'

'I haven't! Where did they fish that one up from? What a tale!'

The Muhtar grasped his wrists. 'D'you mean to say you really don't know? Don't you see what this is leading to?'

'No, I don't,' Tashbash said. 'And anyway why make such a fuss? It's always been like this with these villagers. There's no end to the stories they can concoct.'

Sefer could not detect the slightest trace of duplicity in Tashbash's eyes. Well, he thought to himself, of all the confounded devils! What next? One could expect anything from these villagers!

'Ah, brother, when I tell you, your blood will run cold. You'll curse these villagers from the bottom of your heart. From now on you're my very own brother, the noblest man in this village. Look, my time is passing. In five or ten years you can be Muhtar after me. And I give you my word that this year I'll delegate you and not Bekir to choose the cotton fields. The commission from the landowner will be yours too, all of it. May it choke me if I touch a penny of it!'

'I don't want it,' Tashbash said. 'All I want is that the village shouldn't come to this pass again.'

The Muhtar raised his voice.

'Never again! And truly, so long as there's life in this black soul of mine, the best cotton fields in the Chukurova shall be ours. This village will grow rich. On my honour. But let's get back to the danger that's threatening you.' His face became tragic. He soon forced tears to come into his eyes. 'Brother, you're lost unless you do something quickly. I've tried everything I could. I told them Lokman the Physician was an Arab, so how could he be your grandfather? They only laughed in my face. The situation's desperate. They want to make another Murtaza of you, that's what they're aiming at. And if it breaks into the open, we're lost. Adil is looking for trouble, and the Government's eyes are upon us. They'll throw us into prison for founding a religious sect, and you into the lunatic asylum for passing yourself off as the Mehdi. The pure name of our village will be tarnished abroad. Think, brother Tashbash, think of the shame of such an end, worse than death!'

Tashbash's face had grown pale.

'I suspected something was afoot,' he said. 'But this . . . this is bad. What should I do?'

'Go out and tell them there aren't any holy men or saints in your family.'

'They wouldn't believe me,' Tashbash sighed. 'There must be some other way.'

'Ah, it's a pleasant change talking to a clever man,' the Muhtar exclaimed. 'You've grasped it all, at once. You know better than I how it is in these parts. Holy men have always appeared in times of famine and war and pestilence. When our men were fighting at Sarikamish, there was a new Mehdi cropping up in these mountains every other day. You're too young to have seen those days, but you've heard about them, how every village had its Mehdi and the people clung to them and worshipped them more than they did Allah. Then the big war was over and the war with the Greeks ended too, and suddenly all these Mehdis fell into oblivion. Many died of grief when the people who had idolized them began to look on them with disdain. Some took themselves off to other countries, others committed murder. One Mehdi managed to muster fifty men and he organized a rebellion, but the Government caught and hanged them all. I'm telling you, Tashbash brother, the villagers are in a bad way this winter, desperate. And now they've found you to cling to. They'll exalt you while it suits them, and when it doesn't any more they'll cast you off into the mud. You will be left alone, in the cold, provided you haven't already been thrown into prison or the madhouse. They'll mock you behind your back, saying, there goes the saint! I'm telling you this for the good of all.'

Tashbash felt oppressed.

'All you say is true,' he admitted. 'But if the villagers have got this into their heads, what are we to do?'

Sefer looked fixedly into Tashbash's eyes.

'There's only one thing to do. You must get out of here at once. Leave the village and go to the Chukurova.'

Tashbash laughed. 'That's worse. Talk of saints then! Jesus's ascension will be nothing to it!'

They fell into a brooding silence, their eyes on the fire.

Tashbash was thinking: Sefer's afraid. He's afraid that I'll make use of all this to get rid of him. He'll do everything in his power to discredit me. He's tossed out some threats already. Let's see what he'll do now.

Sefer was thinking: He's feigning innocence, the son of a bitch. He's at the bottom of it all. For seven years he's been doing everything in his power to destroy me. This is his final thrust. Let's see what he'll do now.

A sudden volley of shots roused them from their thoughts.

The Muhtar jumped up. 'It's a raid,' he shouted. 'They're raiding the village! Quick, a gun! Get your gun.'

'What would I have a gun in this house for?' Tashbash said.

'Then I'll run home and hold them up from there, or they'll butcher us all.'

He dashed out.

From the window of his house he was firing at random into the night, but his heart was not in it. It was no use. He had to think of something else, something much more dramatic to turn the villagers away from Tashbash. Suddenly it came to him. He threw his gun down and rushed out. Batty Bekir, getting no response from Sefer, stopped firing too.

He burst into Tashbash's house, panting.

'There, brother Memet! See? Whoever it was, I've knocked the breath out of them. And in half an hour too! You've seen with your own eyes that I'd give my life for my villagers.' He embraced Tashbash in a rush of sentiment. 'I've found a way of getting you out of this trouble,' he cried. 'No one can make a saint of you, if you do as I say.'

'Well, thank you, Sefer,' Tashbash said. 'I know how concerned you always are about the villagers, and myself especially.'

Sefer pretended not to notice the irony in Tashbash's voice.

'I'm thinking of you only,' he said. 'What should a man do to avoid being looked upon as a saint?' His eyes gleamed with the crafty look of a man about to ensnare his enemy. 'If a man did something particularly bad, like thieving or rape, or lying with a beast, or murder, would that man be considered as a saint?'

Tashbash saw what he was driving at. 'That's as may be,' he said coldly.

Sefer took fire.

'If they catch you copulating with a donkey, if a dozen people in this village see you in that position, will they make a saint of you?'

'One never knows what people will do.'

'Well, anyway, this business with donkeys and dogs is a dirty business, the kind of thing we'd do in our youth. The easiest would be stealing. But you wouldn't want that. So what's left? Adultery! Ah, that you can do, and with pleasure.' He laughed. 'And just at the right moment we'll come on you by surprise, the whole Village Council. No danger of there being a trace of saintliness left about you then. So you'll be saved and with a pleasant night gained. The woman's all ready too. That beauty among beauties, Batty Bekir's wife. Bekir knows about her fancies, so he'll hold no grudge against you. I'll have a word with him beforehand.'

Tashbash was white with rage. Suddenly he exploded.

'Have you no shame?' he cried. 'No feeling of honour? I knew you weren't human, but that you could be such a monster . . . Now look here, Sefer, I'd rather die than have my honour stained in this village. I don't care about being a saint or a prophet or a Mehdi. And I don't care if it gets me into trouble either. I can guess the real reason for your panic. It's always the meek simple fellows they pick on, so they can drive them this way and that, but don't worry, nobody's going to make a saint out of me. So don't ever come to this house again with your dirty suggestions.'

Sefer saw that Tashbash was past listening to reason. 'The villagers would never make a saint of you, that's certain,' he said, 'if it weren't for your spreading all those fairytales to your cronies at night and sending them abroad the next day to repeat all that stuff!'

'It's a lie!' Tashbash shouted.

'I know it for a fact,' Sefer retorted. 'Well, "he who falls doesn't cry!" At this rate you'll never be able to save your neck from the rope.'

Tashbash longed to grab Sefer by the collar and shake the life out of him. But the man was in his house. He held himself in check.

'It's my life!' he hissed out. 'I'll do what I like. I can only die once. Have you anything more to say?'

'If you're so far gone as to brave the hangman's noose, then I've nothing more to say. If you've considered what will happen to this village, to your wife and children, how we'll all be sent into exile, far beyond the vast steppe, how the graves of our fathers, of our dear ones will be left desolate, untended, then I've nothing more to say.'

Tashbash was beside himself now. 'I've considered everything,' he thundered.

Sefer recoiled. Suddenly, the man before him was growing in stature, swelling, swelling. Quickly, Sefer threw himself out of the house.

Chapter 19

Let's see what the new day has in store for us. A new day, a new hope. Would last night's shooting have any effect?

Early in the morning Sefer had dispatched his emissaries into the village. Then he had interpreted a dream of Zaladja's against Tashbash and had sent her forth to spread it abroad. But Zaladja had not found the heart to tell a soul. What kind of a man was this Sefer anyway, she thought indignantly. She hadn't dreamed anything like that at all. Just to think of it made her ashamed. On the other hand, Sefer's men gave full rein to their tongues, spreading the most hair-raising stories about Tashbash. No crime was too extravagant; theft, despoiling of orphans, rape of a twelve-year-old girl . . . In his youth Tashbash had copulated only with animals, wild and domestic, and he'd have been at it still but for the prayers of the Hodja of Karatopak. Thanks to the Hodja he had given up that dirty business, yes, but only to molest young children, little girls, and boys too! A terror to the whole neighbourhood!

'How can such a creature be connected with a saint? And one like Lokman the Physician too! A creature who's not worthy of living among human beings, how could it be?'

As for Spellbound Ahmet's kissing the ground before his feet, they had an explanation for that too. 'That day, Spellbound went from house to house, flinging truths at people's faces, but when he came to Tashbash he only kissed the ground before him. Now, what does that mean? Aha, it means this: everyone has his faults, but you, o Tashbash, you're so rotten that you'll go straight to Hell, no questions asked. So, in this world, the only thing one can do for you is to kiss the ground before your feet. Nothing else. You're a lost soul.'

Sefer's men combed the village, talking wildly, but people only listened with half an ear.

Let's see what the new day has in store for us. A new day, a new hope. Tashbash's attitude last night had been a dagger planted in the Muhtar's heart. This time it was open war. Not just the usual skirmish, but a pitched battle. This time it was a question of whose head would fall. And for the moment it looked as though Tashbash had scored.

What news would his emissaries bring, his dear friends, his cronies?

Tiny Musa was the first to come in. He had been an orphan dependent on charity until the Muhtar had taken him in, married him off and got the villagers to build him a home. He was one of Sefer's warmest partisans.

'What news, Musa?' Sefer asked. 'What are they saying in the village about last night's raid by the bandits?'

With the body of a child of ten, his yellow skin sticking to his bones, Tiny Musa had the flurried look of a man living on hot coals, as though every minute of his life somebody was after him, bent on doing him a bad turn.

'They're saying, what kind of a bandit is this who picks on a village everyone knows is up to its neck in debt? What a stupid bandit to look for coals in an empty hearth! And that's all they have to say about the shooting.' He sighed. 'All they can talk about is Tashbash and his family. One of them said, it was Ökkesh Dagkurdu, a man who's got such holy ancestors can't be entirely empty himself, and all the others agreed with him and said they were sure there was something special about Tashbash.'

'So that's what they're saying now, eh? That's the worst so far, the first spark to the powder barrel. Because I know my man, that sanctimonious Ökkesh, making his prayers five times a day! It's Tashbash he serves, the sham, and not Allah at all. Ah, Tashbash has picked the right man to use as the first spark. There are oceans of cunning in that man. But I won't let him get away with this. Oh no, I won't. And tell me, Musa my child, there must be some new stories circulating about Tashbash's famous forbears. If he wants to keep this up, he's bound to produce a fresh story every day. Tell me now, what saints have they discovered in his family today? What new exploits have they performed, these ancestors of his? But first, have you been able to find out who is spreading all this?'

'I've tried my best,' Tiny Musa said, 'but it's no use. It's as though these stories spring of themselves, from the earth, the rocks, the trees, as though they stream into the village from that great wide steppe yonder . . .'

Far out in the west is a mountain by the sea called Mount Ida. There, on its summit, you will find the shrine of the Golden Maid. In those days there were two holy persons in this world. One was the Golden Maid of Mount Ida and the other dwelt in these very Taurus Mountains – the forefather of our own Tashbash, the great Holy Tashbash! From their separate mountains, these two souls were in constant contact, and each knew all there was to know about the other.

The Golden Maid was the Lady of the Birds and our Holy Tashbash was the Lord of the Deer. When the Golden Maid moved from one part of her mountain to another, the sky above her became a flashing, teeming riot of birds of every kind and colour. And thus, escorted by her birds, the Golden Maid wandered about her mountain, her golden hair flowing like sparkling water down her shoulders. She had large, bright blue eyes and her lips were the colour of the pomegranate flower. The Golden Maid was a pure virgin in her sixteenth spring.

Our Tashbash was young too, and handsome! Tall and broad-shouldered with a light brown wavy beard that flowed over his breast. On the back of a horned stag he would ride from peak to peak, and sometimes, with a flock of deer, he would descend right down into the Chukurova plain. He would sleep with his deer in their shelters and eat and drink with them. What did he eat? Just a little deer's milk, wild honey, a handful of corn, a drop or two of water . . .

One day a bird alighted on a rock just in front of the Lord of the Deer, so beautiful, with colours so bright you'd have thought it came straight out of Paradise. The Holy Tashbash put out his

hand to caress it and what should he see? A tiny gold box concealed under the bird's wing! In the box, on a tuft of pure white
cotton, was one single golden thread of hair. The Holy Tashbash
knew at once where the bird had come from. He twined the
yellow hair about an olive sprig and hung it over his breast. Then
stretching out his hand into the invisible where the everlasting
fire of the Forty Holy Men burns, the fire that will never go out
till the Day of Doom, he took a live coal and laid it over the
cotton. He put the box back under the bird's wing and sent it
forth. Such was the magic of the coal from the holy fire that it did
not burn the Golden Maid's cotton. And by this, the Lord of the
Deer meant to say, your message to me is that you are as soft as
cotton, and mine is that I burn for you with the everlasting fire
of the Holy Forties' hearth, but my fire will never singe your
cotton-soft love.

When the bird came back to the Golden Maid, she opened the
box and was struck with admiration. Ah, she thought, his love for
me is even greater than mine. He is the saintlier of the two of us.
I must go and prostrate myself before him.

And straight away, in his heart's eye, the Lord of the Deer had a
vision of the Golden Maid, the sky and earth about her swarming
with birds, a whirling cloud of many colours streaming towards
him. Swiftly, he sprang on to his stag and set off to forestall her,
the stag bounding from peak to peak like a shooting star. Then
he cast a glance behind him and he saw thousands of deer and
hundreds and thousands of stars, all tumbling over each other to
keep up with him! After a while he looked again and what should
he see this time? The huge mountain of the Taurus itself, with its
earth and stones, its trees and rocks and running waters, its every
living creature, rolling along behind him, a whole wide world
coming to greet the Golden Maid! This won't do, he told himself.
What will the Golden Maid think of me! She'll think I'm doing
this on purpose to show what a great saint I am. So he turned and
spoke to the Taurus, saying, stop here, o holy mountain, I forbid
you to come with me. So the mountain came no farther, which
is why the western foothills of the Taurus stretch right out into
the country of Izmir, end and there. And he spoke to the host of

stars in his wake, saying, lovely stars, you too stop where you are. And they were arrested in their course, which is why the heavens over the Chukurova are always so thickly studded with stars.

At last the holy lovers met at the Burning Stone of Chimaera, near Antalya, the stone whose eternal flames are a testimonial until the end of time to the place where the two saints became man and wife. After that, they travelled first to Mount Ida and then to the Taurus, and everywhere they went the birds and deer came teeming after them.

The Lord of the Deer said to the Golden Maid: 'When we die our shrines will be apart, yours on the peak of Mount Ida and mine on the Taurus, you among your birds and I among my deer.'

And the Golden Maid said: 'Since the children I will bear will remain here in the south with you, allow me to bestow a gift on your domain.' And she took a handful of earth from Mount Ida and strewed it over the flanks of the Taurus, saying: 'Let this soil yield crops all the year round. Let it be so fertile that its very stones shall sprout and bloom.'

And indeed the soil of the Chukurova plain has ever been the most bountiful on earth.

Then she took a walnut sapling from Mount Ida and planted it on the flanks of the Taurus. 'Let this tree be a help to those in need, a light in their darkness,' she said, and the tree grew, and at night it turned into a tree of light. People still come with their wishes and their troubles to visit the Holy Walnut. And so it will be till the end of time.

Well, this Lord of the Deer, the husband of the Golden Maid, is the Holy Tashbash, the ancestor of our Memet Tashbash! And ever since then it's been a sin to kill a deer in the villages of the Taurus. If you ask why, it's because the Lord of the Deer is one of us.

Let's see what the new day has in store for us, the Muhtar had said. A new day, a new hope. But it had not turned out well. Things were going from bad to worse with every passing hour.

By the time darkness fell, a great fear had seized the Muhtar. Tashbash would never forgive him after all this. He would take the first opportunity to kill him.

He signalled to Tiny Musa and those who were sitting about the room that he wanted to be left alone. Silent and gloomy, they filed out as though from a house of mourning.

'You stay, Ömer my child,' he said. 'I've something to say to you.'

Ömer turned back and sat by the fire, his eyes on the ground. He was not given to talking. Pale Ismail's daughter came in with the evening meal. They ate in silence.

'Ömer, my child,' Sefer began when they had finished, 'we've got to take this matter into our own hands. They want to lay low the great and noble house of my father, the Headman Hidir, a house that has been a haven for the poor many years, a house so often graced by Osmanli Pashas . . . Tashbash is the enemy who is working for our downfall. For seven years he has been trying, but this time he has hit on an idea, incredible, unheard-of, and he's getting it across to the villagers. He's convincing them that he's a saint! For days now I've been watching him with the eyes of an eagle as he weaves his monstrous plan. Look, Ömer, you're a clever lad, almost one of the Hidir family, tell me, what will this man do, once he's got them all under his thumb? Will he spare us? Will he hesitate to wipe out the house of Hidir? Tell me!'

'He won't,' Ömer said bluntly.

'That's why, before he does away with us . . .'

'We kill him!'

'That's it. But how?'

'I'll go and kill him,' Ömer said. 'It's enough that you should accept me as one of the noble house of Hidir . . .'

'I have! Indeed, you're its noblest member,' the Muhtar cried. 'Only you must be very careful in this matter of Tashbash. Your right hand shouldn't know what your left is doing.'

'That's my concern. I'll do whatever you say.'

'You see, Ömer my child, I don't like the idea of taking a life. The human being is Allah's most perfect work. How can I destroy it? But what can I do? You heard what Spellbound

Ahmet said, that my death would be at the hands of Tashbash. You heard it with your own ears and so did the whole wide world. But I won't let it come to that. Never!' He was stirred. The veins in his neck swelled. 'He must be got rid of before he is crowned a saint. Tonight! Listen, my child, I have a plan, and with you by my side it'll be smooth running. All this sainthood business will make it easier too. Can you mimic Long Ali's voice?'

Ömer had one great gift. He could use his voice at will and there was not a person in the village he could not impersonate, man or woman, from Shirtless to Old Meryemdje.

'Of course I can!'

'Good. We'll smear our faces with soot and wrap ourselves in long white sheets and at midnight we'll go to Tashbash's house. You'll knock at the door and call out to him in Long Ali's voice. As soon as he opens, we'll pull this sack down over his head and carry him down into the valley. There we'll strangle him and throw his body into the Dry Well. In the village, we'll spread the rumour that the Forty Holy Men have taken him away. How's that?'

'It's all right,' Ömer said. 'But what about his wife? Somebody must hold her, while we take Tashbash away, and stuff a rag into her mouth so she won't rouse the whole village.'

'I hadn't thought of that,' Sefer admitted. 'We can't trust this job to an oustider. It must be one of us.'

'There's no one else,' Ömer said, with a touch of swagger.

'What has this family come to?' Sefer groaned. 'To think there isn't a single man to hold one woman.'

'And if it weren't for me . . .' Ömer bragged.

'You're right, my child,' the Muhtar sighed. 'But for you, I'd be alone, and Tashbash would wipe out our race.'

'No,' Ömer said, 'let's not mix a third party into this business, even if he be our own brother.'

'True, this is a matter of life and death . . .'

'Let's take his wife and throw her into the Dry Well too.'

'But isn't that hard on the poor woman?' Sefer said. 'After all, it isn't her fault.'

'She's his wife, isn't she?' Ömer retorted. 'Why didn't she do

anything to stop him being a saint? And a saint who wants to wipe
out the house of Hidir too . . .'

Sefer was tired.

'Ömer,' he said, 'it's a wicked thing to kill a man, isn't it?'

'Why?'

'Oh, but it is! Very wicked.'

'Well, it isn't . . .'

'Have you ever killed a man, Ömer?'

'No, but I want to kill Tashbash for you. And five or six years
later I'll be able to tell everyone about it.'

'Are you mad?' Sefer shouted. 'Is that a thing to boast about?
Look, if you're going to let your tongue run away with you, let's
call the whole thing off.'

'I was only joking,' Ömer said.

Sefer relaxed. 'Well, go and see to the guns now, just in case
they should get clogged or something. I'm going to take a rest.
Wake me up as the midnight cocks crow.'

He stretched himself on the couch and closed his eyes. He was
overwrought. What was it like, this business of killing a man?
You grab the neck and squeeze, you keep on squeezing, harder
and harder, the eyes bulge, the limbs become taut, a mad straining
and struggling, one last effort and the body drops limply. It
grows cold. You cast it into the Dry Well, and that's all there is
to it. One slaughters sheep and goats and cows and every creature
without turning a hair, but when it comes to killing a man . . .
He began to tremble. What if they discovered Tashbash's body
in the Dry Well? What if someone saw them as they carried him
away? It would be prison then, the hangman's noose even! Why
not give the whole thing up and let Tashbash live? Let him live!
On the very first day he was acknowledged as a saint, he would
rouse up the villagers. 'Get hold of that Muhtar, tear him to
pieces!'

How long ago was it? Sefer recalled it all too clearly. Perhaps
ten, perhaps fifteen years ago . . . They were picking cotton for
an Agha in one of the border villages of the Chukurova plain
where the mountain begins. It was a village where everything
belonged to the Agha, the land, the houses, everything. The Agha

wanted to turn the peasants out of their homes so as to sow more cotton, and for the past two years they had been in constant conflict. All about the village the Agha had planted cotton, in the lanes, the yards, right into the village square itself.

One afternoon Sefer and his villagers were picking cotton in the very centre of the village when a terrible noise broke out. They heard the sound of hundreds of screaming voices and suddenly they saw the Agha running for his life, a huge crowd of women at his heels, pelting him with stones. And then he vanished. The women had caught up and closed over him like a horde of eagles. After a while the crowd opened up, still shrieking, and streaked off. In a deathlike silence, the villagers drew near, and what did they see! A leg, an arm and half a lung still bleeding in the dust . . . Where had the rest of the Agha gone to? They searched and searched in order to bury him, but they found nothing.

This had happened in broad daylight, in the populated Chukurova, before everyone! And the women had got off with a sentence of only three months each. All through the cotton picking that year, the half lung, oozing blood into the dust, remained before their eyes. The lynching of the Agha was a thing they could never forget.

Spellbound Ahmet had said his death would be by Tashbash's hand, and a madman's word has more truth than a saint's . . . No, he had no choice! It must be done, and tonight. But then, God damn it, why this trembling, this tightening of the heart, this urge to vomit? He despised himself. Pah, Sefer! he mocked, who are you to kill a man! Ah, if only it hadn't got to be tonight, if only he had a week, just one short week before him, he'd go and find Chello, the bandit, in his mountain lair and get him to do it . . .

Suddenly, he leaped up from the couch.

'Ömer!'

'Yes?'

'Have the cocks crowed?'

'No, but it's nearly time.'

'All right, let's get ready.'

They had prepared the soot in a basin. Swiftly, they smeared it over their face, neck and hands.

'And now the sheets,' the Muhtar said. 'It's a good trick for sowing fear in a man's heart.'

Outside there was a howling blizzard. The night was like a dark wall. Sefer staggered and fell. Ömer dragged him up.

'Have you got the torch?' He was trembling again now.

'I've got it.'

'Cartridges?'

'Plenty.'

'Perhaps we'd better not use the torch. D'you think we can find our way in this pitch darkness?'

'Of course.'

Sefer felt weak in the legs and less than ever inclined to commit a murder. But as they struggled on against the blizzard, the hatred in him grew, his anger revived. He had thought he would never be able to go through with it, but now it was different. By the time they came to Tashbash's house he was calm and determined. He could have strangled Tashbash on the spot without a qualm. At the sound of Long Ali's voice, he gave a start and grasped his gun more tightly. Then he remembered it was Ömer.

From inside they heard Tashbash's wife.

'Is that you, Ali? Memet isn't home. He hasn't been in all night. I'm worried.'

She opened the door, a burning brand in her hand. At the sight of the two white-shrouded figures, she gave a scream and tried to close the door, but Ömer was too quick for her. He pushed his way in.

'Uncle Halil,' he said to Sefer, 'you wait outside at the door and see he doesn't escape. Now, you bitch, where's he hiding, that dog of a husband of yours?'

Torch in hand, he began to search. He looked everywhere, in the hold, among the livestock, in the sacks, in every nook and cranny. He even held the torch up into the chimney.

'Where's he gone to?'

The woman was frozen with fright. She could not say a word.

'Speak! Where is he? I'll kill you if you don't speak.'

With one blow of his gun he struck her down. She uttered a moan, but did not speak.

It was then that Ömer lost his nerve. He threw himself out of the house, pulling the door shut behind him.

'Let's run,' he said to the Muhtar.

They did not stop until they were safely back in Sefer's house. Trembling, they crouched before the fire. In Ömer a dreadful suspicion was growing.

'I searched everywhere, in the hold, among the bedding, inside the grain sacks, everywhere. I even looked up the chimney. Where can he be in the dead of night?' His breath came in short gasps, his eyes were large with fear.

Sefer was now resigned to the worst. Where indeed could he be on such a night of devils?

Chapter 20

'Last night, just as the midnight cocks were crowing, there was a rapping on our door and I heard Long Ali's voice calling. What can he want at this time of the night? I thought. I opened the door and there before me stood two giants draped in white robes, with faces black as the night and rifles slung over their shoulders. One was like Long Ali, only three times as tall. The other looked like Old Halil, only ten times larger. The Long Ali man said: "Where's Tashbash?" And I said: "He's asleep inside." He came in and held a torch to the bed. It was empty! And would you believe it, Memet had been there a minute ago, sound asleep, his flesh touching mine! The long man said: "He's slipped through our fingers." And I said: "How could he? There's no way out except that door." "Then I'll search the house," he said. He was so huge that he had to move about bent double. He looked everywhere, in the hold, in the stable, up the chimney . . . He ransacked the whole house, but Memet was nowhere to be found! I could not believe my eyes. Where could he have gone to? "Ah," said the man, "if I'd caught him, I'd have sent his soul straight to Hell." And I said: "Who are you? Are you man or *jinn*? You come in the guise of Long Ali, but your face is coal-black and anyway would Long Ali ever harm his dear friend Tashbash?" He ground his teeth with a noise like thunder. I was terrified. "Ah," he said, "if I'd laid my hands on him . . ." Then he went out into the raging blizzard and I saw the two of them make off in the direction of Mount Tekech. As soon as they were out of sight I began looking for Memet myself. Had the earth opened and swallowed him? Or the roof lifted and he flown into the sky? It was nearly dawn when there was a knock on the door. I couldn't move for fright. Then Memet's voice called. I hesitated. What if it were someone in the shape of Memet this time? The knocking persisted. "Woman, are you dead! Open up!" shouted Memet's voice. Come what may, I thought, and I went to the door. And there was Memet in the flesh, trembling with cold, covered with snow. I told him what had happened. For a long time, he stood there and thought, then suddenly he went out again. "Where are you going?" I asked. "Not far," he said. He came back only when it was day, quite frozen this time. He's been sitting by the fire ever since, not eating or drinking, just thinking.'

Tashbash's wife first told her story to Meryemdje. Then she repeated it all over the village. There was not a doubt about it, Tashbash had been visited by holy beings from the netherworld. But why the guns then?

'It must be the souls of his ancestors come to help the village in need.'

'Then why did he run away?'

'Who else can it be? Only the spirits can be so tall. They came to do us good.'

'Then why the guns? Why should spirits use guns when they can blast a man with a single spell?'

'Maybe they're the spirits' bandits. Why shouldn't spirits have their bandits too?'

'Would spirits go hunting for Tashbash all over the place? They'd know where he was.'

'But the black faces? And anyway, Long Ali was at home all night and Old Halil disappeared weeks ago.'

'There's no doubt about it. They were spirits.'

'Then why did Tashbash run away?'

'But he didn't, that's just it! He became invisible himself and went with the spirits to Mount Tekech.'

The conviction took root. Two white-shrouded spirits had visited Tashbash in the night, had made him invisible and carried him off to their palace on Mount Tekech. There they had conversed till dawn. And then they had brought him back, covering him with snow on purpose to make people think he had been walking in the storm.

On hearing this, the Muhtar went mad. Spirits indeed! He had just learnt from his spies that Tashbash had spent the night with

Long Ali, the two of them plotting God knows what against him. This accursed man must have been born on the Holy Night of the Revelation or how could he have got wind of what was afoot? What had made him stay away from home that very night? And how cleverly he was making the most of the incident! Sending his wife all over the village to stuff those gullible fools with fairy-tales!

One step, one small step and these stupid villagers would declare him not simply a saint, but a prophet as well! Ah, if only there could be an earthquake now, just as Tashbash had been prophesying! An earthquake that would devastate the village. He visualized the smoking ruins, and suddenly Meryemdje's voice: 'Help! Save me, I'm Meryemdje.' 'Meryemdje, is it? So you've found your tongue now? Who would want to save you! Stay there and croak, spiteful old woman!' Rafters sticking out of the snow-covered ruins. It is snowing . . . from the depths of a wreckage a faint moaning. Ökkesh Dagkurdu! 'Wasn't it you who craved for Paradise? You who didn't eat and drink to save money for the Haj? Who hardly slept for making the *namaz* prayers day and night? Well, there you are, straight on the way to your Paradise! So you don't want to die, eh? Oh well, I'll save you this time. You'll go to Paradise just a little later . . .' And this voice? The dying voice of a man trapped under mounds and mounds of earth? Oh, how pleasant to the ear! It is the voice of our saintly Tashbash, who held communion with spirits nightly, who caroused in their palace on Mount Tekech! 'How did you ever get stuck down there? Where are your spirits now? Why don't they come and dig you out, you prince of liars?' That's one man Sefer will never save! Let him choke to death down there.

In a fever of delectation he was living through it all, the horror of the earthquake, the deaths, as though it had really come to pass.

'Ömer,' he said.

'Yes?'

'This man must be killed tonight.'

'We'll never find him tonight, Uncle.'

'Why not?'

'He'll go into hiding.'

'What shall we do then? This is your job, Ömer. What do you say?'

'He can't be killed.'

'Why not? You can do it right away. He's there in his house, sitting by the fire.'

'What! In broad daylight?'

'Why not? I'll see that you get off. At the most they'll give you a year or two. I'll bring the whole village to witness that you killed him in self-defence. Come on. Now!'

'In broad daylight? Murder . . .'

'So you're backing out?'

'But this is killing a man! It isn't like cutting a chicken's throat.'

'So you're afraid? Or is it you too believe he's a saint?'

'Nooo . . .'

'Well then?'

Ömer was silent.

'Cowards, all of you!' Sefer shouted. 'Turncoats! Why, you saw it all with your own eyes. Even you and I became saints when we went to his house to kill him! And you heard with your own ears that he was in Long Ali's house and nowhere else. What are you afraid of?'

Ömer bowed his head.

So you too, Ömer? You in whom I put all my faith, you whom I fed and clothed and protected like my own son . . . An immense loneliness, worse than death, enveloped him. Everyone was deserting him. It was a dirty loathsome world this, not worth living in. There was just one last hope now, the news the members of the Village Council would bring from town. If that was bad, then . . . Why not do it himself? Why didn't he go straight to Tashbash's house now and kill him with his own hand. Yes, but he would get at least fifteen years for it and who would be Muhtar while he served his sentence? Who but that Long Ali, may he be struck down! He was behind it all, egging Tashbash on against him, setting them at odds in order to reap the benefits himself.

That night Sefer could not sleep a wink. His bed was a rack on which he turned and twisted, inveighing against the worthlessness of this world, its ingratitude, its inhumanity.

'Why don't they come back?' he complained. 'Good or bad, I must have news from town. Then I'll think up some other plan for Tashbash. Why don't you come, my brothers?'

Chapter 21

A furious storm shook the whole world. No living creature was abroad that morning, not so much as a cat or a dog. Even the mighty eagles must have retreated into their high mountain eyries, drawing their proud heads under their wings and listening to the frenzied tumult outside. The wolves and foxes must have taken refuge in their lairs, curled up against each other to keep from freezing. They might go hungry for days without being able to venture into the open. No living creature could brave this storm.

The thin snow already turning to ice as it fell was piling up again like sand, the driving wind forming ephemeral heaps of ice about the village. Such a freezing blizzard had never been known before, and yet someone was out and about, flitting like lightning from one door to the next, head hunched between the shoulders, eyes narrowed against the sleety snow. It was Memidik, the hunter, the one person in the village who owned neither sheep nor goats, nor cows, but who made a better living than most thanks to his craft as hunter, or so he alleged, and indeed no man in the whole land of the Taurus knew how to set a better trap for martens than he.

Memidik was short, the shortest man in the village. When the girls chaffed him saying, 'Isn't it time you grew a little taller, Memidik? You're old enough. If you grew by just a finger or two, I'd marry you straight away,' he would pretend he had not heard and make off, his head hanging. Surely he too would gain height in good time. A man doesn't grow just like that, in one day! It comes slowly, gradually. Anyway, Memidik didn't wish to be like those two giants, Long Ali and Shirtless. Never! God forbid! What kind of a height was that, reaching up to the skies as it were . . .

Memidik was six months old when his father died and his mother had never remarried. She would comfort him, saying: 'Don't fret yourself, my child. Your father was tall as a poplar. You're young still. You'll grow yet.'

'Who cares!' Memidik would answer. 'And anyway, being short comes in handy for a hunter. You lie low on the ground and neither the martens nor the birds can see you . . .'

But he did care. The girls' teasing drove him crazy. And as the years went by and he did not put on an inch, he began to shun people and to spend more and more of his time up in the mountains.

However, this was no weather to go hunting! What was he doing, rushing about the village?

He burst in on his mother, a frozen ball, shouting, 'I saw it, I really did!' His eyes were wide, his jaw trembling.

'Shake off all that snow first, Memidik,' his mother said, 'and sit down by the fire. You'll die, out all night in this terrible weather.'

Memidik did not even hear her.

'I saw it,' he kept on repeating. 'I really did! May my two eyes drop down before me if I'm lying.' He pressed his eyes with two fingers. 'With these eyes I saw it. Who'll believe me? No one. But I did see it . . . I had set my traps for martens, four separate traps. It was a proper night for martens. And then the storm broke, such a storm up there, shaking earth and sky, that I had to take shelter in the Peri Caves. I lit a big fire, for it was freezing, the rocks themselves were splitting with the cold. And then . . . I must say it, I must! Even if they cut my throat, even if they cast the crippling spell on me . . . A moan rose from the earth. It does sometimes, you know, when you're alone, but never like this. It grew and grew until it became deafening, until it filled the whole world. My heart leaped right into my mouth and I would have died of fright but suddenly the noise stopped; no storm, no blizzard, and it wasn't cold any more, but warm and pleasant like a night in May, with the smell of fresh spring flowers wafting over from somewhere. I had no time to think or wonder before, down below the village, I saw seven balls of light come bouncing up the hill. And all at once the whole world was so flooded with light you could have seen the trail of an ant. And then what should I see! In front of the seven balls of light was a man in long white robes and his head was green![1] Such a great brightness he shed about him that even the seven balls of light faded into gloom. He was coming nearer and nearer. I began to tremble. Who can it be? I thought. Only some very holy person could make the world in winter become like spring, could bring light into the night. But then I thought, no, I must be dreaming. So I pricked my leg with the tip of my knife. And sure enough, it hurt. The green-headed man, with the seven bouncing balls of light behind him, passed before me and glided off towards Mount Tekech. I lost sight of them and the world was plunged into darkness again. And then! . . . I saw it with these eyes I tell you, a blaze of light, so brilliant, so strong that I fell down. For a while I thought I had gone blind. I dared not look up. I could hear my heart beat, fit to burst. Then, out of the corner of my eye I stole a glance, and there was the tall man, standing right in front of me. He had a face so beautiful you could not look upon it. A tall tall man followed by seven balls of light that danced behind him, frisky as young colts, shooting out blinding sparks into the night. And as the light hit him, the green-headed man shone greenly, his head, his eyes, his garments, the very ground he stepped on. And then the night, the snow, the summit of Mount Tekech, the rocks, the whole world was aglow with a green brightness. It gushed out from within the snow, blinding me. I could not move for fright. But I looked, and who should I see? His face so beautiful I could hardly bear to look . . . Who? Our Lord Tashbash! Yes, our Lord Tashbash himself! He it was, all swathed in a green glow, with the seven balls of light at his heels, like seven purebred Arabs. I wanted to go and throw myself at his feet. I wanted to say to him: Forgive us, Lord Tashbash. Be merciful to us, to me, to my mother, to the villagers . . . But I couldn't move, as though I no longer had any legs. And then, like the north wind he swept off, with the balls of light hurrying after him. Just like the north wind, I tell you, he streaked off

[1] Green is the holy colour of Islam.

towards Mount Tekech, and soon after I saw the peak of the mountain all radiant with light.'

As soon as he had finished, he rushed out of the house without heeding his mother's cries.

It was mid-morning and the blizzard raged on wilder than ever, but the village was astir with comings and goings from house to house, Memidik the centre of it all, his tale told and retold. The groups gathered about the hearths swelled. It was a happy day for the villagers.

Chapter 22

Memidik was on the point of going to the Muhtar to tell his tale when Lone Duran stopped him.

'Are you mad, Memidik?' he said. 'If the Muhtar hears just one of the things you've been saying he'll kill you.'

But the news had reached Sefer already. And he was pawing the ground.

'Quick!' he shouted to the watchman. 'Run and bring me Memidik, by hook or by crook. Go with him Ömer and carry the son of a bitch here if he won't come. I had a feeling it would break out today! Now we're in for it.'

He waited, itching to get Memidik under his feet and grind his bones to pulp. Tashbash indeed! What he's babbling about is the Holy Man of the Lights. Everyone knows about him and his balls of light. What's that got to do with Tashbash, Memidik you fool? Was it Tashbash who had put him up to it? Or could this little runt have made the whole thing up just to show off? Well, he'd soon find out. He must make an example of Memidik so that no one would want to invent such stories again. But of what avail would that be? Memidik had dealt him the finishing blow. As he waited his anger grew. He clenched his fists and gnawed at his knuckles.

When the door opened and the watchman and Ömer appeared herding in Memidik, he rushed at them with such a look of thunder on his face that Memidik promptly ducked into a corner and crouched there, trembling. But Sefer checked himself just in time. If he'd struck the blow, Memidik would have been killed on the spot or crippled at the very least. God! he thought, what are you doing, Sefer? You're ruining everything.

He went to Memidik. 'Welcome, my child,' he said. 'How is it possible you should go to everyone and not come to your Uncle

Sefer's house? That's why I've called you, so you can tell me too what you saw last night.'

Memidik blinked, dazed, not knowing what to do, his body still shaking.

'What's the matter, my child? Why are you crouching there? Come, tell me all you saw.'

Memidik was recovering from his fright. Sefer took his hand and led him to the fire.

'Woman,' he shouted. 'Pale Ismail's daughter! A glass of tea for our son Memidik.'

She came and poured out the tea from the pot over the fire, dropped two lumps of sugar into it and handed the glass to Memidik.

Sefer was smiling now and Memidik smiled back at him as he drank his tea. What the villagers say must be all lies, he thought. They're always ready to speak ill of anyone. Look at Uncle Sefer now! At first, from a distance, he frightens you, but when you get to know him he's a man after your own heart. See how he laughs. How can he be bad, a man who laughs so pleasantly? From now on I'll stand up for him always. He gazed at Sefer with tears in his eyes. If his father were alive, he couldn't have loved him more. He wanted to fly into his arms, to kiss his hands . . .

'Uncle Sefer,' he said, 'you're my mother's own uncle, so you're mine too. From now on, until I die, I'll do whatever you say.'

He was a child again, a child of seven.

Sefer extended his hand and stroked Memidik's hair. 'Of course, we're the closest of kin,' he said. 'But you and your mother have always kept away from me, I don't know why, because to me you're like my own children.'

It came to him like lightning. He'd play such a trick on these villagers Fortune herself would be amazed. He held Memidik in the palm of his hand now, thanks be to God. 'Yes, my little Memidik, my good clever boy, it's our enemies who have kept us apart or how could the flesh be severed from the bone? We're of the same blood, the same stock, you and I. Whatever the enemy may say, or invent, we can never be separated, can we, my child?'

Memidik was melting with bliss. Never in his life had anyone treated him like this or talked to him so kindly. Ah, it was different when it came to your own flesh and blood! Curse the enemies . . .

'Please forgive me, Uncle Sefer. It's just that nobody knows how good you are, how kind . . .'

Sefer sighed. 'People can think what they like, my child,' he said. 'For me it's enough that the great God above should know. Now tell me all about this business of Tashbash's. What you saw, what you heard, everything. It's very important for us all and especially for the democratic Government of Turkey.'

Memidik was in seventh heaven. The head of the village, his new-found Uncle Sefer was telling him that what he had to say was of real importance to the great Government in Ankara! Promptly he launched into his tale. The words poured out like a flood. The balls of light grew in size from man-tall to the height of a poplar, in number from seven to twenty-five then to fifty . . . Soon they had covered the whole distance between the village and the snowy slopes of Mount Tekech, thousands of them, a vast forest of lights, led by the Holy Lord Tashbash, gliding behind him towards the peak of Mount Tekech . . . It was all Memidik could do not to say there were a thousand Tashbashes as well, he was so exalted. Somehow Tashbash remained one, but his stature soared by a yard or two.

When he had finished, Memidik drew a deep breath. He was sweating. 'And that's how it happened, Uncle Sefer. That's exactly how I saw it. Isn't it wonderful?'

'It's very wonderful, my little Memidik, only it's not true.'

Memidik had not bargained for this. Up to now no one in the village had doubted a word of what he had said.

'But it is true!' he protested. 'I swear it. May my two eyes drop down before me if . . .'

'Hush, don't swear, Memidik. Look, I'm your very own uncle, so I know you've made it all up. And beautifully too.'

Memidik flushed to the roots of his hair. His face began to burn.

'As God's my witness, it's true,' he said. 'I saw it all with these two eyes.'

Sefer decided to change his tactics. 'My child, my little Memidik, I'm not saying you made it up on purpose. What I mean is you fell asleep in the cave there, before the fire, and dreamed it.'

'I thought that too,' Memidik said, 'so I pricked myself with my knife. It hurt and bled and then I knew it was all as real as real could be. I knew it wasn't a dream but our Lord Tashbash himself there before me.'

Sefer lost his temper. 'Don't go calling that dog our Lord Tashbash!'

'God forbid, God forbid!' Memidik muttered a rapid prayer. 'Don't say such things, Uncle Sefer, or your mouth will be twisted. Say you didn't mean it. Quick, quick!'

Suddenly Sefer was afraid. What if the lad really had seen it all? What if Tashbash . . . Nonsense! He collected himself and smiled.

'Nothing's going to happen to me, my child. Tashbash isn't a holy man. He's got so many sins . . . You dreamed the whole story.'

'But I didn't! Look, this is where I pricked myself with my knife . . .' He rolled up his shalvar-trousers and pointed to a raw cut.

Sefer flared up. 'It's a lie!'

'But it isn't, Uncle,' Memidik said wheedlingly. 'How can it be a lie when I tell you I saw it with these very eyes?'

Sefer tried another tack. 'Look, my child,' he said, 'say we believe you. Say we accept that everything you tell us is true. Still, it wasn't Tashbash you saw in front of those lights. You mistook him for Tashbash, but later you thought he looked more like someone else . . . Like me, for instance, that man who glowed so greenly.'

But Memidik was not to be hooked so easily. 'Oh no, Uncle Sefer! No, it was Tashbash himself. My eyes wouldn't deceive me.'

'Well, even if it was, you'll go out now and tell everyone what I'm telling you.'

Memidik smiled. 'But how can I, Uncle?'

'Aren't you my nephew, my son, the apple of my eye? You'll do this for me.'

'How can I forswear myself before the whole village? I'll be branded as a liar for ever. Even my mother would never speak to me again. Look, Uncle Sefer, I love you like my father and more. I'll do anything for you, only don't ask this of me.'

'But if you don't then our whole family will be as good as dead, the family of the Headman Hidir . . .' And the Muhtar went on to explain in detail what Tashbash would do to them. 'And there's worse. What about the good name of our village? The Government will throw us all into prison.' He told Memidik about the Mehdis and the religious sects, and how the authorities wiped them out ruthlessly. 'So you see, Memidik,' he concluded, 'if such a thing happens, if they hang Tashbash, it'll be all because of this fairytale of yours.'

Memidik was basking in self-complacency. 'But I saw it with my own eyes,' he said importantly. 'The forest of lights with our Lord Tashbash leading it along . . .'

Sefer was goaded into threats. Memidik was his mother's only son. Wouldn't it be a pity if something happened to him?

'I can't do it,' Memidik said, with the air of one ready to go through fire and water.

Suddenly Sefer found himself pleading with the lad.

'Look, Memidik, you're young. Young enough to be my son. And yet here I am at your feet, your own Uncle Sefer begging a favour of you. Do this for me and whatever you wish will be yours for the asking.'

'I can't do it,' Memidik said again.

The Muhtar insisted. He promised to marry Memidik off, to give him land and goods, even to make him Muhtar of the village.

But Memidik remained obdurate. 'I can't do it,' he repeated simply.

The Muhtar realized that it was no use. He would have to use sterner methods.

'Ömer!' he called.

Memidik was startled at the violence of his tone.

'Yes, Agha?'

'Ömer, my child, our friend Memidik here refuses to say the one word that will save our family, you, me, the whole village. You two are of the same generation. He'll understand you better. Take him down into the back room and have a little chat with him. But mind you, I don't want any fighting. And no noise either. Just have a pleasant little chat.'

He made a sign and Ömer went out, returning a minute later, a stout oak club in his hand.

'Come,' he said, jerking Memidik up by the arm. 'Let's have a little talk, cousin.'

Ömer's face and the huge club spoke for themselves. Memidik was still looking at Sefer for help as Ömer dragged him away, cursing under his breath. When they reached the downstairs room, Ömer gave him such a shove that he was projected, sprawling, into the room. Coolly, Ömer picked him up and stuffed a large handkerchief into his mouth. Before Memidik had time to offer the slightest resistance he had rammed the club on to his back. Memidik fell to the ground. Ömer struck again. And again. And with each blow, anger rose within him and the stick came down faster and faster. Through the gag Memidik emitted hoarse sounds like a man strangling. Tired, Ömer threw away the club and began to stamp on his victim. Soon there was no more sound from Memidik. Ömer stopped and removed the gag. Memidik opened his eyes and looked up vacantly. Then his senses came alive and he moaned feebly. Ömer propped him up into a sitting position against the wall.

'Now we can talk. Those lights, were they real or a dream? You're in my hands now. Was Tashbash real or a dream?'

Memidik's eyes were open, but quite blank and revulsed, like a dead man's.

'Speak, you muckworm! Was it a dream or was it real?'

A corpse would have made more sound than Memidik.

'So you won't talk, eh cousin? A little while ago though, when you were telling all those lies you were warbling away like a nightingale. But you'll speak yet, or I'll kill you. I'll kill you and throw your carcass into the Peri Caves. Come, brother, there's a brave lad. All it amounts to is that you'll say you had a dream and thought it was real. And Tashbash will back you up too. How could it have been anything but a dream, he'll say, when I was home all night and sound asleep? Well, why don't you say something, you mangy dog? Just like a mangy dog you are, with its tail between its legs. Come brother, say it, just one little word. It won't kill you. You won't be lying. Anyone can have a dream . . . Why, you liar, you yarn-spinner, how can there be a forest of lights moving behind a man? And in this snowstorm too . . . So you won't speak, eh? Then I'm going to kill you, brother. I'm going to skin you alive and stuff you with straw. You know I can do it, so why don't you speak?'

Memidik was trembling like a leaf. His teeth were locked fast.

'Is it because you can't open your mouth?' He rushed out and returned with a tumbler. 'Drink,' he said. 'Come on, drink. Open your mouth.'

Memidik was trying, that was plain, but he could not loosen his teeth. Pulling his head back, Ömer pressed the tumbler to his mouth. The water spilled all over his chin and neck.

'Why the son of a bitch!' Ömer muttered. 'I've never seen such a stubborn creature. But I'm going to make you drink. And talk too.'

He was wet with perspiration, his whole body afire. What kind of a man was this? A madman, who was ready to give up his life, when one word would save him?

'You just wait and see how I'll open that mouth of yours!'

He produced an old blunted knife and, holding Memidik's lips apart, endeavoured to pry his teeth open. Memidik was trembling more than ever, his jaws even more tightly clamped together. Soon there was blood all over him, staining his shirt and shalvar-trousers.

Ömer sat back. He was tired.

'Why are you doing this to me, Memidik?' he said, his voice tearful. 'What have I done to you? Why don't you speak, brother? Who are you afraid of? Say it, brother! I don't want to kill you. It isn't good to kill a man . . . Come on . . .'

He begged and pleaded, for how long he himself did not know.

Suddenly, he set upon Memidik and began to bite him like a rabid wolf, in a berserk fury. After a while Memidik went quite limp. Ömer lost his head. He prowled about the room distractedly, then rushed out and brought a pail of water which he tilted full over the prostrate body. Holding his breath he waited, his eyes fixed on the still, lifeless face. At last there was a flutter of the eyelids. Ömer threw himself at Memidik in a paroxysm of joy and began to kiss him.

'You're alive!' he cried. 'You didn't die, thank God. You're alive, bless you! Don't speak at all if you don't want to. What's it to me? Maybe you did see it. Maybe Tashbash . . . Don't hold it against me, brother, please!'

Memidik's eyes were still closed. Ömer fell into a panic again. What if he died? Ömer would be thrown into prison. He'd get ten or fifteen years at the least. And what if Tashbash turned out to be a real saint and cast the spell on him? His body would dry up like a dead tree . . . Saints have terrible vengeances . . .

'Memidik! Brother! Open your eyes, please . . . Please don't die . . .'

He waited, his heart beating, unable to take his eyes off the pale blood-streaked face. Then Memidik moaned and opened his eyes. Ömer went wild with joy.

'Hooray, Memidik! I'll see my hands broken before I touch you again. You can go. I set you free.'

He ran upstairs to the Muhtar. 'Memidik was dead,' he panted, 'but now he's breathing again. Only just.'

Sefer smiled. 'Look at you!' he mocked. 'A big strapping man quaking with fear. By your size I'd have thought you had some mettle in you. Let me tell you this, Ömer, the human being is tougher than any creature on earth. A man doesn't die so easily.'

Ömer was disconcerted. 'But I gave him such a beating that he died three times, I tell you.'

Sefer smiled more broadly. 'Ömer, my child, you're just a raw recruit. Any old policeman in these parts would have had him singing like a nightingale in no time. You need some training from me. Go now. Let's see this hard-hearted Memidik!'

Memidik was still lying where Ömer had left him. The Muhtar

gave him one look and smiled again. Then his face changed and he began to shout.

'Wretched, wretched man! What have you done to the child? Didn't I tell you I wanted no fighting? Why, you've nearly killed the poor lad.'

Ömer blinked, taken aback. Then he saw that Sefer was winking at him.

'You foul creature,' the Muhtar continued. 'You'll pay for this. I'm a man of the law, yes, the keeper of the high law, if something happens to this child here, I'll deliver you into the claws of justice and see that you go straight to the rope. And truly, that's what I shall do!' He patted Memidik's head and would have forced a tear or two had Memidik's eyes not been closed. 'My poor brave child, what has this monster done to you? Ah, it's all my fault for delivering you into the hands of such a savage. But then, why didn't you say what he wanted and be done with it, you foolish child, instead of taking such a beating? You could always have denied everything when you came out.' He straightened up and turned to Ömer. 'As for you, you've disgraced my house. What will people say when they hear of this! That the Muhtar lures people into his house and beats them to pulp . . . No, you can't get away with this, my fine friend. You can't play with my honour. Now, wipe the blood off the lad's face and have them prepare some poultice for his wounds.'

He went out, Ömer following him.

'There's nothing the matter with the son of a bitch. He's just shamming.'

'Really?' Ömer cried with relief.

'Don't be stupid. Now tell me, what do you think, will he say it?'

'He'll never say it.'

'Well, we'll see. Wipe him clean. Then take a rag and soak it with oil and wedge it between his toes.'

'I see!'

'Wait! That's not all. You'll do the same for the other foot but with paper this time. Then set a match to it. If this doesn't make him open his eyes and talk . . .'

Ömer went back. He cleared the mess and wiped Memidik clean.

'You just wait,' he muttered between his teeth. 'Wait and see what's what! Deceiving me like that . . . Tashbash's dog . . . Just you wait!'

He moistened a bit of cloth with oil. Then he did the same with a scrap of paper. He clamped the rag between the toes of the right foot and the paper on the other foot and set them afire. What happened then even Ömer had not looked for. Memidik jumped to his feet as though catapulted from a sling, then fell back, screaming and thrashing like mad. Sefer was waiting outside. He came in shouting.

'What's this? Now what have you done to the boy?'

'Nothing,' Ömer replied innocently. 'He just got up and then fell down by himself.'

'Well, help him up and let him go home now. I don't want to see such doings in my house again.'

Ömer heaved Memidik to his feet. Memidik swayed, but managed to take one or two steps to the door.

'So!' Ömer growled. 'So you're going home just as if nothing had happened, you son of a bitch? So you didn't dream it? So it was Tashbash you saw, eh?' He advanced upon him menacingly, but Sefer stopped him.

'Don't touch the child. I want no fighting in my house.' He took Memidik's hand in his. 'My brave little Memidik,' he said, 'it was a dream, wasn't it?'

Memidik realized he must do something to save his life. 'Please Uncle Sefer,' he said, 'don't let Ömer kill me!'

'He can't do anything to you,' Sefer said. 'I'll wring his neck first. It was a dream, wasn't it?'

'I don't know. I didn't see anything.'

'Will you tell the villagers that tomorrow?'

'I will.'

The Muhtar clasped Memidik in his arms. Then he turned to Ömer. 'Bring the Koran.'

Ömer returned immediately with the book.

'Say it now. It was just a dream, not Tashbash at all. Swear to it on the Koran. Come on, say it and put your hand on the book.'

'I can't,' Memidik said. 'I can't swear to it. I did see it, Uncle, I did. With these two eyes . . .'

Sefer shook his head. 'So you were trying to trick me? Just to get away from Ömer . . .'

And so they began all over again. All through the night, they tried everything, blows, pleading, torture. Memidik was at his last gasp, but still he would not put his hand to the Koran. In between the blows, whenever he came to, he kept on trying to convince Sefer.

'The forest of lights . . . May my two eyes drop out . . . I saw it with these two eyes.'

During the night Memidik's mother knocked twice at Sefer's door to ask after her son.

'He did come in the evening,' Sefer told her. 'But he left long ago, going to set his traps for martens, he said. He told me his tale too. A pretty dream he dreamed, your son.'

Chapter 23

The baking sheets had been set over the fire and the house reeked with smoke. Three women were rolling out the dough while another laid the flat *yufka* bread to bake on the sheets. Their eyes were streaming, their hands and faces and clothes white with flour. Little flames shot out from under the sheets. The smell of burning flour spread far and wide so that the whole village was aware it was baking day in that household.

This morning, after his sleepless night, Sefer's eyes were swollen, his face puffy and yellow. Everywhere he went there was smoke stinging his eyes.

'God damn this baking day!' he muttered. 'A man doesn't know where to put himself.'

He hung around, restless, thinking how it was all over with him, how Tashbash was now firmly enthroned among the saints, and a bitter wave of envy swept through him. A man can have just so much luck. Many of these small hamlets, nestling on the slopes of the Taurus Mountains had produced holy men, but there had never been one out of Yalak village. And why pick on Tashbash? Why not Spellbound Ahmet, the ideal holy man, with his hardy half-naked body tanned by sun and snow, his large, mournful, haunted black eyes, his tawny shaggy beard? And this business of Memidik's? That baffled all description! There he was, ready to give his life rather than betray Tashbash. Obviously, he had made up this story of the lights and then worked himself into believing it was true, and now he would not recant. But why? What was it to him? What an unlucky star-crossed man Sefer was! Everything had conspired against him, Adil, the villagers, his own men, everything.

He wandered into the room where Pale Ismail's daughter was tending Memidik's wounds.

'Has he come to?' he asked.

'He opened his eyes and said a few words,' she replied. There was pity in her voice. 'But he's burning. He asked for water and drank a little. He won't die.'

'Well, it's his fault,' Sefer said as he went out. 'I can't help it if he does die.'

But, he thought, was it Memidik's fault? Wouldn't anybody else have come out with something sooner or later? People were always ready to make up such tales, deluding themselves and eager to convince the rest of the world too. That was human nature.

'Damn this smoke! These women always hit on the worst possible day for their baking.'

He drifted out of the house. The sky had cleared today. Even the weather had been against him, favouring Tashbash. Was there really something in that man? His throat tightened. A weight had settled on his chest. A strange dread was spreading like poison into the very marrow of his bones. He slumped down against the sunny wall of the house and held his head between his hands. How would it all end?

Suddenly, moved by a feeling, he raised his head and nearly choked with excitement. There before him were the long-awaited members of the Village Council, and they were smiling at him happily.

He rose with difficulty. 'Say it,' he cried. 'Quickly. Good news or bad?'

'Good. Very good,' Mealy Muslu said. 'He's acquitted us of all our debts. What's more, the villagers can go and take whatever they need from his shop this winter, and on credit too. Adil Effendi told us to tell you that you're his deputy here. Whatever's mine is Sefer's too, he said. Look!' He swung down a bundle from his back and opened it. 'Look what I got!'

Sefer stared at the lengths of cloth, transfixed. His lips were trembling. 'Thanks be to God!' he murmured. 'Praise be to the almighty God for allowing me to see this day!'

He sank down and held his head in his hands again. The four members of the Village Council squatted about him, waiting.

After a while Sefer leaped up and rushed inside to Memidik.
'My little Memidik,' he said, patting his head, 'you're all right
now. No fever, nothing. You can go. Don't hold it against me if
that dog roughed you up a little in my house. I didn't know what
he was up to. But then, why begrudge me what I asked of you?
Anyway, it doesn't matter now. You can go out into the village
right away if you like and invent all the stories you fancy. Tell
them you saw Tashbash on Mount Tekech with fifty thousand
suns at his heels. It's all right with me. Nobody needs you any
more.' He turned to his wife. 'Send him back to his mother. Let
him dress and go at once.'

He went back outside.

'Aghas,' he said, 'the good tidings you bring me today are like
telling a condemned man standing under the gallows, go, you're
free, we won't hang you. That's what this news means to me.
God bless you all. Still, my friends, I'm a little hurt. Wouldn't a
man do everything in his power to bring this news a moment
earlier?'

'But we did try!' Mealy Muslu protested. 'Only the road was
impassable. I set out three times and got buried in snow up to my
neck. The flying bird couldn't have got to the village in this
storm.'

'Well, anyway, that's all past and done with,' Sefer said. 'Now
we've got to plan how to make the most of this news.'

'That's exactly what we must do,' Muslu concurred.

'Let's not act hastily,' Sefer said. 'The villagers will go mad
with joy when they hear this. As for Tashbash, he's done for. I'll
show him how to be a saint! Listen, this calls for a big feast. I'm
going to kill a calf. Each of you will contribute a goat. This will
be like an offering to God for having delivered us from evil, and
the villagers will eat their fill too. Only you mustn't breathe a
word to anyone. Just spread it around that you've come back
with great news. Set them wondering, itching to know. And
tomorrow . . . Now, go home and send those goats to me at
once.'

They departed with alacrity, eager to show their wives and
children the things they had brought back.

'Watchman!' Sefer shouted.

The watchman had been around the corner all the time.

'Yes, Agha!'

'You heard, didn't you?'

'Every single word.'

'Well then, run out into the village now. Tell them . . . Just say this. Our Muhtar has tidings for you of the greatest importance. Tomorrow at break of day you'll hear the good news from Sefer's own golden tongue . . .'

In an instant the whole village was astir. For the first time in days Tashbash was forgotten and people spent the evening wondering what the news could be.

Early next morning they were all there, young and old. Even Memidik had come, supported by his mother.

The Muhtar cleared his throat, threw his chest forward and began to speak with the air of a general who has just put the enemy to rout. He made the most of what he had to say, adding flourish and detail, praising Adil to high heaven and enlarging on his own role in the affair. It was getting on for midday when he wound up and invited everyone to partake of the feast.

The villagers pressed about the big cauldrons. They were in seventh heaven. This was a feast indeed, such as they had never seen before, with meat and *pilaff* enough for five villages and to spare.

Sefer looked for Tashbash, but he was nowhere to be seen. This irritated him. 'Well, anyway, I've broken your wings, my friend,' he muttered to himself. 'I've cooked your goose, once and for all . . .'

For a full three days a white bird had perched on Tashbash's house, huge and motionless, the size of two eagles, a bird such as had never been known before in the Taurus Mountains, or in the Chukurova, with one of its eyes blue and the other golden. The minute the news of Adil's munificence came, the bird vanished . . .

'Hah! If it hadn't been for Tashbash . . .'

'If he hadn't breathed mercy into Adil's heart of stone . . .'

'Adil's still the same Adil!'

'One night Tashbash turned himself into a white dove and came to settle on Adil's windowsill. Listen, o Adil! spoke the white dove, and sparks darted out of his eyes, have you heard what the women of Sakarjali did to that Agha? If you love your life, don't come to Yalak village! Forget about those debts. Your shop abounds with goods. Minister to the needs of those poor villagers . . .'

'And here's Sefer bragging . . .'

'When we all know it's for the grace of Tashbash . . .'

'If it weren't for him, it would be all over with this village.'

'The white dove fixed its flashing eyes on Adil, and Adil wetted his pants with fear.'

'And that's the reason why, my good neighbours, we've all been able to sleep soundly for the past three days.'

'As long as our Lord Tashbash is among us, we'll be safe from all evil.'

'Adil won't come . . .'

'There will be no pestilences.'

'The serpents won't attack us.'

'The earth will yield in plenty.'

'The women won't be barren.'

'They'll even give birth to twins.'

'And here's Sefer preening and swaggering, as if he had anything to do with it!'

'Ungrateful man!'

'Where would he be, the lousy brute, without Tashbash!'

As usual, all this was reported to the Muhtar in double quick time. His rage knew no limits and he began whirling about his house like a madman, cursing the villagers.

'I'm choking! Quick, water,' he cried out suddenly. His face was purple.

Outside the blizzard was raging with renewed fury.

When he had recovered from his faint, Sefer summoned the watchman. 'Go and fetch the members of the Village Council,' he panted.

'But for the grace of Tashbash, Adil would have seized everything, down to our last rag.'

'He did it once, remember!'

'He'd have taken the cooking pots . . .'

'Even the spoons!'

'The little *bulgur* we have left . . .'

'Down to our women's drawers!'

'I'm going!' Sefer shouted the minute the members of the Village Council had filed into his house, their clothes white with snow. 'I'm going straight to Adil. I'll show them white doves and Tashbash miracles!'

'Don't,' they begged him. 'These people have gone through a lot this year. They're not in their right minds.'

Sefer did not even hear them. 'Women,' he cried, 'bring me my sheepskin cloak, my woollen hood, my snow-glasses. I'm setting out now, without letting a moment pass.'

'But how can you, in this blizzard?' they begged him. 'You'll freeze to death before you've even crossed the Long Valley. Look what happened to Old Halil. And Rejep and Hüsneh . . . Wait until it clears up a little . . .'

'I can't wait! There's a fire in my heart, stifling me. I can't wait to get to Adil and show those ungrateful villagers what's what.'

He flung himself out of the house and vanished into the whirling blizzard, oblivious to the pleas and screams of his wives and friends.

'So it's for the grace of Tashbash is it, you idiots?'

He was going at breakneck speed and was soon in the Long Valley. There was a rushing in his skull, as though a hive of bees had been stuffed into it. By dawn the next day he had reached the Mortar Stone. The storm raged on more violently than ever.

'I ought to stop awhile in the cave by the Mortar Stone,' he told himself, 'and light a fire . . .'

His legs were giving way under him. He hesitated, then spurted on towards the cave, the snow lashing at his back like a whip. The cave was alive with bats, hanging in clusters from the roof and walls. It made him sick. He dashed out again into the teeth of the unrelenting blizzard.

'I must get to Adil by this evening. White doves, eh? The rats!

Let them see how that soft heart of Adil's can be turned to stone again!'

He pressed on, almost running, slipping, falling, getting up again, stumbling, running, the flame of vengeance fanned at every step, the corroding poison of anger lending him strength to battle against all the blizzards in the world.

Chapter 24

'And you see what they did to me,' Memidik said, as he finished his story.

'Now look at me carefully,' Tashbash said. 'Was I the man you saw with all those lights behind him?'

Memidik considered him gravely. 'It was you,' he said with finality.

'Well, let me tell you something, Memidik,' Tashbash said. 'That night I was right here, sleeping in Ali's house. And when I say sleeping, don't imagine the Forty Holy Men carried me off somewhere unawares, for I really didn't sleep a wink. You must be mistaken. You've mixed me up with someone else. Maybe the green-glowing man was too far from you . . .'

'He was just two paces in front of me,' Memidik replied, 'and you were alike as two peas.' He extended his hand and touched Tashbash's shirt. 'You were wearing this same striped shirt. But your face was a little pale. Maybe because of the green light that shone out of you . . .'

Memidik was standing with awe-struck mien as though in the presence of a holy man, scarcely daring to lift up his eyes and only stealing an occasional timorous glance at Tashbash. This tickled Long Ali enormously. Could it really be, he wondered, that our own Tashbash has become holy? Here's this lad swearing he saw it all with his own eyes. Why should he want to deceive us?

'Memet, brother,' he contended, 'why should Memidik lie? Maybe one of the Forty Holy Men did really assume your shape and showed himself to Memidik like that.'

'I didn't say he was lying,' Tashbash said almost apologetically.

'I swear I saw Uncle Memet as clearly as I see him now. It couldn't have been anyone else,' Memidik reiterated tearfully, like a child deprived of its toy. 'Sefer promised to find a good wife for me if I said it wasn't Tashbash I saw. I'll give you land too, he said, and a house. But I said, how can I tell a lie? I saw him with these two eyes, Tashbash followed by a forest of lights. And look what they did to me, he and Ömer! How it is they didn't kill me, I don't know.'

'The lad's told you again and again that he saw you with his own eyes,' Long Ali said reproachfully. 'What d'you want him to do? Lie to you?'

'It's the truth, Uncle Ali, I swear it. Why should I lie? I'd know my Uncle Tashbash anywhere! And I didn't dream it either. Here's the scar where I pricked myself with my knife.' And Memidik rolled up his trousers for the fourth time.

Tashbash smiled unbelievingly. 'D'you mean to tell me,' he said, 'that I've become a saint without being aware of it?'

'Maybe you're not a saint,' Memidik said, sensing something in Tashbash's voice. 'Maybe you were just passing by and those balls of light dropped in behind you, and as you never looked back you didn't notice them. But it's the truth, please believe me.' He had begun to be afraid. What if they treated him as Sefer had? 'Please don't make me lie! Please! What good will it do you?'

'D'you know what this story of yours is going to do to me, Memidik?' Tashbash said. His face was sombre now.

'I'll die this time,' Memidik cried. 'If you beat me too, I'll die for sure. Please, please don't beat me! Please don't make me lie . . .'

Tashbash drew a deep breath. 'Aaah Memidik, you've destroyed me. Whether you take back your words or not . . .'

Memidik was really scared now. 'Please let me go. I'm ill. They've broken every bone in my body. I want to go home to my mother.'

Long Ali smiled. 'Go, Memidik,' he said. 'Since you're ill and your mother's waiting for you, go, my brave one.'

So they weren't going to do anything to him after all! Leaning heavily on his stick, he dragged himself out of the house as quickly as his aching limbs would let him.

'How could Sefer have done this to that poor child!' Ali exclaimed. 'This business of yours is going to drive him out of his mind in the end. He's been in mortal terror of you for some time.'

'And now he's gone to town,' Tashbash said, 'to try and make Adil change his mind about the debts and stop him giving us goods on credit. Just because the villagers think they owe their good fortune to me . . . As for those villagers, really! They must be mad.'

'How could Sefer be such a fool!' Ali said. 'Once these people get something into their heads nothing can take it out again. Even if Memidik laughed at them now and said, I made it all up, and you mugs went and swallowed it whole, they wouldn't listen to him. But Memet, brother, are you sure there isn't something changed about you? After all, why should the whole village be talking of nothing else?'

Something went 'snap' in Tashbash's heart, like a cord breaking. 'Ali, brother,' he said in a low voice, 'don't make fun of me. This is all Sefer's doing.'

'How can you think that when you see plainly how scared he is of you using your saintly powers against him?'

'I'm destroyed,' Tashbash said gloomily. 'If Sefer's really afraid, he won't rest until he gets me into trouble.' He stopped and thought. 'Now I see!' he went on. 'Now I know who the armed men were who came to my house that night, the white-shrouded ones . . .'

'You're right!' Ali exclaimed. 'We should have thought of that before. From now on you're to sleep here, in my house. We'll keep it secret. I've got an old gun which belonged to my grandfather . . . But what if he denounces you to the authorities as a Mehdi? Perhaps that's why he's gone to town. He'll try to have you arrested, or worse still . . .'

'He'll stop at nothing,' Tashbash said despondently.

'Look, maybe you're holy without knowing it yourself,' Ali said half-seriously. 'Just say a prayer so that brute won't get to town, so he'll be buried under the snow.'

Tashbash laughed. 'For heaven's sake, Ali, stop it! What's holiness got to do with us poor wretches?'

'Who knows, perhaps there's something in you that's pleasing to Allah. Your heart's pure and you never did anyone any wrong. And you've been fighting that Muhtar for seven years now, just for the good of the village. You say that prayer anyway. Maybe . . .'

'Stop it, Ali, I tell you!' Tashbash cried. 'You at least don't do this to me.'

At that moment Hasan appeared at the door. He cast an awe-struck look at Tashbash and gulped.

'Father,' he said, 'we want to go and get wood, Ummahan and I, but Mother won't let us.'

'Well, you can go, if it's stopped snowing.'

Hasan stole another look at Tashbash and ran out to Ummahan who was waiting for him with the axe and rope.

'I saw him,' he whispered. 'I saw Tashbash. He's a saint now. His eyes were strange. He was sitting there with Father, face to face, not talking . . .'

They set out at a run towards the forest. Once out of the village, they slowed down.

'Sefer's afraid for his life,' Hasan said, 'because Tashbash, you know, has an army of *jinn*, a huge army. The *jinn* are very small, they come only up to my knee, but they're so strong, so powerful that . . . Tashbash said, if I just say the word, they'll lift up this mountain and dump it right on top of the next one. I can tell them to grab hold of both Muhtar Sefer and Adil Effendi, and hang them up on the crags of Mount Tekech . . .'

When they came to the forest, Hasan built a fire as usual beneath the jutting rock and settled down to watch the flames. Ummahan fixed her eyes earnestly on the fire too, following every twist and turn of the flames.

'I can't see a thing,' she grumbled in the end. 'I look and look till it makes me squint and still I don't see anything.'

'You wouldn't,' he said with superior scorn. 'Because you need eyes to see. And you're only a witch.'

'It's your mother who's a witch,' she retorted.

'She's your mother too, stupid,' he said. Then he rose. 'Now, turn your back, girl, and don't dare look where I'm going or I'll kill you.'

'Who wants to?' she said crossly. 'You're going to that stone of yours, where else! As if there's a single person left in the village who doesn't know about that! As if there was anything to see there! Just a couple of old roots and plenty of black earth!'

But Hasan only smacked his lips with relish. 'Just you wait a bit, wait and see what'll spring up from under that stone,' he said darkly as he made off towards the boulders.

Ummahan ran after him. 'Please Hasan, let me go with you,' she said. 'Aren't I your sister?'

He softened.

'All right, come along,' he said. Ummahan jumped at his beck. Together they ran to the stone. Hasan lifted it up and left it standing. They squatted side by side without taking their eyes off the black patch of earth, as though something of prime importance were about to take place there. After a while, Hasan rose and eased the stone down again. They were happy. He took his sister's hand.

'Come, Ummahan,' he said. 'It's getting late and cold too. Let's gather some wood and go. We'll come back some other time, very early, and look as long as we like.'

'Oh yes, let's!' she said. 'It wasn't long enough this time.'

The village was all in a ferment again. Why had the Muhtar left for town so suddenly? There was something strange about it.

'My brothers, my own villagers,' Sefer had said that day, 'Adil Effendi's sent word to me that the women are not to enter his shop under any pretext. This year the men'll do the buying. Not a single woman do I want to see, Adil said, not even a five-year-old child, or I won't give you anything. Only the men are to go, and in small groups of five or ten. That's how Adil wants it.'

What did it all mean? A group of men was making ready to set out for town, but the women were uneasy and suspicious. What was Adil plotting now? Did he aim to palm off on the men some old spoiled goods that had been left unsold on his shelves?

As for Tashbash, a strange mood had come upon him. That night, he purified his heart and prayed till morning that the Muhtar should somehow be prevented from reaching town. If

Iron Earth, Copper Sky

something does really happen to him on the way, he thought, then I really will believe everything Memidik said. After all, there is no smoke without fire. Perhaps there really was something in what the villagers were saying . . . What were saints like, he wondered for the first time. Maybe they were only men, just like him . . .

Chapter 25

In the end Tashbash decided to sleep in his own house. If he went to Long Ali's he might get his friend into trouble too. There was no trace in him now of the past few weeks' defiance and thundering abusive anger. He had become as one of those passive dervishes, acquiescent to whatever fate had in store for him, smiling on the world with a strange detachment. He hardly set foot out of his house and the only people he let in were Long Ali and Meryemdje. What upset him most was the peculiar way people had begun to look at him, timorous, wary, fascinated. He had a special affection for his youngest son and often used to hold him on his lap and play with him, so it hurt him when one day as he tried to take him in his arms, the child escaped screaming into his mother's skirts. There they were, his wife and children, huddled as far from him as they could, awe and wonder in their eyes. He felt his isolation more than ever.

'Have you gone mad, all of you?' he shouted suddenly. 'You can't believe all that nonsense too! What business would I have on the top of Mount Tekech in the middle of the night and in this snow and cold too? Why are you staring at me like that? Can I help it if the villagers have gone raving mad? Look at me, a man like any other, no lights in my arse, no forests, nothing! That Memidik's weak in the head. He sees things that aren't there.'

He stopped short, ashamed of himself. What was the use of shouting, nothing would make any difference. He decided to take the situation lightly.

'Listen, woman,' he said with his tongue in his cheek. 'I'm a saint, of course! Such a powerful saint that every morning I lift up Mount Tekech in my right hand and plant it in the middle of the vast Chukurova plain. The people of the plain are astounded when they see the huge snowy mountain rearing up to heaven where there was nothing before. They can't believe their eyes. They come flowing in from far and wide to see this sight. And then, my dear, at sunset I take up Mount Tekech again, in my left hand this time, and put it back where it was before . . . Yes indeed! And I've never told a soul.'

He roared with laughter as he told his tale, not noticing that his wife was taking it differently.

The next day he learnt that his joke was all over the village . . .

'Our Lord Tashbash said . . . He said, each morning I lift up Mount Tekech with this hand of mine, and . . . he said . . . I command the rushing waters, saying, stop o ye sacred waters, and the waters are arrested in their course. Not a drop flows by. I tell them to dry up and they vanish into the earth, which becomes an empty desert . . . When serpents threatened the village, our Lord Tashbash said, stop, don't move, o creatures of God, and we were saved. Our women would have been barren this year, but he prayed to our beautiful Allah and we were saved. Then our Lord Tashbash said, Adil Effendi must not come to the village, lest he die on the way . . .'

'What are you doing, woman? Have you gone mad? Don't you realize all these lies are going to get me into trouble? They'll send me to a madhouse, just as they did with Mad Murtaza of Yonja village. You know perfectly well I'm not a saint or anything like that.'

She untied her kerchief and bent her head towards him.

'What about my wound, then?' she said. 'The minute you laid your hand on it, it healed. Is that a lie too?'

Tashbash lost his temper. 'You goddamn woman, I heal your wound? What about Meryemdje's ointment? The devil take you.'

'But my head . . .'

'Damn your head!' He pushed her away. He had to put a stop to this woman's talk or he was lost. He curbed his anger and began to think.

'All right,' he said at last, very calmly. 'I'm a saint. It's only that I don't want anybody to know.'

'Ah, my Memet,' she cried proudly, 'you are, you are indeed!

Such a saint, you soar high over the seventh heaven. People say that saints never recognize themselves as saints.'

'All right,' he said. 'From now on you're not to speak about me to anyone in this village.'

'But they ask me! And when they ask . . .'

'I tell you, woman, that if you breathe a word about me, if only to say he's in good health or bad, he slept or he didn't sleep, he did this or that, I'll cast the crippling spell on you. I'll do worse. I'll see that it's Hell for you and no other place in the next world.'

She took fright. 'My Memet! My Lord! Please don't do this to me! I swear I won't open my mouth.'

Tashbash was pleased with his stratagem. 'At least let this saint-hood of mine be of some use,' he thought.

But from that moment, his wife changed completely towards him. Even the sound of his voice would send her into trembling fits. There seemed to be no way out for him. The only person left in the village who did not want him to be a saint, who did not believe in it, was Sefer. What if he joined forces with him? Together they might be able to stem the flood.

'O Lord Tashbash, the chosen of the Forty Holies, if this base, this corrupt world is still standing, it is only for the grace of your holy presence! We don't see it, but we know that night and day, before our Lord Tashbash's house, there burns a sacred fire which is never extinguished, for it is kindled by the forty white-clad, green-turbaned Holy Men. And every night, from over yonder ocean-like steppe, from its snow-wasted winter, its flower-decked spring, come thousands of blossom-clad maidens, like white-blooming almond trees. They come and gather before our Lord Tashbash's door and dance all night long, flitting around the sacred fire. And as they dance, thousands of youths, bright as the stars in the sky, come and join them.

'Who can they be, these sprites of the night?

'One night, our Lord Tashbash wished he were in Paradise. No sooner said than done! Out of the blue, before he had time to think, three long-winged maidens stood before him. Close your eyes, Lord Tashbash, they said. And an instant later they told him to open his eyes, and what should he see – Paradise! Our Lord Tashbash said, his own wife told me, he said, I never want to leave this Paradise again. The nights are bright as day, milk and honey pour down its hills as in the land of Canaan. Its waters flow as wine, pleasantly intoxicating, fruit trees abound and it is always spring. But our Lord Tashbash did not stay. He summoned the winged maidens. Quick, he said, take me back to my village, for in my absence a pestilence may strike it or serpents rain upon it. Of what avail is it to me to save my own soul, if my villagers are left alone and wretched. And that's how our own Tashbash gave up Paradise just for our sakes . . .

'Our Lord Tashbash sets out when it's dark and reaches the Kaaba at midnight. He prostrates himself before the *turbeh* of our Holy Prophet, then returns to the village before dawn. His whole body is green now, the sacred green . . . Who's seen it? Only a man whose heart is pure can see that.

'You know the Holy Walnut, the tree the Golden Maid brought from Mount Ida and planted here? Well, one night, one pitch-black winter night, when the snow was softly falling, there was a cracking sound in the west, as though the mountain had split asunder. People ran out of their houses and saw a huge tree all aglow, carving its way through the darkness, gliding nearer and nearer until it came to stand right over our Lord Tashbash's house. And there it began to turn around slowly, just like a whirling dervish. At that moment our Lord Tashbash came out of his house and saw the tree of light, its every leaf and branch aglow, whirling there over his roof! He cast himself to the ground crying, o sacred tree, holy tree of our Mother, the Golden Maid! And the tree came to our Lord Tashbash and prostrated itself before him. Then it straightened up and swept off towards Mount Tekech . . .

'One day our Lord Tashbash had a hankering for honey. He opened his eyes and there before him was a honeycomb. But he could not bring himself to touch it. How can I eat you, honey, he said, when my villagers are hungry, when they've never even tasted honey in all their lives?

'Our Lord Tashbash doesn't eat anything at all. He doesn't

need to. Every day there comes to him, all the way from Baghdad, a single date, and that's all our Lord Tashbash eats. That single date is more than enough for him.

'Oh, my Lord Tashbash, the chosen of the Holy Forties, let me prostrate myself on your threshold! My Lord, my Sultan, my Beautiful One! If this village has not been destroyed by earthquakes, it's for your sake. If the grass greens and the flowers bloom, the crops ear and the waters flow, if spring comes again . . .

'Who was it who went up the mountains of Bingöl in quest of Köroglu's immortal white horse and discovered the fountain of life among the thousand springs of the mountain? And drank of its waters and fell there in a faint for three days and three nights? Our Lord Tashbash himself! And when he came to, he walked down the mountain with a cloud for canopy, and everywhere he stepped the earth grew green and light. And he came to the cave of the Forty Holy Men where they were all seated in a green glow. And the highest among them rose and greeted him. Welcome, he said, take my place, it is yours. And now our Lord Tashbash is the first among the Forty Holies, and the *peris* have built him a palace of pure crystal right on the summit of Mount Tekech . . . But he laughs at all this, our Lord Tashbash, just laughs and says, will you have me be as Spellbound Ahmet and Mad Murtaza? That's how humble he is, our own beloved Lord Tashbash! The mainstay of the earth and the sky and of our blessed religion . . .'

Chapter 26

'Let me be your slave, your victim, my Lord Tashbash!' Fatmadja Woman was saying. 'Allah himself has sent you to us, a cure for our ills, a hope in our distress. Don't deny me your mercy! Don't be mean to me, my beautiful Allah's messenger. You know it too, my good Tashbash, how my girl has been a cripple for seven years now. No faith-healer, hodja, nor exorcizer could do anything for her, not even the Blue-eyed Doctor of the Chukurova. Just as I was giving up hope, Allah sent you to bring life to my poor luckless girl. But here you are, being mean, refusing to do the work He sent you to do. Well, don't then! The great Allah is up there, His eyes wide open, watching you, and He sees your iniquities, and if you're not careful He's going to pass your sainthood on to Ökkesh Dagkurdu. Listen, my Lord Tashbash, may Fatmadja be sacrificed for just the nail you cut off your little finger! Only put your delicate hand on my girl's head. Just do that, my brave one, so she can have her share of life too. What have you got to lose? Come, my Tashbash, do this good deed. Open the door! Here's this poor girl waiting for you to touch her so she will be delivered. She's been waiting outside in the snow since dawn, and it's past noon now. She'll freeze to death. Come, open the door, don't be mean. What have you got to lose?'

It was early morning when Tashbash caught sight of Fatmadja making towards his house with her eighteen-year-old daughter on her back, and he hastened to bolt his door. Everyone knew about Fatmadja and her bed-ridden daughter. She was ready to cling to any straw, and it was with zest and faith that she had spread the stories about Tashbash's holiness, exaggerating them tenfold. But this she had not reckoned with! That he would not even open his door to her!

'Is it because I'm poor? Ah, if a rich man had come to you,

you'd have been ready enough not only to lay your hand on him, but to embrace him even. A saint should know better. He should know it's the rich who'll burn in Hell because of their sins, together with all their wealth and possessions, and the poor who will go straight to Paradise. Come, lay your hand on my girl's head and I'll give you all I earn this year down in the Chukurova. You can have my only cow if you like. Come, don't be mean, my Tashbash.'

Inside, Tashbash was making superhuman efforts to keep himself from bawling out at the top of his voice. The blood rushed to his brain, then drained away leaving him yellow and trembling all over. He knew that if he once put his hand on the girl's head, the villagers would never let go of him again. But the woman was there, outside, in the snow. She had even brought her daughter's pallet and laid it against the wall. She would not go and kept on pleading . . .

'Oh Lord Tashbash, our very own saint, the faithful companion of our Prophet Muhammet, blessed be his name! Open the door! I won't go. I'll not budge from here for a week, a month if need be, and this poor sick girl and I will freeze to death.'

She was banging on the door now with her fists. Tashbash lost his temper. He threw open the door and rushed out, ready to grab the woman and throw her as far from his house as he could. But at the pitiful sight of the two women shivering in the snow his anger melted. Fatmadja was already at his feet, kissing his sandals.

'Fatmadja, sister,' he said with a moan, 'I'm not a saint, I swear it. Leave me alone.'

'Bless your lovely voice!' she cried. 'You spoke to me! Don't be a saint if you don't want to. Only put your holy hand on this girl's head . . .'

'But why, why won't you believe me?' Tashbash cried. 'I'm not a saint. I'm a sinner, just like Sefer said. I did dirty things with animals. I raped little girls. I robbed . . .'

'It's a lie! A lie!' Fatmadja rose to her feet. 'You're as pure as Allah's light. Pure and clean. Now, please put your hand on my girl's head, and I'll sacrifice five cocks for you.'

Tashbash saw it was hopeless. Quickly he escaped back into his house and drew the bolt.

Incensed at having let him slip through her fingers so easily, Fatmadja began to pound on the door again.

'God damn you, what kind of a saint are you anyway?' she howled. 'Son of an infidel! Enemy of our religion! Pig! Whatever possessed Allah to send you as a saint to plague us?'

Suddenly she stopped short. It was a saint she was railing at! And saints were notoriously capricious. One had to be very patient with them. What if Tashbash caused her tongue to wither? What if he turned it into wood? She took fright and began to cry.

'Please, please don't hold it against me, my Tashbash! I've said unforgivable things, I know, but it's your fault. Why don't you put your hand on my girl's head? Please, please! Let me kiss the soles of your feet . . . If you don't forgive me I'll kill myself.'

Her head against the door, she sobbed and howled and her voice rent the skies. A large crowd had gathered in a half-circle about Tashbash's house. They waited, watchful, silent. In the end she dropped down before the door, exhausted. There was a long silence. The crowd stood by. No one spoke, no one moved. Then Fatmadja came to and began all over again.

'Look, Tashbash! Look at the weather,' she wailed. 'There's a storm coming. If you make us stay here tonight, outside your door, my girl and I will freeze and die, and before Allah you'll be our murderer.'

She rattled on while Tashbash from behind the door endeavoured to pacify her. 'You're wasting your time, Fatmadja, sister,' he repeated all the time. 'I swear to you I'm not a saint. May Allah strike me blind if I am. People are saying it on purpose. Go away. Nothing I could do would be of any use.'

'I don't care! Just lay your hand on my poor sick girl's head . . .'

Tashbash already knew he was defeated. This obstinate woman was quite capable of spending the night there, outside his door, and of freezing to death too. And he would be responsible. He would really be the murderer of these two women. But there was something else that plagued him, a question in his mind which he hardly dared put to himself. What if the girl really recovered at the touch of his hand? He stood there, irresolute, ready to cry, alone . . . Then he opened the door and went to the sick girl. He laid his hand on her head and held it there for a while. Suddenly his eyes filled with tears. 'Allah,' he said, 'whatever I may be, this girl is full of faith. Make her well.'

Fatmadja saw his lips moving. She threw herself at his feet.

'Blessed be He who sent you to us, my Tashbash!' she cried. 'It's Allah Himself who's smiled on my poor girl at last.'

She scrambled up and grabbed his hands. Tashbash extricated himself from her clutch and rushed into the house. Whether the girl got well or not, he knew that the sick would begin to flow in on him now. He must do something to prevent it, but what?

Outside, Fatmadja was kissing his door again and again. Finally, she shouldered her daughter, picked up the pallet and made away triumphantly. As soon as she was out of sight, Tashbash dashed out and called to the crowd of onlookers.

'Wait! Don't go. I've got something to say to you all.'

The crowd froze, all eyes on him as though he were a creature no one had ever seen before. Tashbash began to sweat.

'Look,' he began, 'I'm not a saint, believe me. The stories people are spreading about me and my ancestors aren't true. I'm just a poor sinner like all of you. Besides, I'm not even a good Moslem. You know I never make the *namaz* prayers, nor do I keep the Ramazan fast. I've stolen cotton down in the Chukurova, worse than Old Halil ever did. I've drunk *raki* and wine and raped young girls, and I've done things with animals. I've committed the worst sins you can think of. Even Old Halil would make a better saint than me! Why don't you leave me alone? Why don't you pick on someone who'll be of some use to you, like Ökkesh Dagkurdu for instance, a good Moslem who makes the *namaz* not only five times, but ten times a day, who keeps the fast not only during the month of Ramazan, but for six months of the year. As for all that nonsense about me and the balls of light at my heels . . .' He laughed. 'Well, here I am, look at me! Where are they, the lights? Can you see anything at all? Look, neighbours, you've known me so long and we've always got on well together. Don't do this to me. If this thing gets around they'll come and arrest me or they'll drag me off to the madhouse. And what if they hang me? Would you like that?'

More and more people came flocking out of their houses to listen to Tashbash as he stood there reviling himself.

'Is it possible for a person like me to be a saint?' he kept repeating. He was sure now that he was bringing them round and he felt easier.

No one spoke or stirred. It was nearly dark now. Tashbash broke through the crowd and entered his house. The villagers stood there, petrified, looking after him with seething hatred in their eyes. They had built a whole world around Tashbash's holiness, and now it was falling apart, their beautiful, enchanted world of hope . . . Long after he had shut the door in their faces, they still stood there motionless and silent, oblivious of the freezing wind which had risen from the steppe and was lashing ever more forcefully at the village.

It was the old woman's voice, a voice undaunted as life itself, that roused them, or they would have remained there, before Tashbash's house, motionless and silent, all through the night.

'Are you mad, all of you? Whoever heard a saint say he's a saint? These saints are the humblest of creatures, they'll always deny they're saints . . .'

Her words were like a sudden ray of light breaking the darkness.

'Who ever heard a saint say, yes I'm a saint?'

'What fools we are!'

'To think we were all ready to believe Tashbash!'

'We were going to sin . . .'

'Forgive us, Lord Tashbash! Forgive us our sin! But you led us astray . . .'

'Half the sin is yours!'

Chapter 27

Thank God, he'd extricated himself at last! He'd never imagined he could get off so easily. Well, that was that, they would never have let go of him if he'd had the slightest spark of sanctity in him. He recalled all the awful things he'd accused himself of and not a single one among them came forward and said, 'Why are you vilifying yourself in this way, Tashbash? You're not like that. You can't be. We've known you all our lives!' No, they'd just listened and gone away quietly, like lambs. Maybe they'd found another saint for themselves, since it seemed they were determined to have one. Or maybe they'd decided it was better for them to have recourse to the Rain Father, whose shrine lay a long way off on the crest of a bald hill where the steppe ended and the mountains of the Taurus began. In years of drought the peasants of the steppe villages would go to the shrine and sacrifice cocks and pray for rain. The Rain Father accepted only cocks. With any other offering he was liable to do exactly the opposite of what was required of him. The stories and legends about his powers were endless. He held sway over all the forces of nature. Snow fell at his bidding. He raised up storms and floods, he measured out the rain and could bring dearth or plenty. And woe to the Rain Father if it was dearth that year! His shrine would be assailed by hundreds of hungry peasants, praying, weeping, cursing . . . Yes, surely the Rain Father was what Yalak village needed, or maybe Ökkesh Dagkurdu. Well, anyway, they could do what they liked now. He was well out of it.

But what monsters these villagers were, raising a man to high heaven and making a saint of him one moment, then casting him down into the mud the next, at the bidding of the saint himself even. Tashbash could not help being piqued. After all, didn't the villagers know he'd never raped anyone, or robbed, or drunk wine, or done any of the things he'd said? Yet not one of them had uttered a protest.

It was dark in the house though Yalak village was better off than the villages of the steppe, since they had plenty of wood from the nearby forest, pinewood too, and this gave them some light at night. In the steppe, people did not know what wood was. For fuel they used cow dung, which burnt without any flame, so that when night came a heavy unrelieved pall of blackness descended upon the villages up there. It was, as the Kurdish poet had said, a darkness fermented for a thousand years that weighed over their nights. How terrible it must be, Tashbash thought, when even our pinewood here gives out so feeble a light . . .

'Woman,' he called out, 'haven't we got another stick or two of pinewood? It's so dark in here we can't see one another.'

She rose without a word and went to fetch the pinewood. Tashbash thought about the story of the brightly shining Holy Walnut alighting on his roof. If the tree came down my chimney now, he thought, it would at least be of some use . . .

'Eh, woman,' he said aloud, 'thank goodness this sainthood business is over. And if they begin again I know what I'll do to them.'

She was like the others, staring at him as though he were a strange creature from the Taurus forests.

He laughed at her. 'And to think you believed it. The things that have happened this year. Who would have believed that Adil Effendi would acquit us of our debts, and give us credit as well? And the Muhtar leaving in such a hurry, and still not back . . . I don't like that at all. He's going to bring fresh trouble on our heads, I'm sure.' Suddenly he flared up. 'Why don't you say anything, woman?' he shouted. 'Have you lost your tongue?'

She averted her eyes.

Would people never be able to look at him as they had in the past? He saw again the bitter hatred in the villagers' eyes and the slow realization began to dawn that for him there could no longer be a middle road. It had to be one of two extremes now, the crown of the saint or the crown of thorns. What did to-

163

morrow hold for him? Maybe people would just snub him. Maybe they would insult him, swear at him . . . But never, never would they forgive and forget. To them he would always be the man who had played them false, who had dashed their fondest hopes, a murderer just as surely as if he had killed their children. And one day, at the bottom of a gully, the shepherds would find his dead body, his head crushed by a stone, and everyone would believe it was the *jinn* and *peris* who had done it . . .

He shivered. What a fool he'd been! 'You're an ass Tashbash,' he told himself. 'Did you have to look a gift-horse in the mouth? Here you were, all-powerful, the villagers ready to come and go at your command, and you had to destroy it all with that accursed tongue of yours. You fool, how d'you know you're not a saint when all the villagers are sure you are?'

The strain of the past few days had been too much for him. 'God,' he said, suddenly tired, 'come what may now! Let them arrest me for a Mehdi and hang me tomorrow morning. I don't care. . . .

Then he relaxed for the first time in days. The children were fast asleep and his wife sitting by the fire, beautiful in the light of the flames. She was still one of the prettiest women of the village, her body virginal, her breasts firm, her slanting eyes dark and soft. Desire stirred within him. Quickly he went and took her in his arms, but she twisted away and escaped into a far corner, cowering, trembling, she who used to melt at his very touch, giving herself without restraint, eager, warm and soft and loving.

He realized what was happening and laughed.

'Woman, are you mad?' he said. 'Even prophets go to bed with their wives! All the saints had wives, even Hizir, the patron of all saints. He went with his wife so often that she had enough of him and ran away. As for our Holy Prophet, he possessed a spate of wives and forty concubines as well and he went to bed with all of them too.'

He grabbed her again, but she broke loose and ran to the door.

'Woman, are you mad?'

This time he held her fast, pulling off her clothes, kissing her breasts, while she struggled for dear life and tossed and threshed about like one possessed. Suddenly she went limp. There was foam around her mouth. He let go then, frightened, and sprinkled water over her face, hovering about her anxiously. After a while she came to and he drew a deep breath.

'What came over you?' he whispered. 'Have you gone mad?' He tried to take her hand, but she began to tremble again.

They did not sleep until morning and all through the night Tashbash argued with her. With a few words he had convinced the whole village that he was not a saint, but this woman of his would not be swayed.

He was still talking as the day began to dawn and light seeped in through their tiny window.

'Aaah, if only I really were a saint, I'd show you! I'd cast the crippling spell on you. Or better still I'd turn you into an old woman of seventy. The least I could do would be to stick some sense into that stupid head of yours. But I'm not a saint, more's the pity. I can't do anything, neither for good nor for bad.'

He went out, but almost instantly he threw himself inside again, his face pale.

'What's happened? What is it?' she gasped, frightened at the change in him.

'The sick!' he moaned.

She went to the door. They had laid them on pallets on the snow against the wall of the house and were waiting there, patient and silent. It was snowing softly, insubstantially. From afar, she saw more of them approaching, men and women bearing the sick on their backs.

She looked back at Tashbash, proud, expectant. His eyes were fixed on the ash-soiled fire. After a while he turned to her.

'Bring them in,' he said. 'It's no use . . .'

Soon the house was filled with a foul-smelling tattered crowd of sick and invalid, some bed-ridden for years, others at their last gasp, all of them pinning their ultimate hope on Tashbash.

He joined his hands and prayed to God with all his heart and soul. Then going to each in turn, he blew his breath over them.

There was faith and gratitude in the eyes that opened weakly on him. He laid his hand over each one's head and passed on.

They had brought presents, but he would not take them. 'I will accept nothing but a pinch of salt from those who come,' he declared. 'Otherwise my prayers will not find grace in the eyes of Allah.'

A pinch of salt is half a thimbleful.

Chapter 28

Her skirts swirling in the keen blast from the steppe, her white headscarf fluttering like a flag, Meryemdje sped towards the village square. Those women who caught sight of her at once smelled something in the wind and fell in behind her. She reached the square and looked about her fiercely; obviously, she was in a tearing rage. Then she bent down and dug up a heavy stone from under the snow. The women imitated her, and when she whirled about and directed her steps towards Sefer's house, they followed her. Others joined them on the way. They were quiet as a deep-swelling sea. Meryemdje went straight up to Sefer's door and threw herself against it. It did not yield. Sefer had seen the angry horde of women and had not only drawn the bolt but propped a huge log against the door too. The women heaved with all their might, but it held fast. Then they retreated to a certain distance and began to pelt the door with stones.

Inside, Sefer held his rifle ready, but he had only five bullets left. He could hit five women at the most, but what about the rest of them, swarming out there like ants? They would make short work of him and his family, as wolves run wild and devour each other at the smell of one drop of blood. He knew he was lost. Only a miracle could save him now. Already a large stone had crashed through the door and had hit Pale Ismail's daughter in the leg. She was writhing on the ground, screaming with pain.

A group of ten villagers had reached the town a day later than the Muhtar. They had gone straight to Adil Effendi's shop, rejoicing in their good fortune and blessing Tashbash for it. But they were met by Adil's brother, Riza Bey, who had stared at them in surprise.

'Aren't you from Yalak village? Why have you come? To pay your debts?'

'But Adil Effendi promised . . .'

'Look, friends, you'd better disappear before he sees you, because he's very angry now. In fact as soon as the snows melt, he's going to come to your village and seize all you have, down to your wives' drawers.'

And he had told them all about the Muhtar's visit the day before . . .

It was past noon and still the stones came raining down. They had amassed a man-tall pile, which they did not touch. A reserve. The door was riddled with cracks and holes. It would not hold long now . . .

When it broke open Sefer made his decision. He leaped out and threw himself on the ground beside the house with the left wall for cover. The muzzle of his gun was pointed at the crowd.

The hands holding the stones paused in the very act of throwing. The women had sensed his recklessness. They waited, watching him. Sefer lay there, still as the dead, hardly daring to bat an eyelid. The minutes crept by. An hour, two hours, and still no one moved. His life was held by a thread now. A screeching flight of birds in the sky, a sudden storm, a dog barking, the slightest sound breaking the stillness would also break the thread.

He prayed for the night to come quickly. A younger man might have trusted to his rifle and tried to frighten the women off with a shot or two. But Sefer knew that shooting might have just the opposite effect. He knew that a mob seldom gives way before bullets. From somewhere inside the house a cat mewed. His heart jumped. If they had heard it . . . Taut as a bow, he looked at the women who seemed to be growing taller and stronger in the slanting sun. Not a single man! What had happened to them? Where were they?

'Come, brother, come, my beautiful sun, my lion . . . Why don't you set more quickly?' He was sweating and yet it was freezing cold.

And that Meryemdje right in the front of them, erect, motionless as a rock . . . She wasn't one to remain still for long. Any moment now she might make the first move. Well, let her, the old witch! His first bullet would be for her, right in the middle of the forehead . . .

Meryemdje knew it. And the thought rooted her to the spot. If she could only summon up enough courage to take one step, that would be the end of Sefer and his wives and children. Perhaps he would not even have time to fire a single shot, as in the village of Akkisrak when the women had set upon the Bey who had raped so many of them. He had been waiting for them in a ditch, his gun raised. But they had swept on fearlessly and the Bey had thrown away his gun and taken to his heels. In the end they had caught up with him and torn him to pieces . . .

The sun had come to rest upon the peak of Mount Tekech and had stopped there. It seemed to Sefer that it would never move again. A reddish glow lit up the snow and the women loomed larger than ever. He could not take his eyes off Meryemdje, that bloodthirsty old witch bent on drinking his blood.

Now the sun was moving again, and there was only a thin red slice . . . Then it was gone, and twilight began to close in over the crowd. Slowly, the women faded away into the darkness. Sefer did not dare move yet. They could not see him, but they could still feel him. At last there was only darkness, and after a while faint thin murmurings, slow stirrings in the night, bare feet shuffling over the snow. Then he knew they were gone.

'Allah!' he cried, as he struggled to his feet. 'Thank you, Allah, for delivering me from this evil. I swear I'll sacrifice five cocks for you at the Rain Father's shrine.' His eyes searched the night. He could make out nothing but a thin vacillating shadow. 'Who cares about one single woman?' he thought. 'Let her stay there as long as she likes. There's nothing she can do now.'

Meryemdje had not moved. She stood there huddled over her stick, hardly aware that the others had all gone. The defeat was hers alone. Had she been a braver woman, had she given less thought to herself, there would have been no Sefer now.

Inside the house Sefer, exultant, could hardly restrain himself from setting out right away with his offerings to the Rain Father. This was a complete rout for the women. They would never be able to attack him a second time. A single person would try again and again. But it was rare that a defeated crowd would rally once more.

Chapter 29

Sefer realized that he'd made the biggest mistake of his life. The villagers would never forget this. How could he have let his feelings run away with him and get him into this mess? What he'd done was bad, very bad ... To say nothing of all that boot-licking at Adil Effendi's.

'It's a matter of life and death with me, Adil,' he had pleaded. 'You know how I've always been your best friend. You could kill me, but such is my devotion that even then my blood would flow towards you. Don't give them credit. Do your worst to them.'

But Adil Effendi was adamant. 'Never,' he kept saying. 'Never! I'm not one of those who lick what they spit.'

Sefer had begged and wept and kissed his feet to no avail until it had suddenly dawned on him that Adil was afraid. The old wolf could not be doing this out of simple humanity. Something must have happened to put him in such mortal fear of a handful of rustics. The first thing to do was to set his fears at rest.

'Those villagers aren't worthy of what you're doing for them,' he began anew. 'Is there anything on earth as stupid and cowardly as the peasant race? Base, unreliable, biting the hand that feeds them. Timorous as rabbits they are, Adil brother, and when they get together no better than a flock of sheep and just as easily led by the nose. The very sight of a townsman sends them running for their lives. It's as if they'd seen a dragon, that's how stupid they are. How could it be otherwise when for ages and without a murmur they've let us take the very morsel they eat from right out of their mouth? And still they're afraid, like no other creature on earth is afraid, afraid of serpents, of ants, of the forest and the storm, of *jinns* and *peris*, of the darkness and the stars, of the lightning and of fire ... Even the flying bird will scare the wits out of them. But when it comes to townsfolk, that's what they fear most . . .'

He saw Adil's face relax and begin to brighten up. Whatever could have put the man into such a state? Then it came to him in a flash.

'By the way, Adil brother, has Old Halil been seen in town lately? You know Old Halil from our village? He disappeared a while ago . . .'

Adil stared at the floor and made no reply.

Could it really be that the old man had survived, Sefer wondered, survived and frightened Adil out of his wits?

But there was no vestige of fear now in Adil. 'Sefer brother,' he said, 'don't you worry. I'll show these villagers what's what. Not a pin will they get from me. Let them just try to step into this shop! As soon as the snows melt I'll come to the village and claim my due if I have to strip it bare!'

Sefer had left the shop, gloating. Now let them see what Tashbash's power amounted to. Drunk with triumph he had never given a thought to the villagers' reaction. And this had almost cost him his life. A man should never fall prey to his passions. Every single one of his moves should be weighed and considered first. How was he to win the villagers over now? That was the question. He shuddered at the thought of his narrow escape. What if they came again? That would really be the end for him. Nothing would stop them this time, neither guns, nor cannon, nor even Ismet Pasha's jets up on high.

Suddenly he saw three policemen marching into the village and making for his house. His heart jumped and his legs gave way under him. He held on to the doorjamb. Look what he'd brought on his own head and with his own hand too, just because he was jealous of Tashbash, just because he could not bear that the villagers should look upon him as a saint. The monster of jealousy had spurred him on. They were coming to take Tashbash away. And when they had gone, there was no knowing what the women would do to him, with that accursed Meryemdje egging them on. Meryemdje was not one to accept defeat.

She'd bide her time and attack again and again. Why couldn't he have curbed that impulse which had led him to denounce Tashbash?

The young Captain of the police, Shükrü, had been enraged. 'What?' he had shouted. 'Saints in this atom age? Mehdis in this space age? I'll break every bone in his body. I'll show him how to be a Mehdi in the twentieth century.' He had almost wept with rage. 'It's these exploiters, these liars, these Tashbashes who keep our poor people from modern progress. Mehdis in our modern Turkey, eh? Relics of the Ottoman fanatics, eh?'

Even Sefer had quailed before the Captain's wrath.

And now his policemen were here. They would take Tashbash away and beat the life out of him. And suppose he survived, and came back? Like Azrael, the Angel of Death, he would swoop upon Sefer . . . How could he have made so many enemies in this Tashbash business? Memidik, for instance, would he ever forget that thrashing? Little men are apt to have the meanest vengeances.

'Selam to you, Muhtar.'

'And to you too, Corporal Jumali.'

'A prophet has cropped up in your village, Muhtar, and you've denounced him. We've come for him. It can't really be Tashbash, can it? I always knew him for a sensible man. Is it true that the sick flow in to him and that at a touch of his hand, they're restored to health again?'

'Come in first,' Sefer said. 'Come in and rest awhile.'

'We can't wait a minute,' Corporal Jumali said. 'The Captain wants this prophet quickly.'

Sefer was rubbing his hands, unable to make up his mind about what he ought to do. 'Look, Corporal Jumali,' he said with difficulty, 'do you have to arrest him? Tashbash recanted last night. He proclaimed he wasn't a saint, and in the presence of all the villagers too.' Come what may, how he wished they would take him away!

'Is there something wrong with your head, Muhtar?' Corporal Jumali said. 'You're the one who came to inform against him. The Captain's orders are definite. I'm to bring him back at any

173

cost, and if there's any resistance in the village he'll come himself, with the whole platoon.'

Sefer saw his plan of action. 'No!' he screamed. 'No, Corporal Jumali, I'm Muhtar here. I won't give him up to you. Tashbash is our talisman.'

The Corporal laughed. 'I see your game, Muhtar,' he said. 'You're terrified of what they'll do to you after Tashbash's gone, eh? Well, that's easy, twenty-five liras will solve your problem. Otherwise, I'll tell everyone you denounced Tashbash. Twenty-five liras I want, and at once!'

Sefer disappeared into the house and was back almost at once, holding the notes tightly in his fist.

'Take it, Corporal,' he said, 'it's yours.'

'All right, Muhtar,' the Corporal said. 'You can shout now to your heart's content.'

'There's something else I want you to do for me, Corporal,' the Muhtar whispered. 'When we get to Tashbash's, I shall plead and scream and raise hell. Just give me a swing or two with the butt of your rifle. I may fall down in a faint, but don't worry.'

They set off, with Sefer shouting at the top of his voice. 'You can't do this! You can't! We in this village will never give up our Tashbash. Over our dead bodies . . .' A sudden thought came to him. If the villagers defied the police . . . This was worth a hundred liras even. The Captain would come then, with the whole platoon and arrest everyone. He whispered in the Corporal's ear. 'A hundred liras for you, Corporal, if the villagers try to resist.'

The Corporal smiled. 'It's up to you to make them do it,' he said.

A large crowd had assembled about Tashbash's house.

'Move on, you loafers,' the Corporal roared. 'Memet Tashbash, son of Memet, come out of your house. You're wanted at the police station.'

Sefer flung himself against the door. 'Don't come out, Tashbash brother! He hasn't got a warrant to search the house. Just don't come out!'

More and more people came streaming out of the houses to

join the crowd. Meryemdje was there leaning on her stick, at the front of a group of women.

Suddenly Tashbash appeared on the threshold, all spruced up in his best clothes, a smile of defiance on his lips.

'Here I am, Corporal.'

'The Captain wants you.'

'All right, let's go.'

'You can't, no you can't!' Sefer shrieked. 'You can't take away the soul of this village. If you touch him your hand will wither. You can't take him away, you can't! If our village stands as it does, if it isn't ravaged by sickness and serpents and earth-quakes, it's by the grace of Tashbash.' He grabbed Tashbash by the shoulder. 'I won't let him go. Take him away from me if you can.'

Tashbash shrugged him off and fell in before the policemen.

Sefer appealed to the crowd. 'Is there no blood in you? Not a spark of human feeling? Look, they're taking him away, the apple of our eye, our Lord, our very soul? Are you going to just stand there? What are you waiting for?'

No one moved or spoke.

He flung himself into Tashbash's path. 'Stop!' he cried. 'Don't go. Nobody can drag you away to police stations . . . Over my dead body . . .'

At that moment Corporal Jumali swung his rifle and Sefer fell to the ground howling with outraged pain. The blow had been in earnest. He scrambled shakily to his feet, clutching at his shoulder. The crowd was moving now in the wake of the police. Sefer set his teeth and ran after them.

'Why don't you stop them, good Moslems?' he clamoured. 'Are you going to give up your saint without a fight?'

The Corporal lifted his rifle again, tensing himself, and brought it down with all his might.

'They're killing me!' Sefer howled as he dropped writhing on the snow. 'Help! Help me, my villagers!'

'Kill you is what I'm going to do at this rate,' Corporal Jumali smiled at him, 'you rogue!'

Sefer knew that if he moved again he would be crippled for life.

Some of the villagers looked at him pityingly, but they all walked on after Tashbash and the policemen. His eyes rested on Ömer.

'Ömer, my child, have you become an infidel too, like all the others? Help me up. Come, let's get our Tashbash out of the hands of these policemen.'

Without a word Ömer hoisted him to his feet. He knew that the Muhtar was up to something, but he could not fathom what it was.

'Don't let him go, don't! He's our very own saint. If he goes, this village is lost. Lost, lost!'

He dared not draw near again. There was no knowing what that vicious Corporal was capable of. And anyway he had lost all hope of stirring the villagers into action. Nobody was going to offer the slightest resistance, that was plain. He drifted in with the moving crowd. Tashbash was walking ahead, his head held high, trying to put on a show of indifference, but his face was pale.

They were out of the village now. With one last desperate scream, Sefer dashed at the policemen, throwing a cautionary look at Jumali. The Corporal gave back look for look as he raised his rifle again. There was a cracking sound and Sefer dropped down without another sound. This time the villagers gathered around him and helped him up.

'Have they gone?' He opened his eyes weakly. The police and Tashbash were far ahead now. 'Don't you dare beat him!' he shouted after them. 'Nor even touch him. If you do your women will be widowed, your children will be still-born. Earthquakes and floods and fire will ravage the land. There will be wars and plagues . . . Don't say I didn't warn you! Goodbye, Tashbash. Goodbye! You'll come back to us . . .'

His voice died away and he sank down again, judging that a good faint would be just the thing to make a lasting impression on the villagers. They picked him up by the arms and legs and carried him to his house in dead silence.

Away from the crowd, Memidik was watching. He gritted his teeth and cursed. 'Two-faced Sefer! A hundred-faced, a thousand-faced Sefer . . . I'll show you one day!'

Chapter 30

Sefer scoured the village, thundering and cursing and reviling every single person.

'You gave him up,' he ranted. 'Gave him up to three miserable policemen. In front of everyone, before the eyes of a huge village they took him away, Allah's own envoy, the light of our eyes, the bounty of our crops, the milk of our cows, the green of our forests, the fecundity of our women . . . I, only I stood up to them, and they all but killed me!' And he displayed his bandaged arm. The Corporal's final blow had dislocated a bone which the Bald Minstrel had set and dressed, but the pain was enough to bring tears to his eyes. 'It cuts me right to the heart. If you'd backed me, if you'd been men, he would not have ended in the loony-bin, our own Tashbash, or been thrashed black and blue at the police station. Ah, wretched people!' And here he launched upon Tashbash's famous imprecations. 'The women shall be barren, the crops shall wither . . .' With relish he repeated it to whoever he came across, expecting to inflame the villagers and, who knows, perhaps take Tashbash's place on the throne of sainthood.

Modulating his voice soulfully, he poured out the prophetic maledictions, putting all his heart into his performance, but no one turned a hair. What could these wretched people have seen in Tashbash to have made such an idol of him? Sefer was ten times more eloquent. But it was no use. They had shut themselves up like clams. Slowly the very life was draining out of the village. No one stirred abroad. Not a dog barked even, nor a cock crowed. Only the shrill whistling of the mighty wind rushing in from the steppe, sweeping along the empty yards and whirling about the shuttered houses broke the deathly silence, and the sound made by the dreamily falling snow, like the rubbing of an insect's wings.

For perhaps the hundredth time, Sefer walked through the empty village and hurled out Tashbash's imprecations, straining his lungs, shouting himself hoarse, but it seemed as though no one heard him.

'Never since the world began has anyone been mourned like this,' he thought. 'And all for that good-for-nothing Tashbash.' Suddenly he was angry and cursed in earnest at the villagers' wives and mothers, cursed recklessly until a sudden panic fear drove him to his house and he stood panting, gun in hand behind the locked door, waiting for them to come and break into the house, Meryemdje at their head. This time there would be no reprieve for him.

He waited in vain. No one so much as passed before his door.

'They're sore,' he said. 'Sore at the whole world, and they're sulking. Well, I don't care. I'm damned if I'll do anything more for them, the ungrateful dogs.'

And he too retired into his shell.

Not even the rumour about Tashbash and the madhouse had shaken the villagers out of their torpor, how he had been shut up in there, packed with hundreds of lunatics, and how in the twinkling of an eye the building had vanished and all the lunatics had found themselves in the open, freezing in the snow. So they'd hastened to take Tashbash from among them, and in a flash the madhouse had appeared in its former place again. A few days ago, people would have feasted on such a tale. But now . . . The village was like a vast deserted graveyard.

One morning, however, Sefer was awakened by a confused uproar; people shouting, dogs barking, cocks crowing, a din that filled the whole village and roused echoes far in the distant steppe. He jumped out of bed. The sun was not yet up. Thin flashes of light silvered the clouds in the east. A freezing wind lashed at the village.

'What is it? What's the matter?'

But he knew only too well, and with beating heart he sped

straight for Tashbash's house. All the village was there, come to life again, laughing, talking, rejoicing. The door was open wide. He broke through the crowd and burst in. Tashbash was sitting by the hearth, his eyes on the fire.

Sefer threw himself at his feet. 'Welcome back, our Lord, our dear saint!' he cried. 'Welcome back, our Prophet Muhammet's envoy. The flower on the branch, the green of the forest, the flowing of the streams are come back to us with you!'

Tashbash raised his head slowly and looked at him with disgust. Then he turned his eyes to the fire again.

'He didn't speak to him! He ignored him!'

The word spread through the crowd like a paean of joy.

Sefer talked on desperately. 'Our good Tashbash! How did you get away from them? Did they hurt you? Ah, you're back, thank God. This village has been plunged into mourning ever since you left. You've come and brought us to life. You've made the blood in our veins run again . . .'

One word from Tashbash would be enough to change Sefer's position, but he did not even look at him. He seemed turned to stone.

'Look, Tashbash,' Sefer said in the end, 'when they came to arrest you,' he lowered his voice so the others should not hear him, 'you know I was the only one to try to stop them. These people here whom you call your villagers, they couldn't have cared less. The police gave me such a beating that . . . Look, they broke my arm. Come, let's be friends. Forgive me and let by-gones be bygones. I'll do everything you wish from now on, I swear it. Come, just turn your face to me and say a word. Say something so I won't be disgraced here in front of everyone . . . Is there no human feeling, no pity in you? So you're not going to talk, eh?'

People were pressing at the door, eager to hear what was being said. Sefer lowered his voice to a whisper. 'If you don't speak to me, my man, it'll turn out ill for you. Be you saint or even prophet, I'll break you. After this, it'll be either you or me, before Allah that's how it'll be!'

Tashbash never even lifted his face from the fire.

Suddenly Sefer leapt to his feet. 'So,' he hissed, 'I'll pay you back for this!'

He pushed through the throng of villagers and was gone.

A sigh of relief rose from the crowd.

'Sefer kissed his feet, but he never gave him so much as a glance . . .'

'Our own Lord Tashbash!'

The Muhtar dashed into his house chewing at his moustache. He grabbed the gun from the wall and rushed out again. Then he checked himself.

Today, Tashbash had signed Sefer's death warrant. He would never be able to look anyone in the face again. Wasn't this just what the man had been plotting for years, Sefer's utter disgrace?

'I'll get him yet!' he muttered. 'But not this way. No, I must have a plan. Even the Government does nothing without a plan . . .'

He hung the gun back on the wall.

The Captain, when he had come into his presence, was all fire and fury.

'So!' he had roared. 'So we're playing at Mehdis, eh? In this age of the atom, of conquered space? Why, you lout, people are going to the moon now! And not by miracles either, but by the power of science, of technology. And here you are, stuffing our poor ignorant people with fables, nonsense about miracles and spells, so they will be left for another few centuries in the mud and degradation they've been wallowing in so long. But I'll grind you to pulp! This is the twentieth century, and these people still live in the Stone Age as their ancestors did ten thousand, fifty thousand years ago. Nothing has changed for them. And you, with your fairytales and sorceries, you come and try to make them worse than the primitive tribes of Africa even! And why? Just for a little profit, just for a handful of silver! A strong, hale man like you, why don't you do some honest work?'

This had been too much for Tashbash.

'Captain,' he had said, 'you can't hang a man without hearing him first. Let me tell you how they made a Mehdi of me. Listen to the whole story first, and then hang me if you like.'

'Was the Muhtar lying to me then?' the Captain had asked less angrily. 'All right, out with your story, and mind you keep to the truth.'

Tashbash had related all. Gradually, the Captain's face had lost its hardness. He had begun to feel pity for Tashbash.

'This is a bad business, Memet brother,' he had said when Tashbash had finished. 'I wish I could do something to help but . . . How are you going to get out of this mess?'

Tashbash had bowed his head.

'Look, Memet,' the Captain had said, 'I'm a man of the law, but I'm going to let you go this time. You're a sensible person, but somehow you've let yourself be drawn into this. It's up to you to do something, I can't tell you what. But if you're brought here again I'll make you wish you were dead.'

Tashbash had left the police station more dead than alive, racking his brains all the way home as to what he ought to do. Then he had seen the crowd about his house. How, when, had they heard of his release? His first impulse had been to run away, to leave the village, his wife, his children, everything. But suddenly the realization had come to him that he could never do that. He could leave the village, yes, abandon his wife and children too perhaps, yet there was one thing, just one thing he could never bring himself to give up. But this he did not admit even to himself. So he had walked into the crowd and surrendered himself to the demonstrations of love, the kissing of hands and feet, the prostrations . . .

'The Captain, the minute he saw our Lord Tashbash, fell at his feet and begged his forgiveness. And at that instant a ball of light burst from our Lord Tashbash's brow and glided out of the window. And not a minute later, three balls of light came floating in again and settled upon his head. The Captain was dazzled. Ah Tashbash, he said, you're a saint indeed! Go back to your village with your message of hope and bring wealth and plenty to your people . . . Yes, that Captain's as good and clean a man as they make them.'

Tashbash shivered at the thought of what the Captain would do if he heard of those three balls of light!

Night fell and the crowd dispersed, but the sick remained. Tashbash took them in and talked to each in turn. He spoke to them with gentleness and laid his hand on their brow. Then he knelt, facing the Mecca, and prayed aloud.

'Almighty Allah,' he said, 'these people have come to me full of faith. Even if I have no more favour in your eyes than a dog, don't disappoint their hopes, make them well . . .'

Then he rose and blew his breath upon the faces of the sick.

They had begun to come from all over the Taurus now, and even from the distant villages of the steppe, with every kind of disease; epilepsy, rheumatism, asthma, paralysis, tuberculosis, malaria, dysentery, madness . . . It was hard work, and Tashbash was worn out. He treated them at night and slept during the day-time. The villagers saw less and less of him. He had decreed that the only payment he would accept was a pinch of salt, but the salt had now piled up into a tall mound. In Yalak village itself, people had fallen into the habit of coming to him with the flimsiest of trouble, such as bleeding noses or toothache. Some even came hoping he would find their lost cow or donkey.

'From one of the villages of the Taurus they brought her one day, a golden-haired, black-eyed girl. Bed-ridden for years she was, her legs like two withered branches. Our Lord Tashbash laid his hands on her legs and prayed and beseeched Allah to make her well, but nothing happened. So he went up to the summit of Mount Tekech and for three days and three nights he offered up prayers, but when he returned the girl's legs were still like two sticks of wood. He wept with pity, our Tashbash, she was so beautiful, and he bent down his sacred brow, bright with the three balls of light, his brow that never bows to anyone but Allah, and passed it over the girl's legs. And behold she rose and began to walk, and she walked all the way to her village.

'And then there's Dumb Ali, that shepherd from Chukurja village in the steppe, not yet twenty. One snowy night the wolves attacked his flock. He fought them off with his staff for as long as he could, but the next morning they found him lying on the snow, unconscious, and when he came to he could not utter a word. He'd been struck dumb, and dumb he remained until the day they brought him to our Tashbash. Tashbash just spat into his mouth, and there the shepherd was, piping out clear as a nightingale again . . .

'What about Speckled Kemal who's been plagued by the fever every other day for seven years now? He was shaking so much, the poor man, that he couldn't even pick cotton. Tashbash burnt a bit of cotton wool soaked in olive oil and held it to his nose . . . Speckled Kemal has never had a bout of fever since.

'Seventy if he's a day Grim Mustafa is, and blind since the age of thirty-five, but still he wanted to try our Tashbash too . . . Tashbash made a mixture with a handful of willow leaves and the wings of bats, and said a prayer over it. Then he set it afire and the minute the smoke rose to Grim Mustafa's eyes, he could see again.'

These stories, and many more, spread far and wide, all through the Taurus, up into the steppe, in the town itself, and from everywhere sick people who had lost all hope began to come to Tashbash. The saint of Yalak had become famous. Everyone had heard about him except the Government people. Even the Captain's own wife knew what was going on, but she never told her husband.

Not for a moment had Tashbash believed he was a saint, not until the day the paralytic girl had come back to him a week later, walking on her own two legs. Then he had wept for joy. And there had been the dumb talking and the deaf hearing again, and others with sharp pains in their bellies which stopped the instant he laid his hand on them. He had seen all this happen just at the breath of his prayer, the touch of his hand. If he was not a saint, if he was just an ordinary man, then what did it all mean? The insinuating thought preyed on his mind. Could all these people, those who had seen the balls of light and the Holy Walnut, the sick who had been restored to health, could they all be lying? Yet he himself knew very well that he had never gone up Mount Tekech that stormy night, and certainly he had seen no lights, let alone trees and forests of lights. Wouldn't a man know about it if he'd gone somewhere? Wouldn't a man know whether he was a saint or not? Didn't the Prophet know he was a prophet and Hizir that he was a saint? He must wait a little, wait and see . . .

Chapter 31

Now a fresh danger threatened him; the house was about to collapse. A hole deep as a well had been dug right under the threshold, and people had to jump over it to get in. God knows where the rumour had sprung from, but the firm belief had taken root that if the earth from Tashbash's threshold was scattered over a field it would increase the yield ten-fold. People flowed in from as far as the steppe villages for a handful of this earth. As for the Yalak villagers they scooped up whole sackfuls.

If the Captain heard of this and of the hundreds of sick who came to him, he would break every bone in his body. Since the world began who had ever seen a saint or a prophet come to a good end? It was either the scaffold for them or being skinned alive. Tashbash knew this, but still he remained in the village. He told himself he would go as soon as winter was past, but the truth was he simply could not tear himself away from all this adoration.

'Our own Lord Tashbash! If this base dirty world yet stands, it is only for the grace of your dear presence . . . Our own Tashbash! He's taken his rightful place among the Invisible Ones, among the Holy Forties . . .'

The villagers worshipped him. They spoke his name with the same veneration as that of the Prophet Muhammet. He had only to lift a finger now and they would make short work of Muhtar Sefer. And not only the Yalak villagers. He could command all the villages of the Taurus and of the steppe too. He could say to them, gather together, walk upon the town, kill that Adil Effendi, and they would not hesitate one moment. He could make them do anything, even rise up against the Government. They would face death for his sake. And before long his fame would spread all over the country. From Aleppo to Damascus, from Adana to

Istanbul, people would be talking of him. These and other heady fancies would lay their grip on him and at such times there was no doubt in his mind that he really had become holy. Why should so many people all say the same thing? Why should they lie? There could be no smoke without fire. The bright Holy Walnut tree, for instance, that descended on his house every night, flooding the place with light, there wasn't a soul in Yalak who hadn't seen it, down to his wife and children. Could that be an invention too? Still, he had to see it for himself. He must wait up one night and keep watch. Ah, if he could but catch one glimpse of it, then he would fear nothing any more!

At times, the certainty of his holiness was so strong that it was all he could do not to rush out into the village square and give utterance to the winged words he felt called to speak, his message about life and love and light . . . With a tremendous effort he would curb this impulse, but the strain would leave him panting and in a sweat, his body aching all over, as though he had been flogged. He would lie on his bed for an hour, two hours, his eyes fixed on the sooty ceiling. Slowly the tension would leave his body and he would melt back into the pure ecstasy that now filled his days.

It seemed to him as he looked on the luminous snowy peak of Mount Tekech that he could stretch out his hand and caress it. As the dawn drew its streak at the far end of the earth, he felt that if he raised his hand and said, stop o blessed sun, do not rise over the earth today, it would stay right where it was, and the soft lambent hazy earth and dew-scented twilight would last for ever. He could go to the forest even now, in the dead of winter, and say o trees put out your leaves, and in the midst of the snow the forest would suddenly be fresh and green as on a May day. He could lay his hand on the snowbound steppe, close his eyes and say, let the snows melt, let the flowers grow and the birds sing as in spring, and when he opened his eyes all his wishes would have come true . . . And he would laugh out loud with exultation.

His wife and children would fix wide awe-struck eyes on him. She was bursting to tell someone, anyone, about her husband's strange new ways, but he had expressly forbidden her to say a word outside the house and she was afraid that if she disobeyed him he would strike her with the crippling spell.

'Tonight,' he resolved, 'I shall know the whole truth. If I'm a saint I'll go on with this to the bitter end. If not I must get out of here before people begin to mock me and call me Saint Memet, laughing at me behind my back.'

Unable to stand still, he drifted in and out of the house, feeling the weight of the whole village's eyes on him. It was like this always now. His slightest move was watched and a meaning drawn from it. Most of the time he kept to his house and spoke to no one but Long Ali. But even with Long Ali it was not the same any more. He sensed a new reticence in his friend. Now, Ali came to his house as to a shrine and approached him as he would a holy sheikh. The realization of his complete isolation would be brought home to him then and he would sink into fresh depths of despondency.

But not for long. Again the sensation of his new-found power would take the upper hand, the certainty that, as King Solomon, he could if he wished command the birds and beasts, the waters on the earth and the winds in the heavens, the flowers, the trees, the whole of nature. Even Muhtar Sefer, his most bitter enemy, had come to prostrate himself before him like all the others. If he gave himself the trouble he could extend his sway over all the Chukurova, the Taurus and the steppe. He could make men do anything. They believed in him, and they must have seen something to make them believe.

And then there were the dreams, dreams of other worlds, weird far-off worlds where the trees, the birds, the grass, everything was strange, with fantastic colours in the sky and dazzling streams of light gushing forth from the earth. The dreams would linger in his mind long after he had woken up and he would live on in these bright new worlds.

Ever since he had been openly recognized as a saint, there had been a constant din of crowing cocks about his house. Twenty to thirty of them were sacrificed on his threshold each day, and their red-combed heads were hung on his walls, which had become a riot of vary-coloured cocks' heads of all sizes, like a garishly embroidered *kilim*. What's more, after immolating their cock, these mean-hearted villagers would stuff themselves with the meat there and then, or else take it home with them. What kind of a sacrifice was that? A sacrifice should be left where it was offered or should be distributed to the poor. He ought to tell them that. Yet they themselves were so poor. Perhaps they owned just that one cock . . . 'Well then,' he muttered to himself in sudden anger, 'they shouldn't offer sacrifices and think they're fooling Allah! Eating their own offering!' With bitterness he would see his children look on wistfully as the sacrificed cocks would be put to cook and eaten before their eyes, and the injustice of it all would sink like a knife into him.

Tonight would decide everything. Once he had the proof that he was a saint, then he would show them all, he'd show those hypocrites who thought they could cheat Allah! He'd see that they never tasted a morsel of their sacrificed cocks again.

In the afternoon, the head of the long caravan of sick came into view. Some were carried on donkeys or stretchers, others simply on somebody's back. A couple of sheds had been emptied near Tashbash's house as a shelter for the sick while they waited. As for Brisk Dervish, he had been quick to make capital of this opportunity. The minute he'd seen the flow of sick he'd rushed off to town and bought a good stock of raisins, sweetmeats and other things, and had set up shop in a corner of one of the sheds. He was doing a roaring trade and prayed that the whole to-do might last another year or two. By then he'd have made enough money to open a sizeable shop in the town itself. Every morning Brisk Dervish would relate a new miracle of Tashbash's. To the sick from the distant villages, as they waited in the sheds, he'd give long accounts, with names and details of the cures and wonders worked by Tashbash, and his improvised shop in the corner of the shed had become a kindling hearth that radiated Tashbash's reputation for magic to the far corners of the land.

In the evening the sick began to be brought in to him. Tashbash had elaborated his cures now. Through the good services of Brisk Dervish he had ordered a store of candles, and he would pass a lighted candle three times over the sufferer's head, then burn a tuft of cotton and hold it out for him to smell. He had devised other systems as well and would apply them according to the different kinds of complaints. Sometimes he would cast a burning ember into a basin of water and while it sizzled away he would sit in front of the patient with a lighted candle in one hand and gaze unwinkingly into his eyes. He would make some of the sick crawl on all fours from the threshold to the hearth, others he told to hop around the house on one leg. He would have them smell the dried-up remains of a dead bat or else brush their forehead with a bone called serpent's horn. These last had been given to him by Meryemdje. 'These are remedies for all ills. If they're applied by a good man, they can save a life,' she had intimated by signs. It had taken him quite a while to understand her, and the thought had crossed his mind that he could order her to break her vow and talk at last. He knew she would do so at once, but somehow he could not muster up the courage to do this.

It was getting on for midnight and still the flow continued unabated. Some came who were not sick at all, but plagued with little worries and troubles. Those were the worst of all. This world is full of troubles, no man is free of them and once it began to get around that Tashbash was willing to listen and help, they came in swelling numbers; the humiliated, the rejected, the poor and the hungry. Those whose land did not yield enough to maintain them, those who had run foul of society, the thieves, the murderers, they would all come.

He made his plan. A little after midnight he would slip off to Long Ali's and borrow his thick cloak and felt boots, then go and hide himself in an old ruin nearby and set up a watch on his house. But he could not wait. Cutting short his ministrations, he threw himself out of the house. A dry bitter frost nipped at his face and he began to have doubts. How could he wait up all night in this cold? He could not light a fire. People would see him . . .

'Ali,' he said, 'lend me your cloak and boots. And some matches if you can spare them.'

Without uttering a word, not even to ask where Tashbash was

going on this freezing night, Ali hastened to fetch the cloak and boots and also a woollen hood.

Hasan was awake too. There were visitors in the house who had come from a distant village to see Tashbash. He sprang forward, holding out a brand new box of matches filled to the brim.

'Is that for me?' Tashbash asked. He stroked Hasan's hair.

'They're mine and I'm giving them to you,' the boy said proudly, his voice trembling with excitement.

Tashbash slipped into the boots, wrapped the cloak about him and was gone in a flash.

Ali stared after him. 'He's going somewhere, that's plain. May Allah help him, in this cold . . .'

Meryemdje gave him a contemptuous look as though to say, pooh, would he ever feel the cold?

'Father,' Hasan said, 'they never feel the cold or the heat. The lightning cannot strike them. Even the serpent cannot bite them. Nothing can ever touch them.'

Meryemdje embraced her grandson and kissed him.

Tashbash had taken up his position on a stone among the ruins, his eyes riveted on his house, not even daring to blink for fear of missing the coming of the light. The hours passed and he did not move. His eyes watered with the cold and tears trickled down his cheeks, almost turning to ice before he could wipe them away. Why didn't he see the bright Holy Walnut that was said to hover over his house all night long, vividly carved into the darkness, shooting out sparks all over the place? Why didn't he even hear its swishing as it slowly swayed and whirled over the house?

Suddenly he caught sight of shadows moving stealthily about the house. They had come again with picks and spades and were digging away at his threshold.

'Damn it all,' he cursed. 'The house is about to collapse and still they're digging. Oh God, deliver me from all this!'

They were filling up whole sackfuls and carrying them away. In sudden exasperation he jumped up. 'I'll show you,' he muttered. He speeded towards the house by a roundabout way so they should not know where he had been hiding and loomed upon them from behind the wall. The diggers took one look and froze with dread. Then they threw themselves face down on the ground.

'Rise,' he commanded in grave sonorous tones. 'I have something to say to you.'

They scrambled to their feet. He touched each of them on the head with slow solemnity.

'Pour back this earth,' he said, 'and I will tell you where the real blessed earth is to be found, that will make your fields yield ten-fold. But the hand that sprinkles it over the land must be pure, and the earth should be gathered only on the day of the Spring Feast. Go now and come back tomorrow.'

Then he faded into the darkness.

When he looked back there was no one to be seen. He settled down to wait again. Surely the Holy Tree would come at last. It was bitterly cold and his hands and feet had begun to freeze. Should he light a small fire? He had noticed some wood lying nearby during the day. He fetched an armful and set it ablaze, his frozen hands working with difficulty. Then he sat down again with the fire between his legs. But still no light. The villagers alleged that only the good and the pure could see it . . . Well, if he was a saint wouldn't this light that came to glow over his own house be visible to him? He must wait a little longer. After all, the Holy Walnut had a long way to come, over hill and vale. As for the light, there was no place it could not penetrate, the thickest wall, the deepest of waters . . .

He recalled a watercourse which he had seen when he was a soldier. It was called the Murat Stream and it flowed deep and copper-coloured between steep bare red rocks, but at times from the bottom of its depths a mossy green would shine out so clearly that the whole stream would be lit up and the encasing red rocks would glow greenly. Their sergeant had been a man even more terrible than Muhtar Sefer, he beat the men just for the fun of it. Every couple of days the whole squad would be made to run the gauntlet, just in case, the sergeant said, anyone had escaped the weight of his hand.

Suddenly, he heard a rustling like the gliding of a serpent. He sat up eagerly, holding his breath, his heart beating wildly. In vain . . .

'There must be something wrong with my eyes,' he thought. 'After all, I've heard the sound.'

He pricked up his ears. The rustling, now accompanied by short bird-like sounds, seemed to him to be coming from the steppe, then from the Peri Caves, then . . . He whirled this way and that. The rustling was everywhere, swish, swish, swish . . . But the light? God, where was the light?

The fire had long turned to dead ashes, but he was too tired now even to shiver. An irresistible desire to sleep swept over him. If he let himself go, they would find his frozen body in the morning, and who knows, perhaps the villagers would whisper that the Forty Holies had been angry with him and had strangled him to death. Reluctantly, without taking his eyes off the house, he started back.

'There must be something wrong,' he thought. 'What could those sounds have been that I heard? Maybe the light didn't come tonight because of those people digging . . .'

His threshold was like a well. It was impossible to reach the door. He must fill it up first thing in the morning.

'Woman, open the door!' he called to his wife.

She opened up at once. He jumped in and threw himself towards the fire, almost spreading himself over it. All his limbs were trembling.

His wife stared at him. 'God forgive me,' she thought. 'Is it possible a saint should feel the cold so?'

Chapter 32

Tonight the sky was dark and overcast, not clear and frosty like the night before. A furious blizzard tore down from the steppe bent on uprooting all the trees of the forest. This night not a living creature, not a wolf or fox or marten would so much as hazard its head out of its lair. The darkness was like a wall, hard as steel, as though it had been massing since the beginning of time for just this night.

'It was too bright yesterday,' Tashbash said to himself. 'That's why I couldn't see the lights. Tonight . . . Just let me catch a glimpse of those lights tonight and I'll show them in this land of the Taurus! I'll show them how to be a saint!'

He had lit no fire this time. The lights might have been disturbed by that too. For over three hours now he had been waiting without taking his eyes off the house, and suddenly he heard again the rustling and the faint bird-like sounds. In his excitement he jumped up. The blizzard struck him in the face forcefully and at that moment a brief fugitive flash passed before his eyes.

'The light!' he cried out triumphantly. 'I've seen it . . . The light!'

His head whirled. He was drunk with joy, confident now, the flame of holiness burning within him. Through the pounding in his ears he heard again the rustling sound, swish, swish, swish . . . Before his eyes, the green snake-like Murat River, black serpents basking on its warm copper rocks. A white cloud slowly consumed by the heat, its dwindling shadow flowing up, up, struggling against the swift downflow of the stream.

Swish, swish . . . He took a hold on himself. He had seen the light, yes, but only for a fleeting instant, like a blow that makes you see a thousand stars. 'This won't do,' he thought. 'If the light comes just once more and stays just a little longer, then I'll really be sure I'm a saint.'

So he sat down again and waited. The cloak, the woollen hood, the felt boots were nothing against the biting blast from the steppe. He was faint with cold, dizzy with lack of sleep. The roaring in his ears grew louder.

The sudden hooting of an owl roused him with a shock, bringing to his mind the Captain and the promise he had given him. If the Captain saw his house now and the endless flow of the sick, he would break every bone in his body. He was a sharp-tempered man and once he got on to his atom age stuff there was no restraining him. And he was right, thought Tashbash, a hundred times right. In this modern age, with people flying in the skies, to be waiting here for a miraculous light! The owl was an unlucky omen, he was sure of it. The Captain would never listen to him if he tried to explain how people invaded his house and how he could do nothing about it. Ah, if he could but see the light once more, then he would not care a fig about the Captain or the Government or the whole world for that matter! Then, the Captain could pound him to pulp, skin him alive, tear off his nails, anything. Whatever men did to him, it would be to his mortal flesh, they could not touch the holy part of him. And he would not be the only saint to be persecuted on this earth. Men had always dealt cruelly with the saints Allah sent them. Hadn't they done so even to Allah's beautiful prophet, our Lord Jesus, dragging him to Mount Ararat and nailing him to an ebony tree? Nailing him by the hands and feet and leaving him on the cold summit of Mount Ararat, leaving him there to freeze and die . . . He died, our Lord Jesus, without uttering a word of complaint or entreaty to anyone.

'Aaah! If I could just see it once and be really sure, I know what I'd do . . .' He trembled with cold and passion.

Not even the outline of the house was visible now, so complete was the all-engulfing gloom. But he waited on and all the time he heard the sound of the bird, swish, swish, swish! Phewt, phewt, phewt!

He waited until the east began to pale. Then, half-fainting, he dragged himself home. His hands were frozen and the fingers in danger of dropping off. Meryemdje was summoned in a hurry. She applied her secret ointments and salves, muttering to herself all the time. 'Whoever heard of saints freezing like this? Freezing and in need of Meryemdje's medicines?!'

Tashbash detected the doubt in her eyes. 'Tonight I'll wait again,' he resolved. 'And if I do see the light, I'll have a word with you, Meryemdje!'

Prostrate on the ground in the ruin, Tashbash was praying.

'Come Allah, show me this light. Don't let me lose face before everyone. Why don't you let me see this light you've already shown to everyone? If I'm a saint, a holy man, I must be able to see it or I'll be deceiving all those poor people who come to me every day for help, for cure. You're the all-powerful who made the earth and the heavens. You made me a saint, show me the light then, so I can spread your good word among the peoples of the earth.'

Then he kneeled for the *namaz* and said the ritual prayer twice.

The blizzard struck at his face, shaking the breath out of him. This time he had wrapped himself up even more thickly and had made Meryemdje bind up his frozen hands in woollen stockings and old rags.

Loud booming sounds came from the steppe, like an exploding cannon.

'Oh Allah, either you show me the light or I stay here and freeze to death! Show me the light, please Allah, so my heart can believe . . .'

Faint and far away, he thought he heard the rustling sound again. His heart gave a bound. He opened his eyes wide, but there was nothing to be seen.

He was alone, walking in the Chukurova plain. About him were corn fields as far as the eye could see, the corn unripe yet, still in the ear, stirring softly in the warm spring breeze. Under the bright sun, grasshoppers bouncing through the air . . . More and more of them . . . A huge black cloud suddenly darkening the sky . . . The peasant on the roadside on his knees, hands extended to heaven, praying . . . 'Oh Allah, if you are Allah, show your power and turn away the locusts! I have nothing in the world but this field to stave off hunger.' A day later he passed that way again. Clouds of locusts still swarmed blackly over the field. The corn had been shorn to the roots and not a leaf or ear, not even a stalk was left. And in the middle of it all, a man lying face down on the earth. He had gone up to him and seen his face, wet and mud-caked, and he had understood. This is what Allah had done to him, and now he had nothing to live for. Without a sound he had slipped away.

The long slim yellow arrow-snakes of the warm Chukurova land . . . The first time he had seen one was under a fig tree where a fountain gushed forth among jagged rocks. A glinting gold-like rod, lying there at the foot of a rock. Idly, he had stretched out his hand to pick it up but the rod had moved and suddenly it had whirred through the air, plunged into the rocks and vanished. 'That's an arrow-snake,' the peasants had told him. 'That fountain is full of them.' The people of that village avoided the fountain and the huge dark bare rocks about it, that loomed like a small mountain on the flatness of the plain. But some said its waters had healing powers and were good for all kinds of pains like rheumatism and headaches. For the fever, you just spread a thin slice of dough around your throat and poured water from the fountain over it until it dissolved away. And if you spent ten nights stark naked on those rocks sickness would never come near you again . . .

This time he heard the rustling quite clearly. He rose. The wind tore his cloak open. He drew it about him tightly and waited, his whole body tingling with suspense. It would come now, he was sure of it.

When the Lord Muhammet, blessed be his name, walked the earth, a green carpet of moss opened up before him and all the flowers bloomed, and over him a small white cloud hovered and accompanied him wherever he went, a canopy to shield him from the sun . . . Why shouldn't the holy tree of light come to visit the house of a saint at night? There have always been men of good will on this earth, and many who have attained holiness. Saints do not drop down from the heavens like that, they too are born of a mother, like any other human being. So what was wrong with him? In all his life he had never done anyone any wrong, or said a cruel word, except to the Muhtar, and that only for the good of the village . . . Why shouldn't a man like him, who had always followed the path of Allah, be made a saint? And these people, they couldn't all be lying! Even his wife refused to go to bed with him any longer. She couldn't have lost her mind, could she? She wanted him just as much as he wanted her. Well then, why wasn't he satisfied once and for all that he was a saint? Was it because he had promised the Captain? Or was he afraid? Afraid he would end up like all the other saints, on the gallows or in a dungeon? Afraid of being accused of heresy . . .

'But these things can't happen to me,' he thought. 'The villagers will never betray me because I will make them follow the path of righteousness and virtue. I will make those who have much give to those who have little. I will strive for the good of the oppressed, the exploited, for truth and justice.'

But hadn't it been just for this that all saints had striven? For this very reason they had become martyrs. If they had not tried to take from the rich to give to the poor, who would have flayed them alive, who would have touched a hair of their head? No one, that was certain, but then, what poor man would have put his faith in them? It is the poor of this earth who make a saint, looking to him for help in their distress, their sickness, their poverty, who force him to stand up against oppression and slaughter and war . . . For this, they cleave to him, and if the saint won't do what they expect of him, then they look elsewhere. But if he does, then he loses his life, for such things don't suit the Government.

'You're afraid, Tashbash. You're afraid,' he said to himself. 'That's why you're here, waiting night after night to see a light over your house. You're afraid of being a saint. You don't know the worth of this paradise that's being offered you, both in this world and the next. What matter if it costs you your life, when you will live in the hearts of men for ever. They will build shrines for you and come to worship you every day. What are you afraid of,

Tashbash? Saints have achieved eternity, immortality. Why should they fear death? Let the Captain do his worst . . .'

He had seen the light once, what more did he want? Yes, but could he trust that one fugitive flash? And anyway, who was he to presume to sainthood; a miserable ignorant peasant. He could not make up his mind. Should he ask someone? Mother Meryemdje perhaps . . . But how could he? She would laugh in his face.

'No!' he said aloud. 'If Allah has sent me to spread the good word among his creatures, then he must also show me the light. I won't budge till dawn, even if I freeze to death. And if I don't see it, then I'll clear out of this village. I won't believe I'm a saint even if all the people of the Taurus beg me on their knees, even if they say they've seen me flying in the sky, and a hundred thousand virgins dancing at my door. Only when I see the light will I believe. If not I'll take myself off and no one will ever find me . . .'

It was a far cry from here to the Antep villages and Sergeant Müslüm from the hamlet of Kizilkilise was a good chap. They had slept side by side in the barracks during their military service and had rapidly developed a friendship. Together they had learned to read and write, and he recalled their wild joy when they had scribbled down their first word. Then they had attended the sergeants' course and had got their stripes together. And one day they had cut their fingers and sucked each other's blood and so they had become blood brothers . . . If he went there, to Sergeant Müslüm's village, nobody would ever find him again. And it was near the Syrian border too, where a man could make a living out of smuggling, like Müslüm had done before becoming a soldier. Müslüm had sworn he would never do any smuggling again, but one never knows. People say things . . .

The blizzard raged on wilder than ever and it was still several hours to daybreak. Well, if he did not freeze to death this night, there was no need of lights or the like to prove he was a saint! Surely the *peris* and angels would have been watching over him!

Above the roar of the storm, he heard again the swish, swish, swish, drawing nearer and nearer, swelling, surging towards him, and suddenly he was frightened. What if this was the mighty dragon of the steppe? What if it was true? He jumped over the crumbling wall and ran for dear life. Before his door he stopped and listened. The swishing sound came from over his own roof now.

'My God,' he gasped. 'I'm going to miss it. How can I see the light from here?'

He rushed back to the ruin. But the swishing had stopped.

'God damn it,' he cursed. 'Look what I've done now! It's gone, and who knows when it'll come again.'

The biting cold seemed to be corroding his lungs and the cloak about him felt as thin as an onion peel. He could not hold on much longer. Besides, it was no use . . .

'After so much begging and praying, if I really were a saint Allah would have sent not just a light but the sun itself over my house,' he thought, his teeth chattering fitfully. 'I'm going to go home to my warm bed. I'm nothing of a saint and that's all there is to it. Would a saint tremble fit to die from the cold?'

But he could not tear himself away. Now the trembling, the chattering of teeth began to slacken and an easeful drowsiness enveloped him. Visions flitted before his eyes. The sky above him was dark with storks, warm and graceful, blotting out the blue, floating by, one after the other in front of a huge bright globe. Then there were cranes crossing the globe . . . And then storks again . . . Cranes . . . Aeroplanes, cotton fields, even the red-trunked forest of the Taurus. Then a blackness passed over the bright globe, and the forest, the storks, everything vanished and Tashbash sank into darkness.

The dawn was about to break when he was roused by a loud swishing. He opened his eyes and saw for a fraction of a second a huge ball of light bursting over his house in the east. The light! It was the light . . . He struggled to rise, but his numb stiff limbs did not respond. Sleep overwhelmed him. He slept, a huge ball of light behind his eyelids. A moment later he heard his wife's voice, as in a dream. He tried to call to her, then all was blotted out.

When he opened his eyes it was midday. He was by his hearth, in his own house. Crowding about him were Meryemdje, Long Ali, Hasan, Ummahan, his children, his wife . . .

'You would have frozen to death,' Ali told him, 'if your wife hadn't found you in the ruin. I rushed over and found you senseless. Mother has been making ointments for you all morning. You gave us such a fright . . .'

Tashbash only smiled blissfully.

Chapter 33

'Muhtar Sefer,' the Captain said, 'I know very well you're at daggers drawn with that man and I don't believe a word you say. You'd tear him to pieces before my very eyes if you got the chance. But since you insist, I'm going to send three policemen to him, disguised as sick villagers. He promised me he would not dabble in this hocus-pocus any more and he struck me as a man of his word, and sensible too. I've known some so-called holy men in my time and they weren't at all like this one. Anyway we'll see. If you turn out to be right we'll deal with him and he'll never set foot in the Taurus again. I'll break every bone in his body to begin with, then I'll have him sent to prison. Then . . . But, Muhtar, I warn you, if you're lying to me, then I'll do the same to you, and worse.'

'That's a deal, Captain Shükrü,' the Muhtar said in a confident tone. 'If your policemen find I've exaggerated just so much, then do what you like to me!'

The Muhtar knew he should not be doing this, but the demon of revenge had carried him away. He could not swallow his humiliation at Tashbash's hands and rashly he had thrown himself on the road of no return. But an insidious dread kept gnawing at his heart. Wouldn't the villagers know it was he who had denounced Tashbash? Wouldn't they try to avenge him? And Tashbash? He was not a man to take all this lying down. And what if there really was something holy about him? What if it was all true? Then indeed there would be no salvation for Sefer, either in this world or the next. Had he not seen with his own eyes five paralytics rise up and walk after Tashbash had touched them? And Memidik? He could easily have denied everything rather than let himself be thrashed to an inch of his life . . . Even Ömer swore by the book that he had seen the Holy Walnut over

Tashbash's house. The only person in the village who had nothing to say about lights and miracles was Tiny Musa, Tashbash's sworn enemy, but even he was afraid to speak his name without invoking the name of Allah. How could so many people be saying all these things if there were not some measure of truth in them?

'Aaah Tashbash. Damn you, why couldn't we have been friends? The two of us together could have the whole land of the Taurus at our feet. Such a chance can only come once in a lifetime . . .'

The next evening, the police arrived, disguised as sick, ragged peasants, and Tashbash breathed his incantations over them. They had spent the night in the empty shed, together with the sick from the other villages, and they had learnt all there was to know about Tashbash's activities.

Sleep would not come to Sefer. He tossed and moaned in his bed, haunted by dark desperate thoughts. There were moments when he cursed his folly at not having done away with Tashbash at the beginning, when he was not yet a saint and there would have been no great fuss. But then, in his wildest nightmares he could not have imagined that the man would have sprouted into a holy personage, curing the sick, bestowing plenty on the land, attracting miraculous lights over his house. He could only wait and hope that the Captain would send Corporal Jumali again. Fifty liras would be more than enough to shut the Corporal's mouth once more.

And one morning at break of day, Corporal Jumali made his appearance, followed by two policemen.

'Fifty liras?' he exclaimed. 'For this job? A hundred and fifty is what I'll take and nothing less.'

'But Corporal, that's impossible! You can't do this to me after all we've gone through together . . .'

'Nothing less! I'm saving your life, aren't I? Think of what these villagers will do to you once I've taken their saint away.'

'I'd give you the money if I had it, but . . .'

'Don't fool me, Muhtar!'

'As God's my witness, I haven't got it. I swear . . .'

'Well, you know best. If you haven't, you haven't. Makes no difference to me.'

'I'll give you one hundred.'

Corporal Jumali flared up. 'I'm saving your life,' he shouted, 'and you're haggling over a mere fifty liras! Fifty liras for a life! Could anything be cheaper?'

Sefer grabbed his arm. 'Shh! They'll hear you!'

'Give me the hundred and fifty then, if you don't want me to shout. And I won't beat you hard either this time. I'll be careful to bring down my rifle softly. And that takes no end of skill.'

Sefer knew when he was defeated. He disappeared and returned with a wad of money, which he shoved furtively into the Corporal's pocket.

'There! I borrowed the extra fifty for you. But Corporal, for the love of God be careful with your rifle. You nearly killed me last time.'

The Corporal smiled. This Tashbash must indeed be a great and holy man, who shed blessings on one and all. See how fortune had smiled on Corporal Jumali the instant he had come into contact with him!

'Thank you, Muhtar,' he said. 'You were wise not to exasperate me too much. But look! There's a crowd about Tashbash's house . . .'

'Don't worry,' Sefer said. 'They won't make any trouble. Our saint won't let them.'

'But it looks like the whole village . . .'

'I'm telling you, Corporal, you've got nothing to fear. If Tashbash had wanted it, they'd have torn you to pieces long ago, and me too.'

The Corporal started off with wary steps, the two policemen following him, but even before they reached the house, Tashbash appeared at his door and came forward to meet them. On hearing of the Corporal's arrival, he had jumped out of bed and dressed quickly in his best clothes.

It was a cold sunny day, but clouds were gathering high up over the summit of Mount Tekech.

'I'm ready, Corporal,' Tashbash said with a bitter laugh.

'Well, Tashbash Effendi! The Captain's really mad this time. A saint who doesn't keep his word . . . Come on, let's get going at once.'

He took a pair of handcuffs from one of the policemen and clapped them to Tashbash's wrists. A murmur arose from the crowd, which broke and swirled. Meryemdje appeared at the front with her stick.

Tashbash leaned over and spoke into the Corporal's ear. 'Quick, Corporal, take these off or even I won't be able to stop them. Quick!'

The Corporal's face turned red, but he hastened to remove the handcuffs.

Tashbash let his gaze travel slowly over the crowd, then he held out his hands to the Corporal. There was a menacing growl. The Corporal quickly brushed Tashbash's hands away and handed the handcuffs to a policeman.

They set out, Tashbash walking ahead, his face pale, his eyes huge and sad. Those who had come from the other villages rushed up, dragging their sick along and pleading with him to touch them just once, to say his healing incantations over them. He stopped and held his hand long and gently over each in turn as they came up, breathing over them and uttering a prayer.

Silently the people of Yalak, with Meryemdje at their head, followed the procession. As they were crossing the village square Tashbash looked back once, expectantly, then he lowered his head and walked on.

They were leaving the village when his face lit up suddenly. He almost laughed. He had caught sight of the Muhtar running after them, shouting for all he was worth.

Sefer came and threw himself at Tashbash's feet, clasping his knees and raising a loud wail. 'My Lord, my Sultan! They shan't take you away, not while I'm alive. No, I won't give you up to them. If they hadn't played this trick on you . . . If the Captain hadn't sent those three policemen to you disguised as sick peasants . . . If you hadn't taken them in and prayed over them . . . Ah Tashbash, how is it you didn't know they were policemen?

Ah, what a calamity! Does a man ever breathe his incantations over a policeman?'

This was news to Tashbash. It gave him such a shock that, for a moment, he thought he would fall in a faint right there on the snow. With an effort he pulled himself together. If they saw him fall, the crowd would make short work of the three policemen. And that was what he feared most. Then indeed, he would be lost. He shook his leg free of Sefer's clasp and marched on.

Sefer rushed after them, shouting, wailing, in a frenzy. Suddenly Corporal Jumali felt his gorge rise. He hated the man. Swiftly he lifted his rifle and brought it down as hard as he could right in the middle of the Muhtar's back.

'He asked for it, the bastard,' he spat out through his teeth. 'I hope this breaks his backbone and pins him to his bed for months.'

Sefer fell to the ground, wriggling like a beheaded chicken. One or two villagers helped him to his feet.

'They've killed me, my Lord, my Sultan!' he moaned. 'And Captain Shükrü's going to kill you too. Don't go with them. You must escape. Hey, good people, come and take your Lord. Save him . . .'

He dared not draw any nearer. His back hurt as though it had been broken. 'Corporal! Ah, Corporal Jumali, how can you do this to me? After all the times we've spent together in my house . . . After all the mon . . . Is this how you repay me? Is there no spark of honour in you? Kill me!' His voice rose to a shriek. 'Kill me!'

For an instant the villagers were jolted. He threw himself across the policemen's path.

'You can't take him away,' he howled, baring his chest. 'Without him this village is lost, degraded, destroyed . . .'

Corporal Jumali closed his eyes and recommended himself to the Creator as he swung his rifle. Sefer was flung four paces away on the snow, doubled up with pain. But he was aware that the villagers were coming over to his side now. If he could keep this up just a little longer he would have them hurling themselves at the police.

Tashbash saw it too, and he knew that if the crowd made a single move now, there would be no restraining them any more. This was just what Sefer was aiming at. Already he had scrambled to his feet and was coming up to them again, and the Corporal was getting his rifle ready. Tashbash held his arm. Then he pushed back the oncoming Muhtar and signalled to the villagers to gather around him. The seething, explosive crowd obeyed him in silence and surrounded him on all sides like a wall. His eyes moved slowly from face to face. For a long while he looked at them. Then he spoke in a dull dead voice.

'Give up your claim on me and let me go,' he said. 'You have been good to me. You have sanctified me and loved me. May Allah be good to you also. I'm going now. I may come back, and again I may not. I may never even see you again . . .' He paused, his head hanging. Then he looked up. His face was like a rock now. 'I may never see you again!' he repeated in ringing tones. 'But now, as I go, I have one last request to make of you. And I know you will not deny me this. If you do, you will be damned for ever and burn everlastingly in Allah's hell.'

The crowd was all ears.

'There is an evil man among you, one whose murder is sanctioned by all the four Holy Books, and he it is who has denounced me. Because of him, they are taking me away from you . . .'

All eyes turned to the Muhtar.

'This man, this evil, lying, double-faced, hundred-faced man is your Muhtar Sefer, here before you.'

A vengeful rumble rose from the crowd.

'I want you never to speak to him again until the day he dies, no one, not even the ants and dogs and cats of this village, no one, neither his wives nor his children, nor his relatives. You will spread my word to the neighbouring villages, also to the people of the town, to all the creatures of the earth. He is damned, and he who speaks to him shall be damned in his turn and no one shall speak to him either. You will never again accept him as your Muhtar, however much the Government and the parties should wish it. This is all I ask of you. And now, farewell to you all, I may never come back again.'

And he walked off swiftly with a lively step in front of the policemen.

Sefer remained rooted to the spot, his face chalk-white, his eyes starting from their sockets like those of a madman. The crowd flowed past him in Tashbash's wake without giving him so much as a glance.

They were well out of the village when Tashbash turned again. 'Give up your claim on me,' he said again. 'Farewell . . .'

They stopped there, looking after him until he was lost to sight. Then they turned back to the village.

Sefer had not moved, still rooted there like a man bereft of his senses. The crowd shied away from him as though he were the bearer of the plague, of death itself.

Chapter 34

A warm gust came and went like a keen fitful wave, and the sky grew darker. Out of the corner of his eye Corporal Jumali took stock of Tashbash. There was nothing of the crackpot in this man. He was not a hodja or anything religious either. How on earth had he turned into a saint? Of course, every man has something holy in him, but still! . . . Corporal Jumali was a member of the Alevi[1] sects from the region of Sivas. Like all the Alevis, he sported a huge bushy moustache and believed that man was the most precious creature on earth. Allah himself was sometimes manifest in the human form. After Allah, perhaps even before him, man was the lord of the universe. Allah was the light and a portion of that light was immanent in every man. Who knows, maybe one day that light would shine forth in a truly pious person. And so the Alevis always paid worship first and foremost to light and to man.

Tashbash knew about this and sometimes he had thought it must be the light in him that the villagers had seen to make them venerate him so. He had the feeling that whether he was holy or not, there was deep in him something that was sacred, immune, that without him the world could not be, that whatever existed in this world existed only through him. He would strive to capture that sensation more palpably, but in vain. Slowly working himself into a state of winged ecstasy he would come to the very edge of holiness, but then, in an instant, all would fritter away into nothingness. At such moments he recked nothing of the Captain, the madhouse and the prison.

But now he would have to face the Captain. How would he explain his broken promise? A man's a man first, whether he's a saint or not. And a man should keep his word. As he walked on

[1] Alevi: a branch of the Shiite schism in Islam.

ahead of the policemen, his shame became more and more un-bearable. The Captain's dark, moustached countenance never left his eyes. What would he say to him? He could not deny that he had breathed on the sick, that he had allowed people to kiss his feet and worship him. He could only plead that he had taken nothing from them in exchange, nothing but a pinch of salt. No, the Captain would never even listen. He would beat the life out of him. The man had made a name for himself as the most terrible of the flogging policemen that had ever come to that town. And Tashbash simply could not stomach the idea that he, the saint of Yalak, the elect of Allah, of the people, should be thrashed black and blue at the police station like any ordinary man and made to piss blood like all the Captain's victims. He, Tashbash, who had seen the light, and over his own house too! Of that he was firmly convinced now, though at first he had had doubts. But how could he tell the Captain that? He would never believe him.

On leaving the village a large yellow sheepdog, which belonged to his neighbour Blind Durmush, had tagged on after them and had followed them all the way. Tashbash had always loved this dog and it warmed his heart to see it keeping obstinately to his side. As for the policemen, they never uttered a word. Tashbash had noticed their uneasy covert glances at him, and he was highly gratified.

Now they were passing through the forest of Karamuk, all bare in the wintry light, but which was so dark and leafy in the summer. The snow-coated branches glowed whitely in a havoc of light. And suddenly black clouds began to scud overhead blotting out the brightness, and gusts of wind lashed out again. Corporal Jumali looked anxiously towards the summit of Mount Tekech where clouds were gathering, thicker and darker with every passing minute. He knew how it was in these foothills of the Taurus, how the storm would be upon you just like that, without warning, and he cast a whimsical glance at Tashbash, thinking, now's the time to show you're a saint! Stall off this storm if you can.

Not a living creature was to be seen in the all-encompassing

whiteness, neither bird, beast, nor even a plant. The forest
rustled faintly. Now and then, flakes of frozen snow dropped
from the branches like autumn leaves. Softly . . .

They pressed on, fleeing as before an unknown fear, but it was
not long before the lowering clouds from over Mount Tekech
had closed upon them like a black tent and the world was plunged
into a crepuscular gloom, through which only the hoarfrost on
the stiffly frozen trees glistened dimly. A clap of thunder rent the
skies as in an autumn storm and from right and left, from above
and below, from a thousand sides, gusts of wind spurted up,
warm, fresh, then icy cold, and swept the frost off the boughs.
Tiny flakes of snow materialized in the air.

For the first time Corporal Jumali opened his mouth. 'We're in
for it!' he said. 'If this storm lasts . . .'

The yellow dog was right behind Tashbash, almost treading on
his heels.

'Isn't there a cave or some place where we can shelter around
here?' the Corporal asked. 'Memet friend, you know these parts
better . . .'

What warm-hearted people these Alevis are, Tashbash thought.
Theirs is indeed a cult of justice and friendship and love. It isn't
man and light they worship, though they say so, but love, uni-
versal love. And isn't that just what light really is? As his fears
of the Captain increased, Tashbash had begun to pin his hopes
on the Corporal. Who knows but that he might be persuaded to
let him escape?

'Don't worry, Corporal friend,' he said. 'There's a cave not
very far from here, right behind those crags, the Secret Cave.'

The snow fell ever more thickly, the sky darkened still more
and the wild winds battered at them from all sides. Clambering
over the rocks, they reached the cave panting, and quickly lit a
fire to warm themselves. The yellow dog had slipped in too and
was now stretched out on the sand by the fire.

'We've got plenty of provisions, thank God,' Corporal Jumali
said.

Tashbash smiled. 'They gave me enough to last three days.'

They ate their meal. Outside the storm raged even more

furiously whipping up the snow from the trees, the ground, the sky, and flinging it from hill to hill. The trees cracked loudly as though the whole forest were being wrenched by its roots.

'Well!' the Corporal exclaimed. 'What a storm! At this rate we'll be here for a whole week. If Memet friend had not found this cave, our skins would have been only good for salting!'

Tashbash was bursting with impatience. He had made up his mind and was waiting for the night to fall. He could not look the Corporal in the face. They had stocked plenty of wood and built up a big fire of smokeless lambent embers. With a few boulders they had narrowed the entrance to the cave. It was warm and cosy now, and soon they fell asleep.

Tashbash was wide awake. He waited awhile, then rose and tied his pouch of provisions to his belt. Soundlessly, he slipped out through the narrow opening. There was a rustle behind him. He turned and saw the dog.

Outside he was almost struck down by the force of the blizzard. He had no cloak or felt boots to protect him, and up here, on the foothills of Mount Tekech, the cold was nothing like Tashbash had ever encountered before. He clambered down the rocks, hardly able to breathe in the face of the deadly blast.

'It's madness what I'm doing,' he said. 'It's suicide and nothing else.' But then he thought of the Captain. 'Rather than be beaten to death . . .'

But he did not want to die. He sank down on his knees and began to pray. Just let him get out of this alive and he would never again doubt that he was a saint.

'Allah,' he begged, 'show me now that I am your beloved servant. If not take my life right here, tonight . . . You know best.'

He plunged on, but the little strength he had was fast deserting him. He was still not fully recovered after nearly freezing to death that night in the ruin. For an instant he considered going back to the safety of the cave and the companionship of the three policemen. Then it flashed through his memory that there was another cave in these parts, a very small one, called the Cave of the Frozen Men. It ought to be quite near too, but he had lost his bearings. The only thing he knew was that he had found the road again. The rocks that led to the cave must be somewhere farther on. For a long time he walked on without encountering anything. He came upon another path and after taking a few steps he stumbled on to rocky ground. The cave had always been reached from the north, but how to find the north? He recalled some southward-bent trees on the way and advanced slowly, groping at every tree he came across. And now he had found them. He knew the cave must be less than half an hour away and he broke into a run. The yellow dog scurried after him. He stumbled and fell. The blood seemed to be draining from his heart. He was freezing. The cave must be quite near now, but he could not get up. His feet were numb, his body heavy, immovable. And then he felt the dog's hot breath on his nape. With a desperate effort he crawled on over the snow.

The forest roared about him, the trees crashed into each other, straining at their roots. Suddenly, unaccountably, a single flash of lightning lit up the forest and he saw the jagged outline of the Cave of the Frozen Men up there, right before him.

Drenched to the bone, his legs useless, his body numb from the waist down, surrendering to the deathly drowsiness that was slowly seeping into his brain . . . Sleep . . . A mortal fear shook him into consciousness. He was half buried in the snow. With the last remaining strength in his hands, he drew himself up towards the cave. The dog inched along beside him, as though crawling too.

And then he felt the matches in his pocket. 'These are my Hasan's matches,' he thought. 'His keepsake to me.' A warm feeling of love swept through his body.

Chapter 35

It was the time of the thaw. Yellowish rivulets coursed between the houses, bearing a mixture of straw and dung, and all day long the half-naked children played in the dirty polluted waters that poured down the valleys and into the village from their pure crystal-clear beginnings in the snowy mountains. Spring was not far behind.

It was also the time of hunger, when the stores of grain would be exhausted. For the villagers the apprehension of oncoming spring overshadowed even the fear of Adil Effendi. With every passing year the grain ran out earlier and at this rate they would soon find themselves with empty sacks in the middle of the winter. The population of the village kept increasing, but no one did anything to arrest the depletion of the soil. 'In my father's time,' Old Halil would often tell them, 'the land gave thirty to one. Now, all we get is five to one, and soon we'll get nothing at all . . . Ah, this world's going down the drain. All men are bastards now . . .' It was no different in the neighbouring villages and worse still up in the steppe, where sometimes the soil did not even give back the seed that was sown into it. Soon the whole land would turn into a vast blackened desolation.

Shirtless was the first to wake up one morning and find he had no grain left. The thaw was still in full swing and the waters streaming through the village. It was always Shirtless who was hit first and a kind of relief, a release from the anguish which had plagued him all through the winter would sweep over him. This year it had happened earlier than ever, yet there was in him that same lightness, that same feeling of shedding off a heavy burden. At times Shirtless had unwonted bouts of perspicacity. 'It's not the coming of Adil we're afraid of all winter long,' he declared. 'It's this day! The day we have no flour left for our bread. Adil's just a pretext.'

At the end of the winter Shirtless would borrow a little flour from his friend, Köstüoglu. Then, when Köstüoglu had none left either, they would both turn to Slowcoach Halil, and so on. Thus, the whole village would run short of bread at about the same time. Some hid their grain and kept it all to themselves, but these were only a few. No one would ever give them a morsel of bread again even if they were dying of hunger. Come the harvest, everyone would pay back his debt, down to the last handful of flour.

This year was like a year of famine. What did people eat then? How did they manage to keep alive until the harvest? Thank God, spring was nearly here. Soon the earth would sprout forth its blessings, *madimak* which boiled and salted was tastier than lamb, sheep sorrel, chards, and *yalabuk*, peeled off the bark of the pine tree, the very smell of which was enough to infuse life into a man.

The thaw ended at last and with it the dread of famine. The earth emerged in a fresh, moist, lusty greenness. The winds from the steppe blew sunny and warm, wafting sweet scents in place of the wintry blizzard.

Those who searched for Old Halil's dead body in the Long Valley never found a trace of him. People were beginning to think that the wolves had got him when the rumour arose that he had taken up residence in the village of Injejik with an old friend, swearing he would never set foot in Yalak again, cursing its inhabitants from the Muhtar to Tashbash, and spreading grue-some stories about his narrow escape from their clutches. 'They were ready to tear me to pieces, those monsters,' was the burden of his tale. 'To pieces! And hang each piece on a separate tree. Ah, but I don't blame them! I'd have done the same and you too, because, let me tell you, good people, I brought them down late for the cotton and got them into trouble with Adil Effendi. But what they don't know is that it was I who saved them from Adil's wrath as well. How? Ah, that's a secret between Allah and me! A couple of words was enough to make him see reason. So now I'm quits with those Yalak villagers. But still I can never go back, no . . . Those monsters would eat me alive . . .'

Then from Sürmeli came the rumour that Old Halil was there, alive and kicking, inveighing all day long against the people of Yalak. Its women were all whores, and what's more, they always gave birth to quadruplets, and with so many new children there was never enough food for the old people who were left to die of hunger . . . These rumours multiplied and people began to have doubts that the old man had ever frozen to death on the night of his flight.

As for Hüsneh and Rejep, a little boy from the village of Buzdéré came upon them at the time of the first thaw in a little valley only two hundred yards away from the village. There they were, on their knees, folded tightly in each other's arms, broad-shouldered Rejep and Hüsneh with her long, long hair flowing down her back. The little boy hid behind a bush to spy on them as they made love. He waited and waited but there was no movement, not the slightest sign of life from the lovers. So he aimed a little stone at them. Nothing happened. He threw another stone, then another. Suddenly he ran up to them and what should he see? Wedged between the tightly clasped bodies and resting over their intertwined arms were clumps of hard frozen snow! He rushed back to his village with the news.

And so the bodies of Hüsneh and Rejep were brought to Yalak to be buried. The whole village held a wake to keen over the young lovers and many were the dirges that were sung over them by the women and young girls. Even Old Meryemdje was heard to mutter an old lament to herself as she wept.

Of Tashbash nothing was heard any more. He had vanished into the blue, without leaving a trace. There was only Corporal Jumali's testimony, which he swore to before the Captain and repeated to whoever would listen to him. 'A furious snowstorm burst upon us in the forest of Karamuk, and all the world went dark. All of a sudden I heard a voice crying, "Blessed be Ali,[1] blessed be Ali! Blessed be the light of the world . . ." Tashbash

[1] Ali: the fourth Caliph, cousin and son-in-law of the prophet Muhammet, and revered by the Shiites.

had been walking in front of us . . . Then, hard upon the voice a light flared up before our eyes, and glided off swiftly towards the mountains. Tashbash, I called out, Tashbash! Memet Tashbash . . . There was no answer. I waited there till dawn, but he had melted into thin air. May I never see my children again, may Ali Himself drive me from His table if what I say is anything less than the truth!'

And now, in all the villages, the women would be flitting about from house to house, carrying glowing embers on scraps of tin plate. This was a sign that spring had come, for the fires which had burned night and day all winter long were allowed to die out now. Matches are a precious article in the villages and should be saved as much as possible. So the women borrow embers from one another's fires to light their hearths. And in the evenings the villages twinkle as though the stars of heaven had dropped into them.

Chapter 36

And one morning they opened their eyes and spring was there. So it always comes in the steppe, overnight. A delirious spring it turned out to be this year; the rocks, the brooks, the mountains, the whole world suddenly bright green, the vast forest redolent and softly singing, its every tree alive with white birds.

Spring comes late in the steppe and its flowers too are slow to bloom. Squat and blunt, no higher than a finger, they are brightness itself, and whether red or yellow, orange or blue, more brilliant than any other flower on earth, visible even in the night. Their fragrance is heady, piercing, impregnating itself into the earth of the steppe and enduring long after the flowers are faded and gone.

Hasan could not keep still with excitement.

'Hurry up, Ummahan,' he kept urging his sister. 'Can't you be quick, girl? What a slowcoach!'

'What's all the hurry?' she shouted back from inside the house. 'You're not bursting, are you?'

'Come out and I'll show you, you stupid girl!'

'Then I won't come!'

He changed. 'Come out, there's my good sister. Come . . .'

A generous sun caressed the steaming earth, all astir now in the riotous awakening of spring, its myriad insects, birds, wolves, foxes, bears, serpents, tortoises, up and about, mating or chasing each other, spiders after flies, birds after spiders, big birds after small ones . . . In the forest, in the arid steppe itself, a quickening, a rejuvenation, a giving birth, a lusty, frenzied activity. And the earth stretching itself out, joyful, ecstatic, in the throes of resurrection. The soil, the rocks, the trees melting in a paroxysm of surrender, so soft now that a stone would sink deep into them as into a ball of cotton. The ants had opened up their holes and were heaped about the entrances, half-dormant yet, basking in the long-forgotten sunshine. Beady-bees, yellow-jackets, honey-bees, thousands of bees, their bright transparent wings quivering and flashing in tiny sparks, buzzed impatiently around the almost bursting flower-buds, ready to pounce on the first bloom.

The children were running towards the forest.

Hasan was happy. 'I'm going to make a camel,' he said. 'A real sturdy one, out of a laurel tree . . .'

'Make one for me too!' Ummahan begged.

'Gipsy!' he scolded her. 'You shouldn't ask for everything you see.'

'And you're just a silly ass,' she countered, giving him a push. 'If you weren't a silly ass you'd give me my matches, the matches I earned by waiting up with you all those nights in the snow and cold. If it weren't for me anyone could have stolen those matches of yours.'

'They'll take them anyway,' Hasan said, suddenly despondent. 'Adil's going to come now.'

'How d'you know?'

'Don't you see how unhappy Father is? He hasn't talked to anyone for days. He's angry too . . .'

'No,' Ummahan said. 'Adil can't come any more. It's spring now.'

'Shut up!' Hasan shouted. 'Shut up, you stupid girl and don't make me mad. Adil will come, and he'll take all my matches too.' He rummaged in his shirt. 'Here,' he said, 'these two boxes are for you. Adil's going to get them anyway, sooner or later.'

Ummahan hesitated, unable to believe her eyes. She was sure Hasan was teasing her.

'Well? Don't you want them?'

Hasan offering her the matches over which they had quarrelled all through the winter? It was impossible. Why, he wouldn't give her a single stick . . .

'Take them!' he shouted. 'Take them, quick.'

She held out her hand timidly and oh, the matches were in her palm! Tears rose to her eyes. She stood there, irresolute, looking from the matches to Hasan and back at the matches again.

'Are they mine altogether?'

'Altogether,' Hasan said sadly. 'Adil's going to get them anyway . . .'

Ummahan burst out laughing. She laughed and laughed, and Hasan stared at her in bewilderment. Suddenly he broke into laughter too. The more they looked at each other, the more they laughed.

'Are they really, really mine? Both of them?'

'Both of them.'

They reached the forest at a run and immediately Hasan set about heaping brushwood beneath the jutting rock. How good this fire would smell! The scent of burning wood is quite different in the spring. He was seething with excitement after days of waiting for a chance to go to the forest. He sat down, emptied a whole box of matches on the ground before him, picked up half a dozen sticks and struck them all at one go. Then he lit another batch, and another, the bigger the flame the better, and watched the matches burn and flicker out, a strange mixture of pain and pleasure on his face. The box was soon empty. He produced another.

Ummahan was watching him with huge horrified eyes.

'Stop, Hasan, stop!' she cried at last.

It was as though he had not heard her.

Now he had no more matches left. He turned to his sister. 'Give me yours too,' he said.

Ummahan recoiled. 'I won't,' she screamed. 'You're mad, that's what you are! Mad!'

He made a grab for her and a fierce tussle ensued. Hasan wanted the matches with such passion that he fought like a devil and had soon wrung the boxes out of his sister's hands. Panting, his face bleeding where Ummahan had scratched it, he crouched down, oblivious to everything and began to strike the matches again, in larger batches now, the flames spurting forth in crackling bursts. His fingers were getting burnt but he did not even feel it. He held the very last match to the wood and then settled down with his chin in his hand to watch the flames.

Suddenly he gave a shriek. Ummahan jumped.

'Look, look Ummahan! The Holy Walnut Tree! The tree which used to come at night over Uncle Tashbash's house . . . Look, look! Oh, it's slipping away! It's gone . . . Didn't you see it?'

Ummahan was cross. 'No, I didn't! I saw nothing at all.'

Hasan let the fire burn itself out, then he rose and stretched himself. 'Turn your back, Ummahan,' he ordered. 'Don't move and don't dare look or I'll kill you.'

He ran, slipping in and out of the boulders, and came to the great rock that was set like an island among the pines. He found his stone and gazed at it, hope and reverence in his eyes. Then he stroked it gently once or twice and lifted it up. It was as though he had been struck by lightning. He stared at the open space under the stone, unable to take his eyes off it. Slowly, his face lit up, and the mountains, the rocks, the trees, the earth seemed to light up too.

'Ummahan!' he shouted. 'Come here! Come, quick . . .'

His voice was triumphant. Ummahan rushed up, excited, and looked where he was pointing. They held their breaths.

Where the stone had lain there were three freshly blooming flowers, their long stalks trailing over the black earth. One was red, a brilliant crystal red like a flame, the other yellow, yellow as the corn, the sun, a crystal yellow, and the third blue, the blue of the thistle, the sky, the sea, a crystal blue.

Hasan looked into Ummahan's eyes. 'You see?'

'Oh yes, I do!'

'The three of them?'

'I see them all.'

Also in *The Wind from the Plain* trilogy
I THE WIND FROM THE PLAIN

"He speaks for those people for whom no one else is speaking"

JAMES BALDWIN

Each year the wind brings the news to old Halil's keen senses that the cotton is ripe for picking in the plain, and at his word the entire population of his remote village in the Taurus Mountains set out on the arduous trek to earn by their toil enough to pay their debts and buy the necessities of life for the bitter highland winter.

But this year old Halil finds himself too old to go on foot; so does Long Ali's ageing mother Meryemdje, and both clamour for a place on the back of Long Ali's broken-down nag, once a pure-bred Arab steed stolen by Ali's brigand father, now scarcely capable of bearing either of the two old people. Halil's determination to stay on and Meryemdje's to get him off lead to a war of words and cunning which lights with delicious comedy the sombre drama of the march. But when the decrepit animal finally dies, and the group falls behind the rest of the villagers, it is the unfortunate Ali who has to show piety towards his mother and compassion to old Halil, while pressing on with dogged resolution to reach the cotton fields before they are picked bare.

The power of *The Wind from the Plain*, the first volume of *The Wind from the Plain* trilogy, lies in its simplicity, which in turn lies in the handful of down-to-earth characters whose story it tells – the timeless one of survival.

"…has the freshness and vigour of a writer who, one suspects, is the exultant discoverer of virgin territory … it asserts its stature as literature"   *Spectator*

Also in *The Wind from the Plain* trilogy
III THE UNDYING GRASS

"Yashar Kemal is a cauldron where fact, fantasy and folklore are stirred to produce poetry. He is a storyteller in the oldest tradition, that of Homer, spokesman for a people who had no other voice"   ELIA KAZAN

Memidik, the young hunter, is obsessed by the urge to kill the tyrannous headman, Sefer, who has caused him much pain and humiliation. But each time he tries, the figure of Sefer looms many times larger than life, and Memidik freezes in fear. But his accidental slaying of another man fires him with renewed determination. Sefer, meanwhile, has been sentenced to solitude as the villagers refuse to speak to him. Sefer's taunting only strengthens their loyalty to their champion Tashbash whom they come to invest with mythical powers. The web of their fantasy becomes so extensive that when he returns to the village, a worn-out old man, they cannot recognise or accept him.

The Undying Grass, the third volume in *The Wind from the Plain* trilogy and a sequel to *Iron Earth, Copper Sky*, also continues the story of Ali and his mother Meryemdje who, in their different ways, learn the difficult art of survival.

"Yashar Kemal is one of the modern world's great storytellers"
                                            JOHN BERGER

Harvill Paperbacks are published by Collins Harvill,
a Division of the Collins Publishing Group

1. Giuseppe Tomasi di Lampedusa *The Leopard*
2. Boris Pasternak *Doctor Zhivago*
3. Alexander Solzhenitsyn *The Gulag Archipelago 1918–1956*
4. Jonathan Raban *Soft City*
5. Alan Ross *Blindfold Games*
6. Joy Adamson *Queen of Shaba*
7. Vasily Grossman *Forever Flowing*
8. Peter Levi *The Frontiers of Paradise*
9. Ernst Pawel *The Nightmare of Reason*
10. Patrick O'Brian *Joseph Banks*
11. Mikhail Bulgakov *The Master and Margarita*
12. Leonid Borodin *Partings*
13. Salvatore Satta *The Day of Judgment*
14. Peter Matthiessen *At Play in the Fields of the Lord*
15. Alexander Solzhenitsyn *The First Circle*
16. Homer, translated by Robert Fitzgerald *The Odyssey*
17. George MacDonald Fraser *The Steel Bonnets*
18. Peter Matthiessen *The Cloud Forest*
19. Theodore Zeldin *The French*
20. Georges Perec *Life A User's Manual*
21. Nicholas Gage *Eleni*
22. Eugenia Ginzburg *Into the Whirlwind*
23. Eugenia Ginzburg *Within the Whirlwind*
24. Mikhail Bulgakov *The Heart of a Dog*
25. Vincent Cronin *Louis and Antoinette*
26. Alan Ross *The Bandit on the Billiard Table*
27. Fyodor Dostoyevsky *The Double*
28. Alan Ross *Time Was Away*
29. Peter Matthiessen *Under the Mountain Wall*
30. Peter Matthiessen *The Snow Leopard*
31. Peter Matthiessen *Far Tortuga*
32. Jorge Amado *Shepherds of the Night*
33. Jorge Amado *The Violent Land*
34. Jorge Amado *Tent of Miracles*
35. Torgny Lindgren *Bathsheba*
36. Antaeus: *Journals, Notebooks, Diaries*
37. Edmonde Charles-Roux *Chanel*
38. Nadezhda Mandelstam *Hope Against Hope*
39. Nadezhda Mandelstam *Hope Abandoned*
40. Raymond Carver *Elephant and Other Stories*
41. Vincent Cronin *Catherine Empress of Russia*
42. Federico de Roberto *The Viceroys*